Raves for Spider Robinson

"Spider Robinson's the antidote for entropy, the blahs, and the pernicious notion that humor and good grace are absent from the SF field."
—Ben Bova

"Spider Robinson is the Tom Robbins of the 21st century."
—John Varley

"How the hell is any self-respecting author supposed to compete with a soryteller as good as Spider Robinson?"
—David Gerrold

"Robinson knows how to generate tension without losing his sense of humor, a more difficult trick than you might imagine."
—*The New York Times*

Books by Spider Robinson

°Denotes a Tor Book

CALLAHAN'S CON

SPIDER ROBINSON

TOR®

A TOM DOHERTY ASSOCIATES BOOK
NEW YORK

This is a work of fiction. All the characters and events portrayed in this book are either fictitious or are used fictitiously.

CALLAHAN'S CON

Copyright © 2003 by Spider Robinson

Edited by Patrick LoBrutto

A Tor Book
Published by Tom Doherty Associates, LLC
175 Fifth Avenue
New York, NY 10010

www.tor.com

Tor® is a registered trademark of Tom Doherty Associates, LLC.

ISBN 0-765-34165-4
EAN 978-0765-34165-5
Library of Congress Catalog Card Number: 2003040285

First edition: July 2003
First mass market edition: June 2004

Printed in the United States of America

0 9 8 7 6 5 4 3 2

This book is dedicated to Larry Janifer,
known to some as Oudis:
senior colleague, Knave extraordinaire,
and extraordinary friend

ACKNOWLEDGMENTS

For assistance and advice in matters of science and technology, this time around, I am deeply indebted to Douglas Beder, Jaymie Matthews, Ray Maxwell, Jef Raskin, Dave Sloan, and Guy Immega; as always, any mistakes or inaccuracies are my fault for trusting them. Assistance of other kinds, just as valuable and appreciated, was provided by Rod Rempel, Lawrence Justrabo, and Colin MacDonald (the wizards behind my Web site), and by Bob Atkinson, Steve Fahnestalk, Daniel Finger, Stephen Gaskin, Paul Krassner, Alex and Mina Morton, Val Ross, Riley Sparks, the late Laurence M. Janifer, every one of the posters to the Usenet newsgroup alt.callahans, and others too numerous or fugitive to mention.

Particular thanks go to one of my favorite writers, Laurence Shames, for his gracious permission to borrow, for the second time, his splendid creations Bert the Shirt and Don Giovanni. If you find them as delightful as I do, look for Mr. Shames's novels *Florida Straits*, *Sunburn*, and *Mango Squeeze*.

None of my thirty-one books—or anything else I've

done—would have been possible without the advice, ideas, research assistance, not-always-credited collaboration, and ongoing love and support of my wife, Jeanne. This time out, however, she deserves more than the usual thanks; this is the first book I've written since I quit smoking tobacco, and I estimate I was about 15 to 20 percent harder to live with than usual during its creation. (Neither of us is complaining; we both figure it's a good trade. But still—thank you, Spice!) For the same reason and others, special thanks go to my longtime friend and agent, Eleanor Wood, and evenlongertime friend and editor, Pat LoBrutto, for believing in me and being patient.

Howe Sound, British Columbia
8 September 2002

Teach us delight in simple things,
And mirth that has no bitter springs.
—*Rudyard Kipling*

The man who listens to Reason is lost:
Reason enslaves all whose minds are not strong
enough to master her.
—*George Bernard Shaw*

Give up owning things and being somebody.
Quit existing.
—*Jalā ad-Dīnar ar-Rūmī*

When you can laugh at yourself, there is enlightenment.
—*Shunryu Suzuki Roshi*

CALLAHAN'S CON

I

ANOTHER DAY IN PARADISE

The basic condition of human life is happiness.
—the Dalai Lama

Alittle more than ten years after we had all arrived in Key West, saved the universe from annihilation, and settled back to have us some serious fun, bad ugliness and death came into my bar. No place is perfect.

I noticed her as soon as she came through the gate.

I always notice newcomers to The Place, but it was more than that. Before she said a word, even before she was near enough to get a sense of her face, something—body language maybe—told me she was trouble. My subconscious alarm system is fairly sensitive, even for a bartender.

Unfortunately I'm often too stupid to heed it. I did register her arrival, as I said . . . and then I went back to dispensing booze and good cheer to the happy throng. Trouble has walked into my bar more than once over the years, and I'm still here. Admittedly, I did require special help the night the nuclear weapon went off in my hand. And I'm the first to admit that I could never have succeeded in saving the universe that other time without the assistance of my baby daughter. In fact, it would be more accurate to say that she might not have succeeded without my supervision. All I'm trying to say is that in that first glance, even though I recognized the newcomer as Trouble looking for the spot marked X, not a great deal of adrenaline flowed. How was I to know she was my worst nightmare made flesh?

If the Lucky Duck had been around—anywhere in Key West—there probably wouldn't have been any trouble atall, atall. Or else ten times as much. But he was away, trying to help keep Ireland intact that winter, in a town with the unlikely name of An Uaimh. My friend Nikola Tesla might have come up with some way to salvage things, but he was off somewhere, doing something or other with his death ray; nobody'd heard from him in years. Even my wife, Zoey, could probably have straightened everything right out with a few well-chosen words. She had a gig up on Duval Street that evening, though, sitting in with a fado group, and had brought her bass and amp over to the lead singer's place for a rehearsal she assured me was *not* optional.

So I just had to improvise. That only works for me on guitar, as a rule.

It was late afternoon on a particularly perfect day, even by the standards of Key West. The humidity was uncommonly low for the Keys, and thanks in part to the protection of the thick flame-red canopy of poinciana that arched over the compound, we were just hot enough that the gentle steady breezes were welcome as much for their coolness as for the cycling symphony of pleasing scents they carried: sea salt, frangipani, fried conch fritters, Erin's rose garden, iodine, coral dust, lime, sunblock, five different kinds of coffee, the indescribable but distinctive bouquet of a Cuban sandwich being pressed somewhere upwind, excellent marijuana in a wooden pipe, and just a soupçon of distant moped exhaust. The wind was generally from the south, so even though The Place is only a few blocks from the Duval Street tourist crawl, I couldn't detect the usual trace amounts of vomit or testosterone in the mix.

It was the kind of day on which God unmistakably intended that human beings should kick back with their friends and loved ones in some shady place, chill out, get tilted, and say silly things to one another. I've gone to some lengths, over the years, to make The Place a spot conducive to just such activity, so I had rather more customers than usual for a weekday. And they were all certainly doing their part to fulfill God's wishes: I was selling a fair amount of booze, and the general conversation tended to be silly even if it wasn't.

On my left, for instance, Walter was trying to tell Bradley a perfectly ordinary little anecdote—but since they each suffer from unusual neurological disorders, even the mundane became a bit surreal.

"I was down walking Whitehead Street when there was suddenly big this boom, and I'm on my lying back," Walter was saying. Thanks to severe head trauma a year or two ago, his whack order is often out of word: he can say eloquently things, but not right in the way. After you've been listening to him for about five minutes, you get used to it.

Bradley's peculiarity, on the other hand, is congenital, some sort of subtle anomaly in Broca's area. I've always thought of it as Typesetter's Twitch: Brad tends to vocally anagrammatize, scrambling letters within a word rather than scrambling the order of the words themselves like Walter. Sometimes that can be even more challenging to follow. Right now, for instance, he responded to Walter's startling news with, "No this!"

Walter nodded. "I to swear God."

"What went grown?"

"What went wrong some was criminal trying to district the scare attorney who sent jail to him," Walter explained.

"A DA? Which neo?" Brad is a court recorder.

"The new one, Tarara Buhm. He trapped her booby car with a bomb smoke."

Our resident cross to bear, Harry, cackled and yelled one of his usual birdbrained comments: "You're welcome to smoke *these* boobies, bubbelah!" No one ever reacts to Harry anymore, but it doesn't seem to stop him.

"Wow," said Bradley. "I bet she was sacred."

"*Her* scared? I pissed about my just pants!"

"How did it?"

"Some named fool Seven and a Quarter."

"Seven and a Quarter?" Bradley said. "Pretty wired name."

"His apparently mother picked it out of a hat. But if you think *that*'s name a screwy—"

Listen to too much of that sort of conversation without a break and the wiring can start to smoke in your own brain. I let my attention drift over to the piano, where Fast Eddie Costigan was accompanying Maureen and Willard as they improvised a song parody.

> *A nit is a tiny little pain in the ass*
> *The size of a molecule of gas*
> *The average nit's about as smart as you,*
> *Which means that you may be a nitwit too.*
> *. . . and if you don't ever really give a shit*
> *You may grow up to be a nit.*

"Knit this!" Harry screamed at the top of his lungs, and was roundly ignored as always.

Or would you like to swing on your dates
Carry on at ruinous rates
And be better off than Bill Gates
Or would you rather be a jerk

A jerk is an animal whose brain tends to fail
And by definition he is male. . . .

Maureen and her husband both started pelting each other with peanuts at that point, so Fast Eddie went instrumental while they regained control and thought up some more lyrics.

From over on the other side of the bar, Long-Drink McGonnigle's buzz-saw voice cut through the Gordian knot of conversation. Apparently he'd been inspired by a couple of words in the song's chorus. "Coming soon to your local cinema," he declaimed, trying to imitate the plummy tones of a BBC announcer, "the latest entry in the longest-running comedy series in British film history: a romp about air rage titled, *Carry-On Baggage.*" There was general laughter.

Doc Webster jumped in, with a considerably better fake British accent. "Joan Sims will play the baggage—fully packed indeed—Charles Hawtrey will handle 'er, and they'll spend the movie squeezed together, either under the seat or in the overhead compartment, while flight attendant Sidney James offers everyone his nuts." Louder laughter.

Doc has been topping Long-Drink—hell, all of us, except for his wife, Mei-Ling—for decades, now. But the McGonnigle likes to make him work for it a little. "Rest assured that once they get their belts unfastened and locate each other's seat, they'll soon be flying united," he riposted.

"—in the full, upright position, of course," the Doc said at once, "and setting off the smoke detectors. The Hollies will provide the baggage theme song, 'On a Carousel,' performed by Wings in an airy, plain fashion while eight miles high. As the actress told the gym teacher, 'It's first-class, Coach.'"

Long-Drink raised two fingers to his brow to acknowledge a successful hijacking and joined in the round of applause. As it faded, Willard and Maureen tried another take, together this time:

> *A jerk is an animal who's here on spring break*
> *He sure can be difficult to take* (raucous laughter)
> *He has no manners when he swills his ale*
> *He'd sell one kidney for a piece of tail*
> *So if it's years till you have to go to work,*
> *Then don't grow up: just be a jerk*

"Jerk this!" Harry shrieked inevitably. After a brief pause for thought, Maureen launched the next chorus:

> *Hey, would you like to swing on a bed*
> *Try to moon some frat boy named Fred*
> *And be better off when you're dead*
> *Or would you rather get a life?*

"Excuse me," a stranger's voice said, when the cheering had faded enough.

It had taken that long for the newcomer to make it as far as the bar. I'd vaguely noticed her doing a larger-than-usual amount of gawking around at The Place on her way, examining it intently enough to have been grading it by some unknown criteria. I turned to see her now, and a vagrant shaft of sunlight pierced the crimson leaves overhead, forcing me to hold up a hand to block it, with the net effect that I probably looked as though I were saluting.

It seemed appropriate. The short pale Caucasian woman

who stood there was—in that Key West winter heat—so crisp and straight and stiff and in all details inhumanly perfect that I might well have taken her for a member of the military, temporarily out of uniform, an officer perhaps, or an MP. But she wore her severe business suit and glasses as if they *were* a uniform, and in place of a sidearm she carried something much deadlier. From a distance I had taken it for a purse. The moment I recognized it for what it really was, I started to hear a high distant buzzing in my ears.

A briefcase.

With an elaborate crest on it that was unmistakably some sort of official seal.

I felt a cold, clammy sweat spring out on my forehead and testicles. Suddenly I was deep-down terrified, for the first time in over a decade. My ancient enemy was in my house.

The others were oblivious; most of them could not have seen the briefcase from their angle. "No, excuse *me*, ma'am," Long-Drink said politely. "I didn't see you there. Have a seat."

"There's no excuse for either of you dickheads!" Harry said, and shrieked with laughter at his own wit. The stranger ignored him, which impressed me: Harry isn't easy to ignore when you first meet him. He spent a few too many of his formative years in a whorehouse, where the competition for attention must have required strong measures.

"Welcome to The Place, dear," Mei-Ling said. "What are you drinking?"

"Nothing, thank you," the stranger said. She had ignored Long-Drink's invitation to sit, too. Her voice sounded eerily like synthesized speech on a computer, the audio equivalent of Courier font. "I am looking for the parents of the minor child Erin Stonebender-Berkowitz. Would any of you know where they might be found at this point in time?"

My friends are pretty quick on the uptake. By the time she was done speaking, everyone present had grasped the awful truth.

A bureaucrat was among us.

Nobody flinched, or even blinked, but I knew they, too, were all on red alert now, ready to back my play. The small comfort was welcome: I was so terrified, it was hard to get my breath.

She was short, not much over five feet, and fashionably anorexic. I guessed her at fifty-five years old, but could have been low: her greying brown hair was yanked back into a ballerina bun so tightly that there might have been some incidental face-lift effect. Her skin was paler than average for a Floridian, and I could tell by the incipient sunburn on her left arm and the left side of her face that she had just driven down the Keys that morning. But no part of her that I could see was shiny with perspiration . . . even though a business suit is at least two layers of clothing more than is desirable in Key West.

The best way to lie is to tell *part* of the truth, in such a way that your listener fills in the blanks, incorrectly, for herself. That way if you get caught, you can always play dumb. "Her mother's not here right now," I said. "Is there a message I can pass on when I see her?"

"No. Do you know exactly where she presently domiciles?"

About fifty yards away, in the nearest of the five houses within the compound. "Have you tried the phone book?"

"What about her father?" I wasn't the only one who could answer a question with another question.

"Never met the guy," I said, still miniskirting the truth.

I was very glad I still had all my hair, at age fifty-mumble, and still wore it Beatle-style: those greying bangs concealed the icy sweat dripping down behind my sunglasses now. So far, I was still speaking the strict truth—my wife, Zoey, was a few weeks pregnant with Erin when I met her—but I was beginning to pass beyond the area where I could later claim to have innocently misunderstood what this woman was asking. And I already didn't like the direction this was going.

She looked around at the others, one by one. This was a little more complex than it sounds, because she did it like a poorly designed robot: instead of moving her eyes from face to face, she kept her eyes fixed straight ahead and moved her entire body slightly each time. You had the idea she was taking a mental snapshot of each face. "Do any of you know where I might find either of the parents of Erin Stonebender-Berkowitz at this point in time?"

Maybe Mei-Ling guessed my problem. "No offense," she said, "but who are you, and why do you want to know?"

"My name is Czrjghnczl—"

I hastily began drawing her a glass of water to clear her throat—but stopped, because she went on:

" Field Inspector Ludnyola Czrjghnczl—and I am from Tallahassee."

My heart was already hammering. Now it started flailing away with a maul, putting its shoulder into it. I had taken her for a town-level bureaucrat, or at worst someone from Monroe County. But Tallahassee is the capital of Florida. Ms. Czrjghnczl was state-level trouble.

"I am a senior field inspector for the Florida Department of Education," she said, confirming my worst fear, "and I have been tasked with determinating whether Erin Stonebender-Berkowitz is being properly and adequately homeschooled, or is in fact in need of immediational custodial intervention and/or removal from her parents' custody."

Pindrop silence.

The thing to do when you're terrified is to take a step forward and smile. I did both, and when I was done, I had pretty much shot my bolt, so I just stood there, smiling and trying to understand what had gone so horribly wrong.

It was my understanding that Zoey and I were *cool* with the state education people regarding Erin's homeschooling—we certainly had been for the past seven years. And the idea that her education could be deficient in any possible way was ludicrous. To be sure, every single thing we had ever told the state of Florida about her homeschooling had been complete and utter bullshit. But let's be fair: the God's honest truth could only have confused them—at best. Thanks to the intervention of a cybernetic entity named Solace (now deceased) during Erin's gestation, our daughter was born with a higher IQ; a better vocabulary; and a broader, deeper education than either of her parents. Try explaining *that* to a state functionary with a fill-in-the-blank form sometime.

I wished Zoey were there so badly my stomach hurt. She was our family's designated Speaker-to-Bureaucrats, not me. She spoke fluent Bullshit. I speak only American, some Canadian, and a smattering of English, and I've learned from painful experience how dangerous that is around a civil servant. It would be three more years before Erin would turn sixteen and become immune to the dark powers of school boards; in the meantime she was, in the eyes of the law, just like any other child: a slave.

Zoey *wasn't* there. We owned no cell phone. I couldn't recall the last name of the lead singer at whose place she was rehearsing, if I'd ever known it, so I had no way to look up his phone number. It was up to me.

I cleared my throat and said, "Listen, Field Inspector Czrjghnczl, I—excuse me a moment."

The brain behaves oddly under stress. A penny finally dropped. I turned away from her for a moment and directed an accusatory glare down the bar at Walter. He grimaced back, probably with shame. "The district attorney's name was Tarara Buhm?" I asked him.

He hung his head.

"Tarara Buhm, DA?"

He nodded.

I took in a long slow breath, let it out even slower. "Right." I turned back to the Antichrist. "Listen, Field Marshal Von . . . I'm sorry, Field Inspector Czrjghnczl . . . I'd just like to—"

"The accent is on the *rjgh*," she interjected.

Another long slow breath. "Right. As I was saying, I'd like to—"

Harry picked then to shriek, "I'd like to cut the mustard with you and then lick the jar clean afterwards, you spicy slut!"

She turned bright red and spun on her heel, ready to do battle. Then she relaxed a little. "Oh, for God's sake. I thought it was a person."

For once, Harry was speechless. He blinked at her for a moment . . . then rose into the air with a flurry of angry flapping and flew past me. In a place of honor behind the bar sits an old fashioned pull-chain toilet, a little under five inches tall but fully functional. Harry landed, perched on it, put it to its intended use, and flushed it.

"What a disgusting parrot," she said.

"True, but he's not dead."

She didn't get the reference, and I didn't try to pursue it.

"Excuse me, madam," Ralph Von Wau Wau said behind her. "On what basis do you say that my friend Harry is not a person?"

Uh-oh, I thought. You don't often hear Ralph drop that

Colonel Klink accent of his . . . but when he does, it's time to seek cover.

She, of course, had no way of knowing that, and his tone was soft and gentle. She turned around, and whether she intended to debate with him or simply tell him she was too important to do so cannot be known, because when she finished turning, he was not there. Nobody was. She had just heard his voice from two feet behind her, and now nobody was there; she blinked in annoyance.

Then she thought to look down.

She had been opening her mouth to speak as she turned. Now it just kept opening, until she looked like she was using it to pleasure an invisible elephant . . . but nothing could come out of it because she could not stop inhaling.

It was hard to blame her. It's disturbing enough to look down and discover a full-grown, visibly pissed-off German shepherd at your feet. But if it challenges you to argue semantics with it, and you don't lose your cool . . . Jack, you dead. I sighed. I could already tell this was probably going to cost me.

"I vill admit," Ralph told her, "his sense of humor leaves virtually everything to be desired. But by zat criterion zere are very few perzonss present here right now." His fake accent was starting to come back, an encouraging sign.

She yanked her eyes away from him with an almost audible sucking sound and looked quickly around her. I could tell she was looking for the ventriloquist who was causing this dog to appear to talk, and she kept trying even though she kept coming up empty. Again, hard to blame her. The night I met Ralph myself, maybe a quarter of a century ago at the original Callahan's Place, he was working a ventriloquist con, in partnership with a mute guy. We only caught on because the guy wasn't very good at lip synching.

But finally she gave up. You could see that she wanted to

hit a delete key and make Ralph go away. But she couldn't find one. "Vould you mind telling me just vat *your* definition of 'perzonhood' entailss?" he repeated.

Since he persisted in speaking, she would have to answer him, but that didn't necessarily mean she had to concede he existed. She stared straight ahead of her and addressed the empty air. "The abortion controversialization has made the legal definition quite complexitized; it would be imprudent to paraphrase it from memory. I can however direct you to—"

"The hell with the legal definition," Alf yelled. "Answer the damn question, lady."

She froze. This new voice was much higher in pitch and reedier in tone than Ralph's, did not sound even vaguely canine, and had no accent at all—Southern Florida Standard English, if that isn't an oxymoron. But it came from roughly the same *height* as Ralph's voice, so she already sensed she was in trouble.

Again she looked down.

And again performed her Linda Lovelace At The Zoo impression. And once again, I could not find it in my heart to fault her for it. Most people are stunned silent by their first sight of a Key deer.

They look pretty much like any other deer . . . only seen through the wrong end of a telescope: perfect little miniature creatures. One taller than knee-high would be considered a basketball player by his tribe. Tourists who take the trouble to get past the safeguards protecting Key deer and see one up close just about always react with awe. Even without hearing one speak.

Much less speak rudely. "Come on, come on, sugar—we *do* have all day, but we have better things to waste it on than you," Alf snapped, twitching his tail.

The Inspector could not seem to shake off her paralysis;

every time she started to, her eyes refocused on Alfie and her mainspring popped again. Alf's nose is hard to look away from, so big and red he looks like W. C. Fields's lawn ornament—apparently there's an auxiliary brain in there. The bureaucrat tried looking away from it . . . and found herself staring at Ralph; no help there. I felt an impulse to intervene somehow, but many years ago I gave up trying to find ways to cushion fellow humans against that first meeting with people like Ralph or Alf. There *is* no way to cushion it that I've ever found; it's simply a sink-or-swim kind of deal. Best to let the hand play out as dealt.

Long-Drink McGonnigle stood up, frowning.

Shit, where did I put that fifth ace?

He loped over to the chalk line before the fireplace and raised his glass. Silence. "To manners," he said, emptied his drink in a gulp, and flung the glass into the hearth. The smash was loud and musical.

There was a ragged but strong chorus, of, "To manners!" and more than a dozen glasses followed Long-Drink's in a ragged barrage.

Newcomers to our company often find our toasting customs almost as startling as Ralph Von Wau Wau: A sudden thunder of bursting glassware can make some people jump a foot in the air.

"Now, Ms. Belch . . . ," Long-Drink said, turning and advancing on Field Inspector Czrjghnczl. This was not going well. ". . . exactly what the hell makes you think you have the right to saunter in here and make wild insinuations and vile threats about people you've never even met?"

This was something she knew how to deal with: Her blank face congealed. "And you are . . ."

The Drink nodded. "Magnificent. I know."

"Well, in point of fact, Mr. Nificent, I happen to be fully authorized to—"

"Author-ized?" Doc Webster interjected. "Nonsense. Where's your elbow patches? Your coffeemaker? The beads of blood on your forehead? The line of creditors hounding your footsteps? No offense, Ralph."

"I doubt she's authored a thing in her life," Long-Drink agreed. "She looks like more of an editor to me."

She rebooted. "In point of fact, I am fully authorized by the state to investigate and make recommendatory suggestions for disposition vis-à-vis the educational slash residentiary status of minor children deemed to be in a state of potentialized risk."

"Wow," Marty Pignatelli said. "You carry a piece?"

She gave him a withering glare.

"Not even a throwdown?" Marty's an ex-cop.

It had been over a decade since I had last heard someone use the word "slash" in a sentence that did not also have the word "prices" in it. I couldn't help wondering who was responsible for *major* children. And of course, "state of potentialized risk" was one for the archives. But I wasn't thinking about any of those things just then. I was beginning to understand how much trouble I was in.

This was no mere garden-variety bureaucrat. This was the hydroponic monoculture logic-resistant kudzu-gene Franken-food kind. She didn't *need* a damn gun. Sweat ran down my back into my shorts.

It was time to start proffering olive branches. "Field Inspector Czrjghnczl," I said, carefully placing the accent on the *rjgh,* this time, "I don't think anyone here would question your authority, your responsibility, or your probity. Would we, folks?" I put just enough spin on the last three words that the response was a strained silence. I went on, "There's really no need at all to approach this in an adversarial spirit. I'm sure that with open, honest communication we can arrive at a mutually—"

It was working; I could see it in her eyes. My submissive display was pulling her back from the very edge of a snit. There was still hope for negotiation. I was trying to recall everything I knew about stalling, when without warning the situation went completely to hell.

It happened too fast to really grasp, but as I reconstruct things, what started it was Pixel the cat, materializing on the countertop behind me . . . less than a foot from where Harry the parrot still sat on his little porcelain throne. Yes, he's *that* Pixel: the Cat Who Walks Through Walls, former master of Robert A. Heinlein; he wandered into our company and took us captive shortly after Mr. Heinlein's death in 1988. You'd think Harry would be used to his sudden appearances by now, after more than a decade of mutual ballbreaking, but it still gets the little guy every time. He screamed *"Jesus Christ,"* erupted from his commode like a Nike from its launch rack, and made a beeline for whatever he happened to be looking at at the moment. Which was Field Inspector Czr-jghnczl, of course.

From her point of view, she was suddenly under scuz missile attack, albeit a missile trailing feathers and profanity. Her reaction must have been just as automatic as his: She tried to bat Harry out of the air with her deadly briefcase. She had excellent reflexes, too; the only thing that saved Harry a nasty concussion was the twenty-five pounds or so of cat that seemed to be attached to her arm all of a sudden. Painfully attached: I've seen Pixel dice melons with those claws. He doesn't like it when anyone but *him* gives Harry a hard time.

Still operating on hardwired programming, she let go of the briefcase and tried to fling him from her arm. But just as she got to the point where she planned to "snap the whip" and use centrifugal force to unseat him . . . he was just *gone*. She ended up in a spinning, off-balance stagger. Alf just had time to bray, "Hey, I'm walkin' here—*I'm walkin' here*—" before Ludnyola tripped over him. Her brain was lagging three or four crises behind, and her reflexes had done all they could; she would have gone down and landed heavily on that infinitely fragile little animal. But Ralph von Wau Wau roared and reared up on his hind legs, and suddenly all the frenzied high-speed activity congealed into a static tableau.

Ralph and Field Inspector Czrjghnczl appeared to be dancing. A new dance, one I felt definitely had possibilities. Her arms hung limp at her sides, and Ralph was holding her up by the tits.

She stared, from Ralph down to her chest and back up to Ralph, whose muzzle panted and drooled slightly a few inches from her face. Her brain caught up, or perhaps only her reflexes. She screamed, pushed Ralph violently away, and sprang backwards.

Most of us started yelling, but of course the more we yelled, the more determined she became to keep on backpedaling. And she had only been about twelve steps from the pool to start with.

It will be very bad, I thought, *if she falls in the pool.*

She stopped on the eleventh step and planted her feet firmly, oblivious of the water just behind her. By now her brain had definitely caught up, and overruled the reflexes. A civil servant never retreats, no matter what. Not even if it *is* the only sane thing to do. The hounds of Hell can always be slapped with a subpoena or threatened with a seven-year audit. I could see her using fire-extinguisher blasts of anger to smother her fear. She took a deep breath, raised her voice, as if she didn't already have anyone's attention, and said, "Ladies and gentlemen, I require your cooperation. Are either of the parents of Erin Stonebender-Berkowitz here present?"

Gee, this was not going well.

I was out of wiggle room. Outright lying would only make things worse. Time to cop. "I'm Jake Stonebender."

Her target radar locked on to me. "I see. Is your wife present?"

"Uh, no, she's at a rehearsal."

Somewhere on her console a red light came on. "She is an actress?"

I hastened to deny the slander. "A musician."

I could tell from her expression I had added another amber light and a warning buzzer. "I see."

I was wishing I'd thought to lie. Now she was going to ask what instrument, and I was going to have to say bass. Bureaucrats are not likely to be impressed by bass players. Perhaps you've heard the one about the difference between a bass player and a large pepperoni pizza? The pizza can feed a family of four. I wondered if I could phrase it so as to imply that Zoey *bowed* a bass, for a symphony orchestra. Would Field Inspector Czrjghnczl know Key West has no symphony? Maybe I should—

"And where is Erin herself now?"

Cerebral meltdown.

"," I said, not very loudly. How could I have not anticipated this question?

"She is nearby, I presume?"

"Ye-e-es," I agreed cautiously, crossing my fingers hard enough to raise bruises. In a certain sense, Erin is *always* nearby. And it would not be good to admit that I had no clear idea where—or even when—she was, and that she could easily be thousands of miles away . . . or for that matter, thousands of *years*. This woman believed, as an article of faith, that anyone Erin's age was by definition a PINS, a person in need of supervision, and that it was my responsibility to keep tabs on the kid every second.

"Pursuing some sort of educational project at this time of day, no doubt?" she said skeptically.

Here I was on less shaky ground. "Absolutely. Anthropological research."

"Fetch her, please."

"Look," I said desperately, "I don't see any need to—"

"Kindly produce her at once," the Field Inspector said. "If in fact you can."

A couple of people went *woooo*. She had issued fighting words. I considered feigning offense, as a stalling tactic. But stalling until *what?*

Damn it, I might as well bite the bullet.

I sighed deeply and brought my watch up. I pressed the mode button on the lower left and the display changed to a dormant stopwatch labeled CHRONO. I pressed it again and the watch became an alarm clock awaiting instructions. Another press, and the watch offered to tell me the time in some other time zone, arbitrarily designated "T-2." On most watches, the fourth press would have reverted it to default, the current-time readout. On mine, the fourth press caused it to display a crude but recognizable picture of a ladybug.

I hesitated for several more seconds, trying to think of a good way out of this. Then I pressed the button on the upper right, once. The ladybug began flashing—

Erin materialized, immediately between me and Field Inspector Czrjghnczl. "Hi, Papa!" she said cheerily. "What's up?" Her pitch dropped several notes. "Why are you holding your face in your hands like that?"

Behind her, there was a large, loud splash.

Part of it, of course, was that Erin was hovering about a foot and a half over the bar, with no more visible means of support than a bass player. Another part of the problem was probably that she had just Transited—traveled home from some other ficton, some other place-and-time. For technical reasons I don't understand, living and dead matter can't Transit in the same load . . . so those who travel that way necessarily arrive stark naked.

But I think the icing on the cake must have been that whatever ficton Erin had just been visiting, they had a war going on there—well, that doesn't rule out many, does it?—and she was soaked with blood, apparently so recently spilled that it still qualified as living matter. Even I found the sight unnerving, and I knew for sure that none of the blood was hers.

Small wonder Field Inspector Czrjghnczl suffered system crash and fell over backwards into the pool.

Other people hurried to pull her out. I was way too busy. I had five or ten seconds max to bring Erin up to speed. This was going to get ugly, now, and fast.

Fortunately my little girl has always had a tendency to hit the ground running. "Tell it, Papa."

"That splashing behind you is a government employee—"

"Which agency? NSA?"

"No, no, state educa—*Why would you expect the NSA?*"

"Later, Pop, later. She's here about homeschooling, then?" She got the hose, adjusted the sprinkler head to hold still, and began sluicing blood off herself. "But why? We're current with the state."

I shrugged. "Beats me. You know I don't speak Bureaucrat."

In another year or two, long hair would become very important to her, but at thirteen she was keeping hers cut short enough that rinsing it took no time at all, and afterward all she needed to do was shake her head and let the sun do the rest. Clothes appeared next to her, Transited from her nearby bedroom; she began dressing. "How bad is it?"

"She started out by talking about maybe removing you from our custody. From there, the situation deteriorated."

Erin grinned, visualizing it. "She demanded that you produce me forthwith, and then when she suddenly found my bare bum in her face, she went for a swim."

I nodded. "You have the thing in a nutshell. Be careful: surprises frighten her."

"You *said* she's a bureaucrat. What's her name?"

I told her.

Erin frowned. "Accent on the *rjgh*?" she asked, and I nodded. "Aha," she said.

I heard her, but it didn't register right away; I was distracted.

God damn it.

I really don't want anyone but friends in my pool.

No, I mean I really *really* don't want anyone but friends in my pool—and certainly not enemies.

"*There's a corpse down there,*" she screamed as she broached. "A *dead bod—*" and by then she had fallen back below the surface of the water again.

See what I mean?

No friend would leap to a conclusion like that. Not even a fair-minded stranger. The only corpselike thing about Lex at all is his custom of taking naps at the bottom of the pool. And why shouldn't he? Perfectly normal thing for a merman to do, especially at that time of the day.

All right, he doesn't look much like someone raised on a diet of movies and cartoons would expect a merman to look.

Specifically, he has no tail. Unlike Daryl Hannah in *Splash,* even when he's immersed in water, Lex has two legs, just like thee and me—they're just a lot scalier, that's all. Well . . . and they bend in a few directions ours don't. And the toes are webbed. Other details of his lower anatomy I leave to you to imagine for yourself, except to say that while he may not have a tail himself, my understanding is that he gets plenty of it.

Also unlike Daryl Hannah, he is *not* amphibian. If you kept him out of the water long enough to dry off, he would not metamorphose into a smooth pink human being; he would *die*. And would probably soon smell like dead fish.

Lex has lived in the waters around Key West for most of his life. Most of the old-time Conchs know him, especially the fishermen, guides, charter boat skippers, divers, the Houseboat Row gang, and other water people. Nobody actually discusses him at any length, you understand; the word just went around a long time ago that if you got into trouble out there on the briny, and you weren't an asshole, help might just come to you if you were to lean over the side and slap the water in a certain manner. And that if that did happen, the next time you went out, it would be a good idea to toss a large sack of saltwater taffy overboard at the same spot. Then there was the fishing boat skipper who accidentally dropped a waterproof Walkman with a cassette of *Rubber Soul* in it over the side, and from that day forward could *not* go out without catching large, sought-after fish in great quantity. For years afterwards the word was that leaving a cassette tape on a buoy on your way to sea was good luck. Word of another kind also went around about Lex from time to time, but only in the scuba community, and only among the ladies.

I'd been hearing about him since I moved to the Rock, and wanted to meet him, but I'm not any kind of a boat guy, and my wife is crazy about me, and anyway hates to scuba, so there was no occasion for our paths to cross. Then a few weeks ago my friends William Williams and Doc Webster (you'd *expect* a doctor and a guy called Double Bill to get along, wouldn't you?) came to me and asked if it would be all right if Lex moved into The Place's pool for a while, while the Doc experimented with a couple of possible treatments. It seems that in recent years, the water around Key West has finally become so befouled by the crap we dump into it that Lex had developed a really serious rash on his upper half, and some sort of scale infection on his lower half. If The Place is about anything, it's Welcoming the Weird, so I agreed at once to help. I had the pool filled with salt water and raised a volunteer crew to help transport him, and one dark Tuesday night we did it.

Double Bill lined the back of his pickup truck with plastic, filled it with seawater, and we transported Lex in that. At one point Bill stopped a little short at a traffic light on Truman Street, and I guess Lex bonked his head back there, because he let out a bubbly shout loud enough to be heard in the cab. A couple of tourist college boys standing nearby came over and looked in the back of the truck, and the last I saw of them they were still standing there, solemnly assuring each other in hushed voices that the stuff definitely *was* worth three hundred an ounce.

Anyway, I'd had Lex as a houseguest (well, poolguest) for a few weeks now, and he'd been no trouble at all. He spent a lot of his time at the bottom of the deep end, listening to his Walkman, and unfortunately, while engaged in that harmless pursuit he bore a slight but persuasive resemblance to a waterlogged corpse.

Which is why Field Inspector Czrjghnczl left the pool

very much like a Trident nuclear missile leaving an atomic sub: straight up, and with a great deal of foam, fuss, and noise.

Folks hauled her out of the pool—fun new game: Bobbing for Bureaucrats—and set her on her feet, and passed her a few towels, earning not a particle of gratitude from her. Her mouth opened and she gestured with her hands, but she was so terrified and enraged, words failed her.

"God, I love it when she's wet!" Harry the Parrot shrieked, flying in a circle around her head.

She swiveled her head to glare at him, raised a hand—

Suddenly there was a cat on her head.

She removed Pixel's tail from her mouth, spit a fine spray of orange cat hair, and tried very hard to hit him, very hard. Slow learner. She very nearly knocked herself back into the pool when he vanished just before her fist arrived.

"What a knockout," Harry squawked.

When it comes to mollifying monumentally pissed-off women, any man alive can use some advice. "What should I do?" I asked Erin.

She shrugged. "Survive."

It wasn't what I wanted to hear, but she was right. Nothing I could possibly have said or done would have been of the slightest possible use.

The soaked civil servant *did* say things, a number of them—and I'm pretty sure they were in English—but since her voice had gone hypersonic by that point, I'm not sure what they were. It doesn't matter, because she said them over her shoulder on her way to the gate, and she probably summarized them effectively with the violent slam that cracked the gate itself down the center and knocked it off its hinges.

Not one of my best days, so far. Zoey wasn't going to think so, anyway.

The sudden departure left a silence.

It seemed a shame to break it. But Long-Drink McGonnigle managed to find the right words.

"I'm not going in that pool again until it's been drained and scrubbed."

He brought the house down.

"Oughta get Nikky to oil it with his breath day," Doc Webster said.

"Huh?"

"I say, we ought to get Nikola Tesla to boil it with his death ray."

I blinked at him, wondering if he was pulling my leg or my ears were starting to go—then got distracted by the sudden recollection of what Erin had said to me just as the Field Inspector had emerged from the water.

"You said 'aha!' " I said to her.

"Yes, Papa."

I like to think I'd have thought of it myself, in time. Erin has often told Zoey and me that she isn't really any smarter than we are, just quicker at it. I've never been sure if the distinction means anything. "*Aha* what, honey?"

"Well, I can't be sure, of course," she said. "But how much do you want to bet that she's a relative of either Nyjmnckra or Jorjhk Grtozkzhnyi?"

Thunderbolt.

2

LITTLE NUTS

Some recap may be useful here.

I met most of my friends while we were all patrons of a tavern on Long Island, New York, named Callahan's Place, owned and operated by a man who called himself Mike Callahan. It was an unusual tavern in many ways—customers were permitted to make their own change, for instance, and were welcome to smash their glasses in the fireplace . . . *if* they were willing to propose a toast first. Enough interesting things happened there that I'd need three books this size just to hit some of the highlights—and then, one fateful night, it fell to us to defend the planet from destruction by hostile extraterrestrials. In the course of that evening, Mike found it necessary to reveal to us all that he was a time traveler named Justin from the far-distant future . . . and we all found it necessary to enter telepathic rapport together . . . and I found it necessary to set off an atom bomb I was holding in my hand at the time. Busy night.

When the dust settled, Mike Callahan was gone back home to his own ficton, Callahan's Place was a radioactive hole in the ground, and I had started another bar for us all to hang out in just down the road: Mary's Place, named after Mike's daughter. There we all spent an almost indecently happy year together, during which I met and successfully wooed my Zoey.

Then the night our daughter was being born, there was another of those annoying alien-destruction-of-Earth attempts—don't you hate when that happens?—and we managed another of those group telepathic hookups to stave it off . . . only this time our group included Solace, a silicon person. Solace was, in fact, the Internet itself, become alive and self-aware . . . and that night, just before she sacrificed her own life to save the human race that had unknowingly birthed her, she took the opportunity to interface directly with my baby Erin's brain, as Zoey was in the act of birthing her. Erin emerged from Zoey's womb with an IQ and vocabulary better than those of a university graduate. Hell, a university *professor*, these days.

Unfortunately, under the stress of saving the world and birthing a supergenius, my friends and I—well, mostly I—managed to mortally offend our next-door neighbor, Nyjmnckra Grtozkzhnyi, an infected pimple of a human being and a finalist in the Ugliest Person That Ever Lived sweepstakes. The problem with offending her was her nephew Jorjhk. By evil chance, he was a town inspector . . . for our town . . . and there turned out to be some deficiencies in my liquor license, business license, operating permit, and fifty-'leven other required forms; namely, their nonexistence. In establishing Mary's Place, I had seen no reason to waste anybody's time, particularly my own, on paperwork. This turned out to be a fatal mistake. Bureaucracy, I ended up proving, is way more dangerous than nuclear weapons.

In 1989, after a year of sulking, I was seized by either inspiration or madness—you pick—and moved my family and myself out of Long Island, all the way down the coast to Key West. To my astonishment and joy, just about every one of my former customers opted to follow me, in a caravan of school buses, and I ended up opening yet another tavern, a little south of Duval Street, which I called simply The Place.

My mistake was in assuming that the entire Eastern seaboard was enough distance to place between my bar and the vindictiveness of a pissed-off petty official. There was, it appeared, an unofficial Old Pricks' Network—as slow as a glacier, maybe, but just as deadly. The long arm of Clan Grtozkzhnyi had finally reached all the way down to the ass end of the Florida Keys.

And fallen into my pool.

"Oh, shit—*of course.*"

"Ukrainians have long memories," my daughter said.

From the pool came a splash, and then a series of sounds familiar to me but probably not familiar to you. In order for Lex to speak, in air, it's necessary for him to empty his windpipe of whatever water is in it at the time, and then dry out his larynx by flexing his gills and breathing in and out—as quickly as possible since breathing air hurts his lungs. The net effect is that conversations with him generally begin with the sound of a man vomiting, and then hawking and swallowing extremely juicy boogers for ten or twenty seconds. The resulting tone poem has driven tougher people than the Field Inspector to depart the premises at high speed, even *before* they saw Lex's legs. In a weird way, it's been a boon for Lex:

not one of his friends is a silly, shallow person, distracted by trivia.

Perhaps in consequence, he speaks with a distinct Bahama Village accent—a strange lilting creole that borrows quirks from Jamaica, Bermuda, Cuba, and other places I don't know. "I beg your humble pahdon, Jake—but who was dat gray-yut styoupid harse? She look like a jumbee, bahd ting to see wakin' from a nap."

"Sorry about that, Lex. I wish she *were* a jumbee; a simple charm'd get me off the hook then. She's a bureaucrat."

Sploot. He was gone.

You wouldn't think someone like Lex would know enough about bureaucrats to be properly afraid of them. But he knows the movie *Splash* real well—I believe that's why he chose the name Lexington, actually—and there are several bureaucrats in that.

"Well," I said to Erin, "I guess the first thing to do is try and get hold of your mother."

"The first thing to do," Erin said, double-knotting a shoelace, "is make a few phone calls and find out what the hell's actually going on, how much trouble we're actually in. Mom's better with clearly defined problems."

I refrained from comment.

She straightened up from tying her shoes. "Okay, the first—damn." She had just noted the position of the sun in the sky. "It's after three P.M. Every state employee in Florida has gone home by now. Ah well, that's why they invented the Net. Excuse me, Papa." She left and went in the house. On foot: Zoey and I have impressed on her that teleporting is not something to be done casually, especially not in public. (Sure, only family were present in The Place at the moment—but at any time a really tall tourist standing up on the seat of a bicycle could glance over our hedge.) Our house is less than fifty yards from my bar, and the windows are pretty much always open in the daytime, so I could hear the chiming chord of the Mac booting up in the study.

"Hey, Jake," Jim Omar called from the other direction, "I can fix this."

He referred to the gate. He was holding it up against its ruined hinges experimentally, the way a girl holds a dress up in front of herself to judge how it will look if she puts it on. He was using a thumb and two fingers to do so. Omar looks like a normal, if large-size, person, but I've seen him lift up the front of a school bus and set it down on its jack. The gate itself was badly cracked, but Omar was right; it was repairable. Seeing it made me think of a man decades dead, with the unlikely name of Big Beef McCaffrey. "Okay," I called back to him. "But do a mediocre job, will you?"

He pantomimed puzzlement.

"Tradition," I told him.

He continued to look uncomprehending for a moment— and then he smiled. "Big Beef."

I nodded.

There were smiles all around. Nearly everyone either remembered Big Beef McCaffrey or had heard the story. Our original home, Callahan's Place, had featured a big poorly repaired crack right down the center of its front door, too. It had been put there in the late 1940s by the head of the McCaffrey, the night he tried to stiff Mike with a bogus ten-spot. Now I had a crack to match it in my own tavern door. For some reason I found that absurdly pleasing, and a quick glance around told me I wasn't the only one.

"You got it," Omar called. He inspected the door again. "Still rather use my own tools, though. I'll have it back tomorrow." He left with it, carrying it in one hand as if it were an empty pizza box.

I put my elbows on the bar, my face in my hands, closed my eyes, and briefly left the world. (That's the kind of clientele I got: I can do that when I need to, and my bar will still be intact when I get back.)

Okay, Jake: let's compact our feces, here. The hammer of doom hangs over you, the forces of darkness are mad enough to shit thumbtacks, and it's time to establish priorities. You won't be able to get hold of Zoey for hours yet. It's too late to phone your lawyer, or anyone in the government who could offer info or advice. So your optimum move right now is . . . what, again?

Well, I have a default answer for that question.

I turned to The Machine and found that Long-Drink McGonnigle was way ahead of me. While I had been staring into space, he had come around behind the bar and taken over for me. A whipped-cream-capped mug was already emerging from the right side of The Machine, the air above it shimmering slightly; he picked it up and handed it to me. The first sip told me that he'd gotten my prescription right. Tanzanian Peaberry coffee, the Black Bush, two sugars and 18 percent cream. "Thank you, Drink."

"My pleasure," he said, dialing a different prescription. His own empty mug was just disappearing into the left side of The Machine. The barely audible sound of the conveyor belt stopped and was replaced by the gurgle-bubble sound of magic taking place inside. When it emerged, I knew, it would contain New Guinea Peaberry, Tullamore Dew, three sugars and whipped Jersey cream. "As your physician, I prescribe intoxication," he told me. "Why don't you let me take the stick awhile, so you can focus?"

"*I'm* Jake's physician," Doc Webster said from his seat behind us.

"As your attorney," Long-Drink told him, "I advise you not to contradict me. Do you dispute my diagnosis?"

"No, no," the Doc said. "You're quite right: she heeds to get nitfaced."

Long-Drink and I looked at each other and rolled our eyes. Spoonerisms—in a company that included Walter and Bradley. The Doc was slipping.

Nonetheless he constituted a qualified second opinion, so I allowed Long-Drink to take over as bartender, found an empty chaise longue near the pool, and consented to the course of treatment he had prescribed. It was delicious.

An hour or so later, Erin came back outside, again walking rather than teleporting since there was no need for haste. I was sitting beside Fast Eddie's piano, holding my guitar on my lap, helping Willard and Maureen Hooker put the finishing touches on their fond desecration of Johnny Burke's lyrics and Jimmy Van Heusen's tune:

> *A duck is animal that flies around town*
> *Try him if you're looking to get down*
> *Named after champagne in a paper cup*
> *When he flies upside down, he sure quacks up*
> *And if you don't mind how badly things will suck*
> *You might grow up to be a duck*

Our listeners liked that one. Three puns in one verse made it their kind of lyric. When the applause had faded, Erin put a hand on my arm to get my attention. "I think I've found the problem, Pop," she said.

"I'm not sure you should call him that," Willard said.

"While I've never been sure what to call the kind of music your father plays, it's definitely not Pop."

She gave him deadpan. So did his wife, Maureen, whose distaste for puns rivals Erin's. No accounting for distaste.

Willard grinned at both of them. "Folkaoke, maybe?"

I was suddenly too agitated for repartee. "You've found the problem," I prompted Erin.

She nodded and offered me some printout. I glanced at it, but one glance was enough. "This is in Bullshit."

"You can say that again," she said, "bearing in mind that if you actually do, I'll bite you. And don't call me Shirley. I'll translate the important bits into Human for you."

"Wait," I said, holding up a hand. "Hey, Drink—hit me again, harder." Behind the bar, Long-Drink waved acknowledgment and turned to The Machine. If I had to be exposed to Gummint Regulations, I wanted fortification. "Okay, honey, go ahead," I said bravely.

"The Home Education Program comes under Florida Statute 232.0201. It says that parents who choose to teach and direct the education of their own children at home must notify their district school superintendent, and, quote, 'meet the other requirements of this law.' It says, 'Parents bear the teaching responsibility in this option . . .'—news flash—'. . . and the child must show educational progress each year.'" She did not glance down at the papers she held, but her voice told me she was quoting.

Long-Drink arrived with my Irish coffee, and I took a big gulp, waving thanks to him with the mug. "What are these *requirements* we're supposed to meet?" I asked Erin.

"The law requires an annual educational evaluation, which the parent or guardian must file with his district school superintendent's office."

"When?"

"The state doesn't say, exactly."

"What *does* it say?"

Again she became Quote-Robot: "'Some superintendents have established deadlines for receiving the evaluation in order to help them with their bookkeeping. While nothing in the law requires families to comply with a particular date, most families do comply unless circumstances make it impossible to do so.'" She went on in her normal voice, "Especially since the superintendent in his or her sole discretion determines whether the evaluation is satisfactory or not."

Already I was beginning to get a headache. This definitely sounded like state law, all right. "I don't think you're doing enough translating, honey: it still sounds like Bullshit. We do have to comply, but we don't, unless we don't want to get screwed, in which case we do. What exactly is this furshlugginer evaluation supposed to consist of?"

She shrugged. "It can be any one of five things. One, individual assessment by a Florida-certified teacher. There are some who do that full-time, like circuit judges."

I pictured the kind of teacher who could be permanently spared from actual teaching duties to do that gig. Like being surgeon general, or vice president: a distinction that disgraces you. "Pass."

"Agreed. Two, a nationally normed student achievement test, administered by a certified teacher. Three, a state student assessment test. Four, a psych evaluation. Or five, 'any other method that is mutually agreed upon by the parent(s) and the superintendent.'"

The first four all sounded horrid; the last didn't sound like anything at all. "So, which method have we been using, so far?"

She kept her features smooth. "None."

"No!" I couldn't believe I had blown off paperwork this

crucial. After losing my first bar for that very mistake, had I really made it again, badly enough to risk costing me the custody and company of my only child? "Oh, *fuck* me—"

"Best offer I've had in half an hour," Harry brayed.

Erin put a hand on my shoulder. "Relax, Daddy—we didn't *need* to do any of those things. We had a waiver. An unofficial one, a special understanding with the district superintendent. Until recently."

"We did? Really? How did I pull that off?"

"Remember that time we all went on that vacation cruise with Uncle Trav for a whole week?"

I smiled just thinking of it. "I'll remember that trip a month after they cremate me."

"Remember the lady Uncle Bbiillll brought with him?"

Nobody but Erin can pronounce Double Bill's name that way. I've heard several try. "Yes, I do. Remarkable woman. Morgan Something."

"Morgan Sorensen. That was her."

"That was who?"

"She was the district superintendent of schools. The operative word being *was*."

I nodded. "I can see how that would be. She was at least an order of magnitude too smart to have that job, and almost certainly too good a teacher to waste on it. What I don't understand is how she ever acquired the post in the first place."

"Inheritance. Her brother died in office, and she agreed to fill out his term. What with one thing and another—Peter Principle, I suspect—she was still there eleven years later. Six months ago, she retired and moved away."

I finished my Irish coffee. "It's *not* just an expression. I can actually feel my eyeballs glazing over."

"Her successor is a professional chairwarmer named Dhozi Pilok."

"If this conversation goes on much longer, they're going to be big glass marbles—"

"You lost your marbles a long time ago!" Harry the Parrot crowed. (Um.)

"He's got you there, Jake," Alf said.

Erin raised her volume just enough to regain control of the discussion. "Nearly done now. Superintendent Pilok's mistress is Field Inspector Ludnyola Czrjghnczl—ah, multiculturalism!—which basically means she has a mandate to do any goddamn thing she feels like doing within the world of Florida education. And as I suspected, Ludnyola turns out to be the third cousin twice removed of Smithtown Town Inspector Jorjhk Grtozkzhnyi. With Ukrainians, that makes them as close as, say, an Italian brother and sister."

"Terrific." I sighed. "Well, at least now I understand why th—what's wrong, honey?"

To my consternation Erin suddenly burst into tears. "Oh, Pop—*it's all my fault.*"

Automatically I got up and put my arms around her. "What the hell are you talking about? The only thing in the round world that's all your fault is that damn tattoo."

In the midst of crying, she couldn't help smiling at that line, which of course was why I'd said it. But the smile lasted for less than a second. "Remember the day we left Long Island?"

"Vividly," I assured her.

"What's the very last thing I did?"

I thought about it. "Uh . . ."

"Just as we were pulling away."

Suddenly I remembered. "Oh, *hell* yeah—that was beautiful! Old Nyjmnckra Grtozkzhnyi came waddling out to the roadside to see us all leave, to gloat over having driven us out of the state, and as I drove past her, you—"

"I gave her the finger."

I laughed out loud remembering it. So did Ralph, who'd been there on our bus at the time. Erin had still been in diapers, back then: Nyjmnckra's expression had been something to see.

"And she fainted dead away, fell over on her back, and made an angel in the snow," Erin said, and I laughed even harder.

And then stopped. I began to see what she meant. "And you think her nephew Jorjhk has been hunting us ever since, planning his revenge."

She nodded against my shoulder. "Oh, Papa, I knew even then. Less than two years old, and I already knew it was a mistake to do that." Her arms tightened around me. "I was just so mad at Ms. Grtozkzhnyi."

"Hell, so was I, honey. That silly woman ruined everything we had. And all I ever did to her was answer the door. Spilling that beaker of piss on her was *totally* accidental—"

"Sure. But don't you remember what Lady Sally said about vengeance?"

I shook my head.

"She said, 'Vengeance is counterproductive, always. Not to mention the fact it gets your soul all sticky.' I should have remembered. But I was too angry at Nyjmnckra, for hurting you and Mom."

I hugged her even harder. "Hard to think straight when you're mad."

"Honest to God, Pop," she said, "sometimes I really wonder about evolution. The whole fight-or-flight business . . . I just don't understand it. I can't remember one time when adrenaline ever *helped* me in a crisis. Usually it spoils my judgment, makes my knees tremble and my hands shake, makes my voice sound quavery and unthreatening, and screws up my reflexes. Wouldn't you think anger would make you *smarter*? Calmer? Instead it's a cliché that if you can get your opponent angry, you have the fight half won. The natural, hardwired human response to sudden crisis is to drop IQ points. How did we ever last this long?"

Fast Eddie spoke up. "Da madder ya get, da less effective ya get. I got no problem wit dat. Maybe dat's ezzackly how we lasted dis long."

Eddie doesn't say much, but when he does, the result is often a short thoughtful silence on the part of those within earshot.

"All right, enough of this," I said finally. "Flipping old Nyjmnckra the Pierre Trudeau Salute may indeed have pissed her off. But she was plenty pissed off at us to begin with. There's no reason to believe the very last thing we did to annoy her had any sort of threshold effect. In any case, the question is irrelevant. The point is, what are we going to do about this?"

"Get me evaluated, somehow," Erin said.

Alf spoke up. "Evaluated in some way that suits . . . Look, let's all just start calling her Ludnyola, okay? My throat hurts when I try to say her name." Agreement was nodded or grunted generally. "In some way that suits Ludnyola."

"She was suited when she got here," Doc Webster said. People blinked at him. "Alf said we had to suit her," he explained. "Well, she was suited to start with. That silly 'power suit.'" He snorted. "Like all other kinds of suits were hand-cranked."

I was starting to wonder about the Doc. Over the years I'd heard him make some very lame puns, sometimes so abstruse it was days before I realized they'd been puns. But I had never heard him explain one before.

Willard Hooker cut to the chase. "Well, we can't figure out

what sort of evaluation we need to fake until we consult some experts tomorrow during business hours. I say the only sensible thing to do now is make supper and then get drunk."

This suggestion met with general approval. I realized I was starving, myself. "Who's cooking tonight?" I asked.

It happens that among the staff and regular clientele of The Place we have, these days, seven people generally deemed competent to cook for the group, each with his or her own unique culinary style. There's no system to the rotation or anything; dinner just tends to get made by whoever consensus agrees should do so that night. Anybody who eats some tosses some cash into the cigar box at the end of the bar before they leave, in whatever amount they deem appropriate. Maybe it wouldn't work with another group. Okay, probably.

Zoey says we're the first commune in history that don't live together. Not the only one, mind you: there are several of them on the Internet right now, and at least one of them has a membership numbered in the high six figures. But our group first achieved telepathic communion back in the 1970s—well before ARPANET evolved into even Usenet, much less the World Wide Web—so I'm pretty sure we hold the record.

"Well," Marty Pignatelli spoke up, "I was planning to make an Italian rabbit stew for everybody, but you managed to find a way to screw that up, Jake."

"Oh, Fifty-Fifty," I said, shaking my head theatrically. We had all started calling Marty Pignatelli Fifty-Fifty that year to break his chops, the logic being that he was a retired policeman—*Five-Oh* in street parlance—and had just turned fifty. I smelled a pun coming, now, chiefly because Marty was *not* one of the seven competent cooks, and I decided to help him out by supplying the shortest distance between two puns: a straight-line. "What could I possibly have done to spoil your cooking plans?"

He didn't let me down. "Not buy the hare of my guinea din-din."

It was decided, by instant consensus, that Marty really ought to be chatting with Lex rather than with us, and he was delivered there airmail by an ad hoc committee. He made an impressive splash, exciting general merriment.

Most important to me, my daughter's dark mood of self-recrimination vanished in a silver cascade of giggles.

That sort of set the tone. The crisis was over now, the emergency past for the moment, problems remained to be solved, but for the moment there was no pressing reason for us to stay sober. First Willard and Maureen and Eddie and I finished our parodic desecration of "Swingin' on a Star" together—

> *Or would you like to swing with your wife?*
> *Eat your beans and peas with a knife?*
> *And be smarter dead than in life?*
> *Or would you rather be a dork?*
>
> *But if you've got some manners and class*
> *And you ain't a pain in the ass*
> *And you've an itch to pitch you a glass*
> *In an amazing state of grace*
> *You could be swinging at The Place!*

—and after that, Eddie and I did one of our usual sets of whatever piano and guitar tunes entered our heads, and by the time we were ready for a break, Willard had finished barbecuing, and about then the evening crowd started to arrive, and what with one thing and another, The Place managed—

in spite of the brief shocking infestation of the Bureaucrat from Hell—to return to what we like to consider normal, at least for the rest of that night.

Zoey came plodding home in the small hours. She looked like an unusually lovely zombie and moved like Lawrence three-quarters of the way to Aqaba. Bass players work *hard*. Especially on Duval Street.

Some of the plodding, of course, was due to the fact that she was towing her ax behind her. Minga is a big brute of a standup bass, which produces a sound so powerful Zoey's never bothered to electrify her, but even in the wheeled case I built for her, she just barely qualifies as portable. Erin keeps offering to just teleport the thing home for her mother after gigs, and I suspect one of these days Zoey's going to take her up on it. Art ain't easy.

By then everyone but me had gone home, and the compound residents—Eddie, Doc and Mei-Ling, Tom Hauptman, Long-Drink, Tommy Janssen, Pixel, Alf, Lex and even, thank God, Harry—had all gone to bed in their various cottages. I still had a few closing-up chores to do behind the bar, but nothing that wouldn't keep until tomorrow. I stopped whatever I was doing, came around the bar, and joined my beloved in the last fifty yards of her March to the Sack.

"Hi," I said.

Pause, several slow strides long. "Mmrm," she agreed finally.

"Glad it went well, Spice." Her face was slack with fatigue, but I could tell it had been a very good gig: the corners of her mouth turned up perceptibly.

She nodded once. Long pause. "Gate."

"Yeah, Omar's fixing it. It got split down the middle. I told him to leave a scar."

Pause. Then one eyebrow twitched. "Big Beef."

"Right."

She grunted approval. We were already in our cottage by then. She let go of Minga's case handle in the middle of the living room and, freed of her weight, seemed to almost float into the bedroom. Where she waited, patient as a horse being unsaddled, while I undressed her. It is, I find, a vastly interesting experience to undress the most beautiful and desirable woman in the world, and to know with equal certainty both that she feels exactly the same about you, and that if you attempt the slightest sexual liberty *now*, she will kill you with a single blow. There ought to be a word for frustration that doesn't make it sound like a bad thing. I stopped chatting to devote my full attention to the task.

As soon as I was done, Zoey toppled over into bed like a felled tree—a fascinating thing to watch, from start to a couple of moments after the finish, when the ripples died down. I heard her eyelids slam shut, and she made a small purring sound deep in her throat. But my wife is a polite person; before surrendering to unconsciousness, she turned her face toward me and murmured, " 'thing 'kay, Spice?"

Tough choice to make. I knew she was physically and mentally exhausted, knew she had earned her rest, knew there was nothing useful she could possibly do about anything until she woke up anyway.

I also knew, to a fair degree of certainty, what she would say tomorrow if I let her go to sleep without telling her. The question was, was I hero enough to accept that penance, in order to give my beloved a good night's rest.

Well, maybe I would have been . . . but I hesitated too long making my choice. One of her eyelids flicked, as if it were thinking about opening, and she repeated, " 'thing 'kay?"

I suppressed a sigh. As casually as I knew how, I said, "A

little hassle came up, but nothing you need worry about now. Erin and I have it covered."

She made a half-inch sketch of a nod. There was a long pause, and just as I'd decided she was under and I was home free, her eyelid twitched again, and she mumbled, "Wha' hassle?"

This time my sigh emerged. "Well—" Further amphigory would only be counterproductive. I wish they made a tasty bullet. "—this afternoon a state education inspector showed up. She says she's going to put Erin in foster care because we're unfit parents. No big deal. Go to sleep."

For about ten seconds I thought I had pulled it off. Then one of her eyes opened wide. "Name."

"Ludnyola Czrjghnczl. Accent on the *rjgh*."

The eye powered up, swiveled to track me. "Oh, my God. A relative of—"

I hastily nodded, to spare her throat. She'd been breathing barroom air all night. "You guessed it."

Both eyes were open now, though the second wasn't tracking yet. "Was she carrying a briefcase?"

"Afraid so."

She was sitting bolt upright in bed. I hadn't seen her move. "Job title."

"Senior Field Inspector, Florida Department of Ed."

Her second eye caught up with the first and locked on to me. "The homeschooling scam came apart?"

I nodded, and she groaned. "Oh, *shit*."

A man has to know when he's in over his head. What kind of coward would wake his teenager in the middle of the night to help him deal with an emergency? This kind. I fiddled with my watch, and Erin materialized next to us, and after that, a whole *lot* of words got said, but I can't think of a reason to burden you with any of them.

It wasn't *that* bad. It could have gone much worse. It was no more than half an hour after dawn when I managed to get the last of us—me—to sleep. But the upshot was, all three of us started the next day feeling unusually tired . . . and of course, it turned out to be a worse day than the one before.

Not that it started out that way.

I was able to sleep in a little, for one thing. I run the kind of bar where it's not strictly necessary for me to be there when it opens. Everybody knows where everything is, and just about any of them is competent to step in and serve a newcomer if need be. (It must be hell to serve alcohol to people you don't trust with your life.)

When I finally emerged, showered and nearly human, from my home into the morning light, Long-Drink McGonnigle was behind the bar, and the dozen or so people in front of it all seemed content with his stewardship. A glance at the sun told me it was early afternoon on a nice day, if that last clause isn't redundant in Key West. Two steps later, I stopped in my tracks, paralyzed by a dilemma that might have killed a lesser man.

Two paths lay before me. The right-hand path led to the pool—where Zoey sprawled in a chaise longue, sunbathing. (Not tanning. Thanks to the Callahans, none of us is capable of it. Our bodies don't believe in ionizing radiation, any more than they believe in bullets. Perhaps this is regrettable—but since it kept us from being toasted by an exploding atom bomb once, I've never quite managed to regret it.) My Zoey has the most beautiful body I've ever seen—have I mentioned this?—as generously lush as my own is parsimoniously scrawny, the kind of body Rubens or Titian would have leapt to paint, the kind they call BBW on Usenet, and when it glistens with perspiration . . . Well, it glistens, that's all.

But the *left*-hand path led to coffee.

I might be standing there now, my nose still pulling me in two different directions, if I hadn't noticed the small bucket of coffee my darling had placed on the flagstone beside her recliner.

"Can I have some of your coffee, Spice?"

She raised her sunglasses. "If it's worth your life to you."

"Thanks." Cuban Peaberry, it was, somewhere between a medium and a dark roast. To forestall my assassination, I took a seat down at the end of the recliner and began rubbing her feet. Young men, forget Dr. Ruth and heed the advice of a middle-aged fart: Rub her tootsies. This is the only Jungle Love Technique you will ever need; done properly, it will melt a Valkyrie.

"Have some more coffee," Zoey murmured shortly. And a little later, "All right, you win; I will tell you of our troop movements." Then nothing but purring for a while.

After I judged enough time had gone by, I said, "Has Erin filled you in?"

"Yes. It *ought* to be manageable. She's working on it now."

As if we'd invoked her, Erin came out of the house just then. From a distance, in shorts and halter and bare feet, she looked pretty enough to make a bishop dance the dirty boogie. Closer up, though, the frown spoiled the effect a little. Nobody can frown like a new teenager.

When she reached us, she dropped like a sack of laundry into the chaise longue next to Zoey's and said, "I think we're screwed."

"I'm just rubbing her feet," I said.

"Good morning to you, too," her mother said, ignoring me.

"Good morning," Erin conceded.

"That's better. How screwed?"

"The *law* says just what I thought it did: We can get me evaluated by quote any Florida-certified teacher unquote."

"But—?"

"Well, to put it in technical terms, Ludnyola has the whammy on us. She didn't just pull some strings; she winched some cables. The deck is not just cold, she's dipped it in liquid nitrogen. I won't tell you the details of how she rigged it, because I'd get too mad. But the ultimate carriage-return is, there's now one and only one person in the state of Florida authorized to evaluate me."

Zoey and I groaned together. How odd that our groans of genuine dismay sounded precisely like the moans of pleasure Zoey had been making as I rubbed her feet.

"You guessed it," Erin confirmed. "Accent on the *rjgh*—as in, 'What a dorjgkh!'"

Zoey and I exchanged a glance. "Screwed," I said, and she nodded.

"Well . . . ," Erin said, and trailed off.

After a while, her mother said, "You won't be well for long if you don't finish the sentence."

"Well, we may have one thing going for us. I'm afraid to trust it, though."

Why does evolution require humans approaching puberty to become exasperating? My theory is, so their parents will go away and let them get some experimenting done. The only defense is to refuse to be exasperated. (Or, of course, to go away.) After another while, Zoey said gently, "I might better advise you if I had some sense of what it is."

"What what is?"

"The one thing we may have going for us that you're afraid to trust."

"Oh, yeah—sorry. It sounds paradoxical, but the only edge we may have is that Ludnyola is a real bureaucrat."

Zoey and I were beginning to be tired of exchanging glances, so we stopped. "This is good?"

"In a twisted way. It could have been much worse: she could have been like half the other people in civil service."

"Who are—?"

"Who are chair-warming buck-passing trough-slurping fakes, *pretending* to be bureaucrats because that's an acceptable excuse for not being a human being. As far as I can tell from study of her record and interrogation of her computer, Ludnyola is the genuine article: a machine with a pulse."

"Yeah, so?" I grasped the distinction, and from my limited acquaintance with the field inspector, agreed with Erin's analysis . . . but I still didn't see how this helped our cause. I suspected caffeine deficiency, and signaled Long-Drink to send a Saint Bernard.

Zoey seemed to get it, though. "Is that true, Jake?" she asked.

"Yeah, she's Mr. Spock without the charm, all right. So what. Why is this good for the Jews?"

"Don't you grok, Daddy? From everything I've been able to learn about her, she's a cyborg. And cyborgs *always* follow their programming. They *have* to."

"Sure. And she's programmed like a Saberhagen Berserker . . . or an Ebola virus molecule."

"She's not an assassin, Daddy; she's a bureaucrat. They live and die by rules. By *the* rules. If we are very lucky, if she's as genuine and as hardcore as we think she is, it just won't be *possible* for her to break the rules, any more than an Asimov robot could punch somebody."

Alf arrived with the drinks cart; I thanked him, gave him a quick scratch around the base of the horns (who doesn't enjoy that, eh?), and traded Zoey's empty for the new coffee. It was Tanzanian Peaberry, roasted by Bean Around The World up in British Columbia, the mere scent of which always kick-starts my cortex. Sure enough, after only one sip—okay, gulp—I saw with crystal clarity that I was still confused.

Zoey saw it, too. "Jake, take it from the top."

"Okay. Ludnyola wants to take our kid away and put her in hell. *Using* the goddamn rules." More coffee. It was literally priceless then. No Tanzanian coffee was sold anywhere in the world that year, because all the Tanzanians who were supposed to harvest the coffee either were butchered or starved to death. The only way to get any was to have a teleport who loved you in your family.

"What is her thesis?" Zoey prompted.

"We're shitty parents."

"And her proof of this is that we—"

Light finally dawned. *"Ah."*

"—that you did a shitty job of educating me," Erin supplied. "And you *didn't.*"

"We didn't do a damn thing!" I felt obliged to point out, though I was already beginning to see what she meant.

"Exactly. You stayed out of my way. How many *universities* have that much sense? It was a terrific education."

"—and we can prove it," Zoey said.

"Exactly," Erin agreed. "If she has any doubts after ten minutes of conversation, let her give me the Mensa test! Or any other test she's capable of comprehending herself—I've got more IQ points on her than she *weighs,* Daddy."

I wanted to agree with them and cheer up, but I just couldn't seem to work it up. "And you think if we just prove to her that she's wrong, she'll go away?"

She sighed. "Well, like I said, I'm afraid to trust it. But if she's a *genuine* bureaucrat—"

"I don't know," I said, finishing my coffee. "I think you may be underestimating the ability of even the most robotic bureaucrat to *interpret* the rules. Remember, she's related by blood to Beelzebub."

"That's the question," Erin agreed. "How important is family to a robot? Cousin Jorjhk, back on Long Island, was as corrupt, venal, and nepotistic as any other public official on Long Island: one glance at his record will tell you that. But Ludnyola here comes across as . . . well, as a laser beam. *Straighter* than any straight arrow. I think she got into this because she believed what her relatives told her, and what she saw yesterday didn't help: she thinks we're all some kind of cult of anarchists and hippies."

"We're not?" I said, and Zoey pinched me. Never mind where. By the poolside, okay?

"She'll never understand us much better than that; she's not equipped. But we don't need her to. If I'm reading her right, the only thing she cares about is whether my education has been neglected. We can demonstrate that it has not, no matter how she may stack the deck. That may be enough to deactivate her—whatever she may privately *wish* she could do to us."

"I follow the logic," I agreed, and looked for words to explain my doubt. "Back in the late sixties, I lived in Boston for a while. There was a drug cop there like you're talking about, Sergeant Holtz. Like Inspector Teal in the Saint stories, he lived by the rules, and as long as he didn't catch you violating any laws, you were safe from him. This made him unique among drug cops, then or ever. Well, this one pot wholesaler who thought he was as slick as the Saint—come to think of it, his name was Simon—used to yank Holtz's chain all the time. Simon was slick enough to get away with it, too, was never on the same *block* as probable cause. But he was unwise enough to rent a third-floor walkup . . . and one night Sergeant Holtz arrested him for coming home.

"He'd turned up the fact that Simon was one-eighth Mohawk—it probably wasn't hard, the guy used to brag about it—and then he'd done a little research. Turned out there was a very old law still on the books in Boston, then—might still be, for all I know—that made it illegal for an Indian to go above the first floor in any public dwelling. Sergeant Holtz explained matters to a judge who was just as much of a stickler for rules as he was, and Simon would have done time if he hadn't jumped bail."

"Okay, I get your point," Erin said. "But Simon really was a drug dealer, Pop. I'm really not an uneducated kid."

"Agreed. The trick will be to overcome Ludnyola's presumption that you are one. Whether we can depends on how thick her blinders are. And I'd have to say in the short time I shared with the Field Inspector, her mind seemed as made up as a bed the second week of boot camp."

"Oh, big deal," Erin said. "I don't see what everybody's worried about, anyway. No matter what, she's not taking me away from you guys."

I didn't say anything. Neither did Zoey. When neither of us had said anything for several seconds, Erin repeated, "She's *not*," with rising pitch and volume.

"Of course not," her mother said gently. "But think it through, honey. If she comes after us, she has the whole machinery of the state behind her."

"So? We can whip 'em all!"

"Sure," I said. "But not without causing talk."

"Oh. Shit."

"If a state cop whips me upside the head with a baton, and I don't seem to mind, he and all the other policeman will become very curious to know why not. Sooner or later they'll learn me and my family are bulletproof, too, and then we'll be talking to a lot of humorless people from Langley, and life will be *much* less fun. Those guys would have uses for bullet-proof people—ugly ones. One way or another, it'd be the end of The Place; I doubt they'd leave us alone to drink in the sun." I reached for an empty mug and started to pour myself a beer.

"I'm not going underground at my age," Zoey said. "I took that class."

"Wait a minute!" Erin said. "So are you saying if we can't head her off, I'm supposed to *go* with that nimrod? To some foster home?" The pitch of her voice began rising on the second word, and by the last it was close to supersonic. I opened my mouth to reply, genuinely curious to hear what I would say, but I never got to, because just then the man monster walked in.

It was as though he had been constructed specifically to refute my belief that a bureaucrat is the scariest thing there is. He was good at it, too.

First of all, he was big as a mastodon. I saw him right away, before he even entered the compound, and I spilled the beer I was pouring myself. I take great care not to spill beer. He had to turn sideways to come through the open gateway, which is not small. I remembered big Jim Omar carrying that gate away in one hand, an hour or two earlier, and estimated that this guy could have carried Omar *and* the gate in the same effortless way.

It wasn't until you got past the sheer mountain-out-for-a-stroll size of him and got a close look at his face that you *really* started to get scared.

Look, he wasn't quite as big as the late great Andre the Giant, okay? And if Andre was ever defeated in the ring, I never heard about it. But the moment I saw this guy's eyes, I knew he could take on an armed squad of angry combat-trained Andres, barehanded, with a high degree of confidence. And probably would have, given the opportunity, for no other reason than to prove he was alpha male. I stared at those eyes of his for several long seconds, and the first human emotion I was able to identify there was a very mild disappointment that none of us men present was enough of a challenge to be any fun to kill. I felt keen relief. He ignored all the women present. I sensed that to him women were interchangeable; when he was ready, he would simply take the nearest one.

Then his eyes went toward the spot where my thirteen-year-old daughter was sitting.

3

BIG STONES

It's funny. I knew, for a fact, that there was no way he could form a real danger to Erin. Try to bear-hug her, he'd end up holding her empty clothes. Try to shoot her, he'd be in serious jeopardy from the ricochet. Try to outsmart her, and gods who'd been dead a thousand years would come back to life just to laugh at him. I knew all that. Do you think it made the slightest difference in how I reacted? If so, you must be childless. Some of the basic human wiring is buried so deep it simply *cannot* be dug up and replaced with fiber-optic cable. I wanted him dead, wanted to do it myself, and knew I would die trying. Every gland in my body went into full production.

But Erin was not where she had been sitting a moment ago. She was *behind* the man monster now, looking at *me*. Her face was expressionless, but her eyes seemed slightly brighter than anything else in my visual field, twin tractor beams locked on my own eyes. Far away, someone said something. I found myself remembering what Erin had said yesterday about the fight-or-flight response. Were those really the only two alternatives? I hoped not. He didn't look like a fight I wanted any part of, and I was not going to flee my home. I'd done that more than once in the past, and I was sick of it.

I perceived that Erin was breathing in and out in long, slow, measured breaths. I could almost hear her voice saying, *We can't afford to give up any IQ points, Pop,* and I knew it was true. I struggled to follow her example, for the ten or twenty seconds it took the man monster to reach the bar area, and by the time he was close enough for me to throw peanuts at, I was getting a pretty good supply of oxygen to the cerebral cortex, and beginning to feel fairly confident of bladder control.

Unfortunately, by then he was close enough to smell. Something about his smell went straight to some atavistic part of my brain that lay even deeper than the basic human wiring. Externally it was as though my friend Nikola Tesla were playing one of his benign practical jokes with electricity on me: every single hair on my body tried to stand on end at once. The silhouette of my head must have expanded by 10 percent.

I forced myself to devote all my energy to my breath, like Captain Kirk telling Sulu to divert all power to the shields. In. *Om mani padme hum.* Out. *Om mani padme hum.* In. *O pinupdi podbe dorhal—*

The man monster reached the bar; cleared a section of debris such as drinks, coasters, ashtrays, and bowls of snack food with his forearms; and leaned forward to rest his weight on them. The groaning of the bar top coincided with a squeal from the foot rail below. Our faces were now two or three feet apart.

In spite of myself, kicking myself for it, I dropped my eyes from his. Only then did I take in how he had dressed to come to south Florida. Dark double-breasted suit. White shirt with button-down collar. Wide necktie. Stingy-brim fedora. I already knew he wasn't local—no way he could live on an island the size of Key West for as long as a week without every Conch hearing about him. In my years as a barkeep, I've become pretty good at guessing where the tourists are from, but this guy was almost too easy: he fit one of the oldest templates I have on file. The way I phrased it to myself was, *from the neighborhood: half a wise guy.* I glanced quickly over at Fast Eddie and saw that he had spotted it, too; he rolled his eyes at me.

So I was less surprised than I might have been when the monster made a perfunctory left-right sketch of looking around the place and said, in a voice like a garbage disposal working on a wristwatch, words anyone else would have realized were a ridiculous cliché:

"This a real nice joint ya got here, chief. Be a fuckin' shame if somep'm bad was ta happena the place, ah?"

Down at the end of the bar, Maureen emitted a gasp that was almost a shriek, and then clapped a hand over her mouth.

I didn't blame her. He was an evolutionary throwback. Go to any museum with a diorama of Early Man, shave the Missing Link down to a ten o'clock shadow like an extremely coarse grade of sandpaper, and you'll have something very like his face. Failing that, there are a couple of Frank Frazetta cover paintings that depict him trying to rip Tarzan's throat out.

Okay, Mr. Sulu—divert a little power to the voice.

To my great relief, it did not quaver when I said, as nonchalantly as I could manage, "I've always thought so." I forced myself to meet his eyes. "Not for nothing, but you're a long way from home, ain't you, pal?" I asked.

He squinted at me and pursed his lips. He was thinking about frowning at me, and if he did, I was going to have to drop my eyes again. "You born inna Bronx, chief?"

I nodded. "Moved out to the Island when I was six."

He aborted the frown. "Oh. For a minute there, I t'ought you was squeezin my shoes, talkin at way." Without warning he smiled, and I needed full impulse power to keep the blood from draining from my head. "Okay. So you unnastan the way things work. Terrific." The smile went away, like a furnace door slamming shut. "Half a the mutts down here, I gotta drawer 'em a pitcher, an then come back inna couple days when they heal up enough to talk again. Waste a fuckin time, nome sane?"

"Yeah, I know what you're saying," I said. "We don't get many guys like you in Key West. You're the first I've seen, and I've been down here ten years."

He shrugged. "All good things come to a end, chief. You own iss dump?"

"On paper," I agreed. "I'm Jake Stonebender. What's your name?"

He smirked. "Fuck difference it make, really? Like you just said, there's only the one of me."

"I have to call you something."

Very slowly, his massive head went left . . . right . . . stopped. "No, ya don't."

"I don't?"

"You ain't gonna be talkin about me. Unna stanwhum sane?"

I sighed. "Aright. You wanna bottom-line this for me or what?" Amazing how easily New Yorkese came back to me, after all those years. Some things you never forget, I guess: like stealing a bicycle.

He took a step back and turned in a slow circle. People

seemed to wither slightly under his gaze, in a wave, like wind passing through a wheatfield. Even Harry the Parrot was silent. The only one who didn't flinch was Fast Eddie, who grew up in darkest Brooklyn back when there were Dodgers there. Willard and Maureen actually ducked their heads and averted their faces.

The man monster took in the entire compound: the bar area with its big freestanding stone fireplace, the nearby pool, the scatter of tables and chairs, the five cottages, the shell and coral gravel parking area to the south that rarely held anything but bikes and mopeds, the flaming canopy of poinciana overhead, the handful of obligatory palm trees here and there, and the tall thick hedge that enclosed and shielded the property on all sides. With no apparent pause for computation, he named a sum. "That's what I figure ya take in, here, an average week."

I shook my head. "You're high. Way high."

He shook his. "Not when I'm workin. Now, I can prackly guarantee ya no trouble here for only a quarter a that."

"Twenty-five percent is pretty stiff," I said evenly. My hands were starting to ache from wishing they held a shotgun.

"Not when ya add it up," he said. "No fire . . . no explosions . . . no armed robberies . . . no random drive-bys . . . no customers mugged or raped onna way in or out . . . no wakin up onna bottom a the pool strapped to a safe . . . ya add it all up, chief, it's a fuckin bargain."

When in doubt, stall. "I have a partner I have to consult first."

"Notify, ya mean. Where's he at?"

I shrugged as eloquently as I could. It wasn't quite a lie: as long as I didn't look at my watch, I couldn't be certain whether Zoey was still rehearsing, or setting up for the gig. I poured a shot of Chivas and slid it across the bar to him. "Give me forty-eight hours."

He thought it over. So far I had not said or done anything disrespectful, even for form's sake. "Okay." He gulped the shot, turned on his heel, and lumbered away, dropping the shot glass onto the cement beside the pool as he passed it. It broke, a musical period to his overture.

It was quite a while after he was gone before anyone moved or spoke.

"Holy this," Brad said finally. "How *saw* that guy, Jake?"

"Yeah," Walter agreed. "And what want he did exactly here?"

"Well, I didn't get his name," I said, "but I bet I can guess the name of the organization he represents."

"You're wrong, Jake," Maureen Hooker said.

Something in her voice made me look down the bar to her. Nearly all of us Callahan's Place alumni tend to tan so poorly that we're always being mistaken by tourists for other tourists. But now Maureen was *pale*, the kind of fish-belly white you usually see only on a night-shift worker from Vladivostok. So, I suddenly realized, was her husband Willard. Since I happened to know them both, from conclusive personal experience, to be about as timid and panicky as your average Navy SEAL, this caught my attention. "You're telling me that guy is *not* mobbed up?"

Willard answered. "You know the way some respectable Italian-American citizens resent the Mafia, for making all Italians look bad?"

"Sure," Fifty-Fifty said, and I nodded Irish agreement.

"Well, that's the way Mafiosi feel about him. They figure a guy like him makes regular Italian murderers and thieves look bad."

"Which is just backwards," Maureen added. "He makes Capone and Mad Dog Coll look good."

Doc Webster cleared his throat loudly. "All right, goddamn

it, if nobody else will ask, I will: Who *was* that massed man?"
He paused a moment for people to resume breathing. "And
where do you two know him from?"

Maybe Maureen's wince was due to the Doc's pun. (Mine
was.) And maybe it wasn't. "I've never seen him before in my
life, Doc. But there's only one person he could possibly be."

Her husband nodded glumly. "And until five minutes ago
I'd have told you, with some confidence, that he couldn't possibly exist."

Maureen half turned in her chair to face him. "But there
isn't any doubt, is there, sweet?"

Willard was frowning so ferociously he looked like a
migraine victim. "Not in my mind," he said, and opened his
arms.

They hugged each other hard.

The Doc cleared his throat again, perhaps half an octave
higher, and said in his very softest, gentlest voice, "The first
one who tells me who that guy is might very well be allowed
to live."

Willard sighed. "That guy," he told us all, stroking his wife's
hair, "pretty much has to be the son of Tony Donuts."

"I believe you," I said. "That's so weird, it almost has to be
true. But it doesn't *tell* me anything, yet. Who exactly is Tony
Donuts?"

"A memory, now." He shuddered, and I don't think it was
theatrical. "Not a good one."

"Well . . . mixed," Maureen said.

"He was a mixed cursing," her husband agreed. "I can't
deny that."

"Willard and I knew each other for years," Maureen said,
"and at various times we were partners, lovers, friends. For a
while we weren't anything at all. Then Tony Donuts came

into our lives and brought us back together . . . and when the dust settled, we were married."

"Whoa," Long-Drink exclaimed. "And that's not enough to make him a good memory? What was he like?"

Willard looked thoughtful. "Picture the monster that just left here."

Long-Drink frowned. "Okay."

"Two inches taller, fifty pounds heavier, ten years older."

With each successive clause, Long-Drink's frown deepened. "O-kay."

"With a permanently abcessed tooth."

Long-Drink's eyes completely disappeared from view beneath his eyebrows. "Ah," he said.

"That was Tony Donuts on a good day."

There was a brief silence, as we all tried to picture such a creature. "I see," Long-Drink said, though it's hard to imagine how he could have; by now even the bags under his eyes were obscured.

Fifty-Fifty spoke up. "How'd he get that name? Was he a cop once?"

Willard briefly sketched a smile. "No, Marty. He was born Antonio Donnazzio, that's part of it."

"And the rest?"

Willard grimaced. "With children present, I hesitate t—"

"One time he was raping a woman named Mary O'Rourke," Erin said, "and her husband kept trying to stop him." She saw Willard's surprise. "Lady Sally told me the story once. So Tony decided to secure Mr. O'Rourke out of the way, and the tools at hand happened to be a mallet and a pair of large spikes. Afterwards, one of the crime-scene cops voiced the opinion that Mr. O'Rourke's scrotum now looked like a pair of donuts, and the name stuck."

"So did O'Rourke, it sounds 1-*oooch*," Long-Drink said,

the last syllable occasioned by the heavy shoe of Doc Webster.

"So how did you two get mixed up with him?" I asked Willard, to change the subject.

He sighed, looked down, and rubbed at the bridge of his nose. "Well . . . this was back in the days when some people called me the Professor."

Yipes. I had a sudden flashback of several decades, and made a clumsy attempt to interrupt him. "Uh, look, we don't really need to go into this level of detail—"

Maureen was shaking her head. "Thanks, Jake, that's sweet—but it's okay. There isn't a single want or warrant outstanding for anyone of that name, in this or any jurisdiction," she said. "There never was." You could hear the pride in her voice. Not many world-class confidence men can make that claim.

"In the course of business," Willard continued, ignoring my interjection, "I found myself in sudden urgent need of a fair amount of really good funny money. Fifty large, to be exact. So sudden and urgent that I was willing to deal with Tony Donuts, who had only recently finished murdering the best counterfeiter in the country and stealing his equipment. I knew better than to do business with Tony. And I was right, too. Almost the *moment* I had put the amusing currency to its intended use, and it was forever gone from my control . . . Tony decided he wanted it back again. The feds had got on to him, and suddenly he didn't want large blocks of evidence in circulation."

"Jesus," I said, "he wanted you to sell him back his counterfeit fifty grand?"

"No." He shook his head. "Just give it back."

"But that's not fair!" Erin exclaimed.

Willard did not smile. "He said he would keep the phony

fifty thousand . . . plus, to cover his time and general aggravation, the five thousand in real money I'd already paid him for
it . . . and in return, I could keep all twenty fingers and toes,
and my genitalia. Sounded like a fair deal to *me*, at the time.
A bargain, in fact."

"A steal," Maureen said. "With the genitalia."

"Ah," Erin said.

"If I could possibly have returned Tony's moneylike paper,
I would have done so without regret—even though it was the
bait in a million-dollar sting I had working. Unfortunately,
that bait was *gone*, already deep in the water with a large
shark's mouth around it. And disobedience was simply too
novel a concept to risk baffling Tony Donuts with. So I
changed my appearance and went underground at Lady
Sally's House . . . which is where I hooked up with Maureen
again." Without looking, he reached his hand toward her;
without looking, she took it. "That complicated things."

"The Professor couldn't hide in a whorehouse and impress
a girl at the same time," Maureen said, "especially not one
who worked in the whorehouse. So he needed to cool Tony."

Willard took the narration back. I was pretty sure they
hadn't rehearsed this story; maybe they were passing cues
through their joined hands somehow. "There just wasn't any
way to come up with another counterfeit fifty large—not of
that high quality, not quickly."

"Besides, all the Professor's seed money was spent," Maureen said.

"There was only one thing to do," Willard agreed.

After the silence had gone on long enough, I finally got it.
I drew a pint of Rickard's Red and slid it down the bar to him.

"Thank you, Jake." He raised his mug to me, took a long
sip, set the mug down, held up one finger, and looked down at
his belt for a long moment. Finally he threw his head back,

belched ringingly, lowered his finger, and said, "We stiffed
Tony Donuts. We gave him real money."

Well, there was a bit of *rooba-rooba-rooba* over that, of
course. All of us simultaneously saying some version of, *I
thought you said you were broke, where'd you come up with
fifty thousand bucks?* Finally I whistled for silence.

And when I got it—I once studied whistling under a traffic
cop—I said, "I thought you said you were broke. Where'd you
manage to come up with fifty kay?"

"Oh, that." The Professor shrugged. "We robbed a bank."

Pause.

"Of course," I said. "Only sensible thing you could have
done." General murmur of agreement.

He nodded. "Unfortunately, the moment Tony examined
the money we brought him, he recognized that it was bogus.
Or rather, *not* bogus: fake counterfeit, if you will."

"How could he tell?"

He sketched a grimace. "It's a long story."[*]

"And it doesn't matter," Maureen said. "The point is, he
was going to tear us limb from limb, and not metaphorically
speaking either. So we brought the problem to Lady Sally,
and she . . . fixed things." She glanced around automatically,
making sure the lodge was tyled, that all present had been
stooled to the rogue. "When it was over, Tony Donuts was
doing life in a maximum security federal facility . . . and there
is no question it was hard time. The Lady had made certain
subtle alterations to his brain."

"What, you mean like a lobotomy?" Doc Webster asked.

Willard's grimace was a grin now. "Way subtler. And way
nastier. A permanent hand-eye coordination problem. When
Her Ladyship was done with Tony, if he tried to hit some-

body, he *always* missed. By at least an inch. The same if he tried to shoot them, or stab them, or throw something at them, or even just grab them. You might say he always aimed to please." His wife jabbed him with an elbow, but he was expecting it.

I was awed. "I can see where a maximum security prison would be an unfortunate place in which to have a condition like that."

Willard nodded wordlessly, and by now the whole front of his head was mostly grin. Maureen was trying to suppress her own grin, and failing. "Especially for someone too stupid to unlearn a lifetime of aggression and arrogance," she agreed. "I can't imagine he survived long, and death was probably a blessing when it came."

"Anyway," Willard said, "the other upshot of the whole business was . . . the other *two* upshots *were*, that I decided to give up screwing people for a living and become an honest prostitute instead . . . and that Maureen consented to park her cotton balls under my bathroom sink." They kissed. "So things worked out in the end."

"Only it wasn't de end," Fast Eddie said.

Willard and Maureen stopped smiling.

"Apparently not," he admitted. "Whatever the nature of Lady Sally's mojo, either it was not hereditary, or—far more likely—Tony had already spawned by then. The man who just left here did not seem as though he'd ever had much trouble hitting anything he wanted to."

"You're sure he's your Tony's kid," I said.

Willard looked at me. "Jake, can you picture random chance producing a set of genes like that *twice?* Not only am I sure that was Little Tony Donuts, I'm prepared to wager twenty bucks that every single gene his mother tried to contribute to the mix was a recessive that died waiting for reinforcements."

"Another twenty says she died in childbirth," Maureen said. "Nobody has that kind of pelvis anymore."

"He resembles his father *so* closely that even though my forebrain knew better, my hindbrain kept insisting he *was* Tony Donuts. I kept turning my face away so he wouldn't recognize me."

"Me, too!" Maureen said. "Somebody like Tony, you see him again thirty years later, you *expect* him to look absolutely unchanged. Like Mount Rushmore."

"This," Alf said, "is an interestingly tricky situation."

"How do you mean?" fellow quadruped Ralph asked.

"You people have to fight a guy even the Mafia is scared to mess with. But not only can't you kill him . . . you can't even let him try to kill you. For the same reason: It'd cause talk."

"Aw, this is Key West," Long-Drink argued. "People are reasonable, here. Nobody'd mind too much if we put down dangerous wildlife like a Tony Donuts Junior."

I had to side with Alf. "The deer's right, Drink. Sure, the community might well decide Little Nuts needed killin' . . . that's not the point. The point is, even this place isn't so laid back that it's safe to display paranormal powers here. If Tony kills one of us and we don't die, it might take a week or two, but sooner or later we're all gonna find ourselves talking to somebody from Langley, Virginia."

"I think you're all overlooking something," Erin said.

If it seems strange to you that a thirteen-year-old girl got the respectful attention of a barroom full of adults, remember that most of them watched her save the entire macrocosmic universe back before she had a single permanent tooth in her head. "Yes, honey?"

"You keep assuming that just because you can't be harmed by gunfire or explosion, you can't be harmed."

"Oh." She had a point. Mickey Finn's Filarii technology—or "magic," if you prefer—is highly selective. Of course, you'd want it to be. It wouldn't be much good if it simply coated you in invisible plastic: How could somebody kiss you? Mickey explained to us once that it's calibrated to stop only lethal force. Don't ask me how it can tell, *instantly,* whether an incoming missile is going to be fatal or not: Mick did explain it, but none of us understood what he said. The point is, you can shoot me with anything from a bow and arrow to a bazooka, or bomb me with anything from a grenade to a nuke, or hit me with anything from a crowbar to a broadsword, without necessarily capturing my attention, if I happen to be working on an especially interesting crossword puzzle at the time. But if you decide to punch me in the mouth, I'm probably going to lose some teeth.

I knew for a fact I had nothing to fear from atomic weapons. Yet there was an excellent chance that a monster like Little Nuts could hospitalize or kill me with his hands, as long as no single blow was deadly in itself. And even if I owned a gun of sufficiently authoritative caliber to annoy him back, I wouldn't dare use it in any but the most dire emergency. It may be a little hard for you to believe, especially if you live in an American city, but in Key West gunplay is considered bad form.

"Well," I said, "when in doubt, consult an expert."

Zoey grimaced. "Terrific. Who's an expert on exterminating mastodons?"

"Hmm," Long-Drink said. "The definition of expert is, 'an ordinary person, a long way from home.' An ordinary person, far from home, who knows about monsters and how to kill them without getting into the papers . . ."

He and I and Doc Webster and Fast Eddie all said it at once: "Bert!"

Bert D'Ambrosio, aka "Bert the Shirt," is believed to be the only man who was ever allowed to retire from the Mafia.

He was well past middle age, on his way up the courthouse steps in Brooklyn to not-testify in some now-forgotten trial or other, when he had a heart attack and died. The medics managed to get him rebooted within a matter of minutes . . . but as soon as he was back on his feet, he went to see his Don. Look, he said, I died for you: Can I go now? The Godfather must have liked him. After some thought, he told Bert to go keep an eye on the family's interests in Key West.

This was Mafia humor, because there *are* no family interests in Key West, because who in his right mind would bother exploiting an end-of-the-world rat hole and college-student-vomitorium the size of a New York City park, with a speed limit of thirty, way more bicycles than cars, and only one road in or out? Bert thanked Don Vincente and retired to southernmost Florida. Today he's edging into his eighties, and I confidently expect him to dance at my funeral. And the ridiculous thing is, he's still as connected as he ever was, in a quiet sort of way. Somehow, he manages to stay in touch, keep plugged in. He sits there in the sun, in his splendid silk and linen shirts, and people come along and tell him things. Specifically because there is no action here, nothing to get killed over, Guys From The Old Neighborhood (as Bert always calls them) will come through on vacation, from time to time. They say the Don himself actually visited once, before my time.

So Bert seemed the ideal choice for an expert consultant in

the matter of how to deal with an extra-large psychotic extortionist without the neighbors noticing.

For some reason, Erin was nowhere to be found. I left the bar in Tom Hauptman's capable hands, and Zoey and I saddled up and pedaled over to the Paradiso Condos on Smathers Beach. At his age, Bert the Shirt doesn't come to you; you go to him. In fact, I seldom approach Bert these days without reflecting how extraordinary it is that you still *can* approach him without first floating down a tunnel toward a very bright light.

We found him where we expected to, sitting in a lounge chair under an umbrella, watching the zoo parade of beach people across the street. Under the chair, in the small pool of shade it and Bert's bony flanks afforded, lay what looked like a heap of bread dough that hadn't risen very well, except that it pulsed in slow rhythm. As we came near, it rose slightly at one end and emitted a sustained baritone fart that any camel would have been proud to claim. Bert leaned sideways slightly and glowered down at it.

"Hi, Bert. Hi, Don Giovanni," Zoey said happily.

The object under the chair lifted its other end enough to reveal a face, and turned it up toward the sound of Zoey's voice. The face made Bert's look young. Well, younger. Both eyes were so heavily cataracted they looked more like immies than eyes. There were about four surviving whiskers, randomly placed. The nose was the only part of him still capable of running. Basically Don Giovanni is one of the very few blind dogs to have a seeing-eye human.

"Hey, kiddo," Bert said to Zoey with real pleasure. "Whadda ya say?" He nodded politely enough to me, but it was clearly my wife's appearance that had made his day. She gets that a lot.

Today the shirt was midnight blue silk, a wide-collar

thing with an almost liquid sheen and real ivory buttons, an impressive garment even by Bert's standards. As usual, it and his pants were covered with a fine mist of white hairs the length of eyelashes; nonetheless he was almost certainly the snazziest-dressed man in Key West, that or any other day.

"It's time to move him," Zoey replied.

Bert grimaced and nodded fatalistically. Without looking down, he reached under the lounger and tugged Don Giovanni a few inches, until the dog was once again completely in the shade. Don Giovanni shuddered briefly in what might have been gratitude or merely relief, and became completely inert once more. "I'm his personal ozone layer. I never laid anybody from Ozone Park in my life. Hello, Zoey; hiya, Jake—what brings ya all around ta this side a the rock?"

"Trouble," Zoey replied, pulling another lounger up alongside his and sitting down. I did the same on the other side, and Erin sat on the edge of my lounger.

Bert nodded again, even more fatalistically. "Everybody could use a little ozone. What'sa beef?"

Zoey looked at me. Discussing homicidal psychopaths with a representative of the Mafia was the husband's job. "Ever hear of a traveling mountain range called Donnazzio?" I asked.

Bert sat up straighter so suddenly that the lounger bounced. Somehow Don Giovanni bounced the same amount at the same instant, so the lounger's feet failed to come down on him anywhere. "Tony Donuts's kid, ya mean? Tony Junior. Little Nuts, they call him. He's your trouble?"

So the kid's name really was the same as his dad's. "Yah."

When a serious man like Bert, who usually looks solemn even when he's having fun, suddenly looks grave, the effect is striking, and a little demoralizing. He looked away from me, sent his gaze out across the Atlantic, and frowned at Portugal. I bet it flinched.

"Ya got a beef with Little Nuts," he said, "my advice is ta shoot yourself right now. Try and run, you'll just die tired."

"Neither one is an option, Bert."

He snorted. "Right, I forgot. You guys don't get shot. You wanna keep somethin' like that quiet. CIA hears about it, you're up shit creek. Okay, ya better explaina situation ta me."

So we did. It took longer than if one person had done it, but not twice as long. Quite. In no time Bert had grokked the essentials.

"So ya can't kill this bastid, and ya don't even want him to figure out he can't kill *you*."

"That's basically it," I agreed. "Either one would be liable to cause talk."

Bert nodded. "We don't want no more a *that* in the world than necessary. Okay, gimme a minute." He sat back in his lounger, aimed his face at the horizon, and closed his eyes.

Zoey and I exchanged a glance.

Finally he opened his eyes, studied the horizon a moment, and nodded. "Okay," he said, "It's risky, but at least it's a shot."

We displayed respectful attentiveness.

"Ya can't take him out, ya can't drop a dime on him, an ya can't let him attack ya. So there's only one thing left ya can do."

"What, Bert?" Zoey asked.

"You're gonna have to con him, dear."

My wife and I smiled.

"We got some people who are pretty good at that," Zoey assured him.

"Really?"

She nodded. "World class."

Bert nodded. "That's gotta help."

"I don't know," I said dubiously. "Their experience has mostly been in conning humans. How do you con a gorilla?"

"Same way ya con a chimp," Bert said, "or a college professor. Ya figure out what he wants bad, and then sell him somethin' that smells just like it."

"That's what I mean," I said. "What Tony Donuts Junior wants bad is *everything.*"

Bert shook his head. "Don't matter. Lotta guys want everythin'. I known a few in my day. But there's always some one thing they want *most.*"

"So how are we going to find out what Tony Junior wants most?" Zoey asked.

"Oh, I know, kid," Bert told her. "Everybody does."

"You do?"

"Sure. He wants a button."

"Huh?"

"He wants to get made. Tony Junior wants ta be a wise guy. Common knowledge."

I was skeptical. "Are you sure, Bert? The way I hear it, the Donnazzio family and the Mafia have always given each other a wide berth. I mean, I met the guy. He's not just a loose cannon; he's a loose nuclear weapon."

"No argument," Bert said, holding up his hands. "I'm not talkin' what he's gonna get, I'm talkin' what he wants. Real bad. I think it's a way ta, like, succeed where his old man couldn't."

Zoey was frowning. "I don't see how this helps us. We can't sell him a counterfeit mob membership card."

Bert's hands were still held up; he turned them both around in a *"beats me"* gesture. "I'm just tellin' ya what he wants most. He talked ta me about it one time, like soundin' me out. I hadda tell him I didn't see it happenin'. He wants ta know, what if he put a couple mil on the table? I told him it ain't money; any asshole in a suit can bring in money. Ta be made, from the outside . . . I ain't sayin' it never happened. But it'd take something special."

"Like what?" I asked.

"I dunno. Somethin' *different*. Outa the ordinary, like. Bringin' in a new territory . . . takin' out a whole police department . . . dreamin' up some new racket . . . somethin' flashy like that. And it's hard to picture Tony Junior pullin' off somethin' that impressive."

Zoey said, "A new territory, you said? How about Key West?"

Bert shook his head. "Nah. Fuck's heah?"

Zoey shrugged with her eyebrows, conceding the point. "Then I don't get it. How is shaking down bars in Key West supposed to help get Little Nuts a button?"

Bert spread his spotted hands. "Why don't sheep shrink when it rains?"

The four of us sat for a silent while together and watched the sea, the sky, and all the sweating, swarming people in the way. Key West is people-watching paradise. You get to see them temporarily freed of nearly all the inhibitions that help define them back home up north, to see them with their wrapper off, so to speak. Well, most of it—despite the lateness of the hour, the sun was so intense today that even drunken college kids slathered with Factor 100 sunblock had had sense enough to put at least a T-shirt on. The sun was dropping fast, though; it was almost time to think about where to watch the sunset from.

"I got a teary," Bert said suddenly.

Teary? "A sad story, you mean?"

"No. A teary."

When I failed to respond, he glanced at me and realized I was clueless. "A guess that's been ta college. Some guy in a white coat makes a guess, he don't wanna admit it's just a guess, so he calls it a teary."

Light dawned. "Of course. Sorry, I didn't hear you right at first. So what's your theory?"

"It just come to me. Maybe there *is* a new territory here. It ties in with somethin' I been thinkin' about for a long time—that *everybody's* been thinkin' about for a long time. Ask yourself: What's the strangest thing in Key West these days?"

"The T-shirt shops on Duval," Zoey and I said simultaneously.

"Fuckin' A," Bert said. Beneath him, Don Giovanni gently farted, possibly in agreement.

Duval Street is the heart of Key West's tourist crawl, over a dozen blocks of road-company French Quarter, and as recently as five years ago, it was still a lively, diverse, eclectic mix of bars, galleries, bars, studios, bars, food outlets, taverns, and shops of every conceivable kind, hawking everything from aardvark-hide upholstery to zabaglione. Then at some point nobody has ever been able to pin down, for reasons no one could explain, it all began to change. Today the bars are pretty much all still there . . . but of the other commercial enterprises on the street, more than half are T-shirt shops now.

We Key West locals have all been trying to make sense of it for a long time, without success. It just doesn't seem reasonable that there could possibly be enough business to support so many competing enterprises with such a narrow product line. Surely when tourists pack to come here, they bring T-shirts?

Yet there the T-shirt shops are—a couple dozen of them. None of them ever seems to have much in the way of customers inside, when you pass by them, but somehow none ever seems to go broke. Even stranger, they seldom put up signs *claiming* to be about to go broke. As far as anyone has ever been able to learn, they mostly seem to be owned by anonymous distant corporations. They're usually managed and staffed by hired transients, with a turnover rate rivaling raw combat troops in a jungle war.

"I spent a little time and money at City Hall," Bert told us, "and got a list a who owns 'em all. Turns out mostly it's companies where the name is just initials annee address is a post office box. So last night I made a call ta Miami, an' got a readin' on who pays for the post office boxes. Come ta find out, it's a buncha different guys, all over the world . . . but they all got one thing in common, sticks right out." As an excuse to pause for effect, he leaned down and tugged Don Giovanni fully back into shade again.

"And that is?" Zoey prompted impatiently.

"Skis and coughs."

Zoey and I exchanged a glance.

"Alla names ended in *ski* or *cough*," Bert explained. "Like Tufshitski or Yubi Chakakov."

"Russians? All of them?"

"Damn near."

That was odd. Why would so many expatriates of the late Soviet Socialist Republic all pick the same eccentric capitalist trade, and all end up in Key West—on the same street? It was as puzzling as how they all managed to earn a living.

Bert said nothing now.

I closed my eyes and thought. But Zoey got there before I did. "Bert—are you telling us the Russian Mafia has been turning Duval Street into a giant money laundry?"

"Vaffanculo!" I exclaimed involuntarily.

"Dis is my teary," he agreed. "I had my suspicions for a while now, but I think the skis an' coughs nails it down."

"Think about it, Jake," Zoey said. "It makes a lot of sense. If you were a Russian gangster, a rat fleeing the sinking country, and you wanted to get a toehold in the U.S., where would you start? Someplace American gangsters won't notice you, right? Somewhere that isn't anybody's turf, so you aren't cutting into anybody else's action. Someplace where *nobody's* liable to notice you, because everybody else around is so weird or so drunk, you can't possibly stand out. How many places like that *are* there?"

Bert smiled fondly at her. "What a consigliere you woulda made, kid."

Zoey smiled back at him, then sobered. "Speaking of which, you haven't passed your suspicions . . . well, back up the chain of command yet, have you Bert?"

Bert sighed. "I been gettin' ready ta," he said. "But once I get on the horn ta Miami, either I'm wrong an' I look like an asshole . . . or I'm right, an' a war starts. Here. In Key West." He spread his hands and shrugged. "There didn't seem ta be any rush."

I was beginning to see metaphorical light at the end of the tunnel. "So Little Nuts—"

"—maybe figures if he can roll up the Russkis and deliver them and their action to Chollie Ponte up in Miami, before Chollie even figures out they're here, maybe it earns Tony Junior a button."

"And he starts out by—"

"—by rollin' up all the little joints on either side a Duval, first. Like you guys. He's encirclin the bastids, get it? Standard strategy; lock up the neighborhood, from the outside in. Then when he finally squeezes *them,* the Russkis got no place ta go. They're surrounded."

Bert's teary made a certain twisted sense. It would be easy enough to check with neighboring businesses and find out which of them had also been visited by Little Nuts recently.

Zoey was shaking her head and groaning. "This is not good news, Bert. Basically what you're saying is, we're not merely being shaken down by the Son of Kong, we're actually at ground zero of an impending international gang war."

Bert pursed his lips. "Yeah."

"This is sounding less and less like something we can keep quiet."

He nodded. "Yeah, it is."

"What would you do if you were me, Bert?" I asked him.

"You said ya had a couple of players in your crew, right? Put them ta work on it."

There are two reasons why Bert survived as long as he did in a dangerous occupation, and only one of them is luck.

4

DOG DEER AFTERNOON

On the way home, we had to bike along half of Duval Street to reach the turnoff for The Place. As I pedaled along—moving slowly, but faster on average than the cars—I couldn't help but glance into every T-shirt shop we passed. There were so many of them, it was nearly as much strain on my neck as watching a tennis match.

It was equally true that not one of them I saw had more than three customers in it, most of whom looked more like browsers than live ones. In nearly every case, clerks outnumbered customers. On a pleasant sunny weekday in tourist season. The bars and the few remaining Duval Street enterprises that were neither bars nor shirt-shops all seemed to be doing reasonably, seasonally brisk business.

Whenever I saw anyone behind a shirt-shop counter who seemed old enough to be an owner and not stupid enough to be a manager, he looked Russian to me. But that could be overactive imagination—how the hell did I know what Russians looked like, really? From movies where they were played by English actors?

I found myself looking at the T-shirts themselves. Each store displayed as many different shirts as physically possible, in windows, doorways and streetside racks. I had long since noticed that just about every store seemed to carry more or less the same basic inventory of shirts and shirt logos. Now that I was paying attention, their stock seemed literally identical. Roughly half the shirts were souvenirs, bearing the name Key West in assorted fonts and sizes, usually accompanied by some lame graphic of vaguely Floridian motif, and not all of them were horrible. The other half were moron labels: attempted-comedy shirts, emblazoned with some of the lousiest jokes ever composed, so brutally stupid, sexist, racist, scatological, and sophomorically obscene that I don't think I'll give any examples. I could not seem to find one joke that wasn't on display in every window.

Then I began to notice the people all around me—and what they were wearing. Just as at Smathers Beach, the vast majority of pedestrians, drivers, and cyclists on Duval Street, whether tourist or local, were wearing T-shirts of some kind. It was the kinds I started noticing. I took a mental tally, and by the time we reached our corner and hung a left, I was bemused by my findings. Roughly 30 percent of the T-shirts I'd seen were Key West souvenirs. Another 25 percent were souvenirs of someplace *else*, most often Disney World. A whopping 5 percent were dirty-joke shirts. And the whole remaining 40 percent were generic plain white undershirts, either T-shirts or the sleeveless kind popularly known in Pittsburgh as "wife-beaters."

I had not seen a single plain white undershirt of either type offered for sale on Duval, as far as I could recall.

"It's weird," Zoey said as we approached The Place. "And

it's even weirder that I never noticed how weird it is before. Each shirt store's the same. Gaudy signage, overkill display, loud rock music, massive air-conditioning with the doors wide open, huge inventory with identical wide selection. Each store says, at the top of its lungs, 'Hey, look at me here, selling the shit out of these T-shirts!' Only—"

"—only nobody's wearing what they're selling."

"That's it," she agreed. "You noticed it, too, huh?"

"Yep." We were home now; I dismounted, feeling the mild rush that comes with effortless exertion. "I also notice Jim Omar is a man of his word." The gate Little Nuts had destroyed was rehung now, as Omar had promised, latched open at the moment—with the crack down the center intact.

It cheered me absurdly, that small silly symbol of continuity with the original Callahan's Place. Drunkard's dharma transmission. The Alcoholic Succession. If the spirit of Mike Callahan was still with us, surely a trivial problem like a crazed killer giant trying to start a Criminals' Cold War in Key West—funded by *us*—was something we could deal with. Hell, we'd stymied interstellar invasion three times out of three, so far, and saved the whole damn universe for an encore. Who knew? It might even be possible, with the right combination of luck, perseverance, delicate diplomacy, and massive bribes, to work something out with the Florida Department of Education. Thinking these hopeful thoughts, I waved my wife through the open gate first, stepped through it myself, bumped *hard* into her, glanced past her, and at once saw Tony Donuts Junior leaning back against my bar with his arms folded, cowing my clientele.

Even Omar looked a little intimidated. Well, that's too strong a word. I suspect if it ever came to it, Jim would be willing to wrassle Satan. But he was certainly still and silent and extremely attentive. The attitudes of the dozen or so others present appeared to cover the spectrum from there down to paralyzed with terror.

Zoey belonged to that latter group. I tried to reassuringly squeeze her tension-stash muscles, right where her shoulders meet the back of her neck, and hurt my fingers—it was like trying to knead rebar. I could not blame her. This was her first encounter with Little Nuts. Sure, she'd been told . . . but actually seeing him, smelling him, was something else again. The brain circuitry involved was *way* older than the cerebral cortex.

I wasn't in a lot better shape myself. I remember thinking, *Waterfall? When did I acquire a waterfall?* and then realizing the thunderous roar I heard was my own bloodstream trying to squirt out my ears. I told my adrenal gland to knock it the hell off; neither fight nor flight was an option here.

No sense trying to push Zoey ahead of me like a shopping cart; she outweighed me. I stepped up beside her, took a deep breath, and—all gods be thanked—a pair of hands came around from behind my head and covered my mouth.

I did *not* jump a foot in the air, despite my hypercharged state, because I'd had a split second of subconscious warning—and more than a decade of conditioning. Materializing behind me without warning is a game my daughter invented the second day of her life, and has never tired of since—and whenever she does it, there's almost always a faint but distinctive *pop* sound of displaced air as she winks into existence. This time was a little unusual, though: usually her hands go over my eyes rather than my mouth.

I thought it was a spectacularly bad idea to let Tony Donuts Junior see Erin teleporting around like this. But as I framed the thought, she whispered urgently in my ear,

"Remember, Daddy: *You don't know his name*," and was gone again. And I realized three things at once: First, Little Nuts hadn't even noticed Zoey and me yet; second, even if he had, Erin would have been concealed behind us; and finally, if she had not done what she just did, I would unquestionably have used the deep breath still sequestered in my lungs to call out, "Hi there, Tony." The Professor and Maureen had assured us that Tony's IQ could not legally order a drink, being under twenty-one—but surely he possessed enough rat shrewdness to notice if someone addressed him by a name he was not giving out.

I learned to deal with the humiliation of being way dumber than my child about the same time she invented materializing behind me without warning. By now her mother and I are just thankful she still chooses us to make look like idiots. She almost never rubs it in unless she absolutely positively feels like it.

"Hi there," I called across the compound, to the vast relief of my lungs, and Tony looked up. "I must have got it wrong: I thought our appointment wasn't until tomorrow."

"That's right," he said. He picked a longneck bottle of Rickard's Red up off the bar top, snapped the neck off the bottle with his other hand, tossed the still-capped stub into the pool, and drank deep. "Fuck appointments."

"Ah. Good point."

A second gulp drained the bottle; he cocked his arm to toss it too into the pool. An attractive young woman down at the far end of the bar said, "Glass goes in the fireplace."

He turned slowly around and stared at her.

"You can pee in the pool if you want," she told him. "Everybody else does. But glass goes in the fireplace. See?"

She pointed, and automatically he looked, and sure enough, the big stone fireplace was full of broken glass. It pretty much always is. He looked back at her, frowned hard as if in thought . . . well, maybe not *that* hard . . . and emitted a belch that made bottles rattle behind the bar. She met his gaze without flinching.

Tony shrugged and flicked the empty bottle into the fireplace; it burst with a musical sound. She awarded him a *Mona Lisa* microsmile and said nothing.

I was confused. She spoke as if she were a regular, and indeed there was something oddly almost-familiar about her . . . but I was fairly sure I did not know her. She was too pretty to forget. Her long curly chestnut hair alone was too pretty to forget. She was tall, shapely, and very young, the youngest person in the compound besides Erin, whom I did not see anywhere. In fact, now that I looked closely with my professional bartender's eyeball, I wasn't even certain she was old enough to buy a drink in the state of Florida. She could be a youthful twenty-three . . . or she might be a late teenager of uncommon poise. Who had she come here with who'd explained our fireplace customs to her? Nobody I could see seemed a plausible candidate to be with anyone that pretty and that young.

She seemed to puzzle Tony, too. For him the speed of thought would always be slower than it was for most other people, or even most mammals, but he stared at her for a few seconds longer than that would account for. It didn't seem to bother her. It was as though there were invisible zoo bars between them.

He shrugged again. He seemed to have asked Tom for a sampler of beers; this time he picked up a big sweating quart can of Foster's from the selection beside him on the bar. He glanced down at the pop top. Then he turned the can upside down and, holding it one-handed, punched a hole in the bottom of it with his thumb. Spray arced high, and part of the sound was people gasping. Omar became still as a statue of a panther. With exaggerated care, Tony reached up with his pinkie and delicately used its nail to cut a smaller hole on the far side of the can. He drank the quart in a single draft. When it was empty, he caught the pretty young girl's eye . . . and tossed the can into the pool. He hadn't even bothered to crush it first; it floated on the surface, gleaming in the sunlight.

The pretty young girl said nothing, didn't so much as blink.

He turned his back on her and faced toward me and Zoey again. He opened his mouth to speak, and another LaBrea Tar Pits belch emerged; from fifty yards away I seemed to feel the breeze, and smell a whiff of primordial decay. Behind him, the girl did blink now. No, in fact, she was *winking*. At me. And grinning.

Okay, so I'm an idiot. I'm sure you would have figured it out much sooner, if you'd been in my sandals. It was only when I saw that impish grin that I finally recognized her. I felt the seismic tremor through the soles of my feet as the shock of recognition went through my wife's body, too. There was no mistaking who that was, even though neither of us had ever seen her before. In my profession I have become fairly expert at telling whether someone is twenty-one or not.

It was our daughter, Erin. Just about twenty-one years old.

There are physical limits to how fast electrical impulses can propagate between neurons. The following sequence of thoughts seemed to arise, uh, sequentially, but I don't believe they could have because when I was all done thinking them, no more than a second of real time had elapsed. I think what happened is that my brain instantly copied itself a large number of times and thought them all simultaneously:

———

—*poker face poker face pokerfacepokerface*—

—Holy Christ, she's as beautiful as her mother! Is that even possible? *Her hair is really amazing, long like that*—

—*I am looking at my daughter at something over age twenty. The universe does not appear to be collapsing. Ergo, the Erin I know—thirteen-year-old Erin—is no longer present in this ficton, this here-and-now. She must have not merely teleported away from here, but also time-hopped to some other ficton, to make room in this one for her older self*—

—*Why the hell is she going through all this? Is it simply because yesterday Little Nuts scared her, made her feel just for once like her calendar age? Temporal shenanigans of this sort are supposed to be a real bad idea, as I understand it . . . which I don't*—

—*If the two Erins simply swapped places, then "my child," the one I know, is presently wandering around 2006 without valid ID. Or she may have opted to go back in time, to any era prior to 1986 that interested her—and that she has not already visited before. I wonder which she picked: forward or back*—

—*Back her play. She wouldn't go to this much trouble frivolously: She's running some kind of scam on Little Nuts, and it already looks like a pip. Whatever it is, back her play . . . or at least try not to screw it up*—

—*poker face poker face poker*—

—*Could Little Nuts possibly notice a resemblance between this Erin and the thirteen-year-old he glanced at here in this compound yesterday? If not, how much danger is there that he'll think of it a little later on?*—

—*Don't be silly, Jake. It took you a while to spot her, and you're her father. Body language says it was the same for Zoey. And the two of you know about and believe in the exis-*

tence of time travel. It's about as likely that Little Nuts will sequence her DNA—

—God, the years between thirteen and twenty-one change so much about a girl! Height . . . voice . . . posture . . . demeanor . . . attitude . . . self-image . . . facial structure . . . walk—

—chest size—

—pokerfacepokerfacepokerfacepokerfacepo—

—Look at that face! My heart sings to behold it. That face says plain as print that she is a strong, confident, kind, and happy young woman. She looks as if she has had, if such a thing is even remotely possible, a great childhood and an endurable adolescence. She looks like I couldn't have been such a rotten parent after all. From the grip of Zoey's hand on my shoulder I know she is as pleased as I—

—Damn it, what the hell is that tall tower of testosterone doing back here a day earlier than he said? I'm not ready for him yet! I intended to spend the rest of today and tonight devising a Special Plan in consultation with all my friends, especially Willard and Maureen. Right now, I got nothing—

—This certainly is a tilted picnic—

—What am I gonna do?—

—Stall.

"So what can we do for you?" I asked him after the above extremely busy second.

He didn't even need a second to choose his answer. "Money," he said, and held out an upturned palm much like a snow shovel.

Shit. "Uh . . . like I said, I wasn't expecting you back until tomorrow."

In response he merely pursed his lips, as if to say, Yeah, life sucks sometimes.

"So I didn't get to the bank today. But tomorrow—"

"Ya partner get back yet?"

For an instant the question baffled me. Zoey was standing there right beside me, big as life. Then I realized that in Little Nuts's universe, *partner* and *woman* simply did not go together. I started to explain . . . and then thought, well, I don't really have any particular reason to lie to him, but why do I need a reason? "Uh, no, actually. My partner's been held up."

As surreptitiously as possible, Zoey stepped on my foot. I find pressure situations an excellent time to make bad puns; my beloved holds a differing view.

"So it's up to you, then," he said. He was still holding out that big snow shovel hand. I had not seen a snow shovel since I'd left Long Island to come down to the Keys.

"Well . . . I can write you a check, if you give me a name to make it out to."

He just snorted.

To negotiate with an Italian you need both hands for gesturing. I used them to emphasize a shrug. "Then I can't come up with anything like the amount you mentioned yesterday. Not until the bank opens again tomorrow."

Little Nuts slowly lowered his hand until it was at his side again. "I unnastan. Any new business relationship, there's gonna be little kinks startin' up. I gotta make allowances. Like ya said, you got the day wrong, so it ain't all your fault. And you ain't gimme no attitude yet." He sighed. "So here's what we do. You empty the register, plus gimme everythin' you got on ya, plus your ATM card and PIN code, plus tell me you're really sorry an' promise not ta fuck up no more. Then I break a coupla unimportant fingers an go away, an we put the whole thing behind us. You can make up the shortage tomorra when ya partner gets back. Sound like a plan, chief?"

I caught Jim Omar's eye, shook my head microscopically. Just in time; he'd been preparing to attack. With his bare hands, and whatever utensils he might find on his way to the enemy. Others were bristling, too; I could sense it. I began whistling loudly through my teeth, as if from nervousness. *"Do Nothing till You Hear from Me."* There are times when it's good to have a clientele who are somewhat musically sophisticated. I felt a slight relaxation in the vibes, and knew everyone would stay calm and let me handle it. All I needed now was a clue how to handle it.

Once again my mind did that business of cloning itself in order to think multiple thoughts in the same split second.

Suppose Tony Donuts Junior decided to punch me in the face. There were basically two possible outcomes.

First, the invisible protective shield given me by Mickey Finn might assess the incoming punch as being of lethal force, and instantly activate to protect me: I'd feel nothing, and Tony would break his hand. This would probably clue him in that there was something unusual about me, which was something I was hoping very much to avoid. If he found out he couldn't hurt me, he would not only become curious, but a little afraid of me, as well. All in all, you'd have to call that a bad outcome.

Alternatively, my magic cyborg defensive system might diagnose the punch as sublethal, and do nothing. That was really the more likely result: Tony in fact did not want to kill me (yet), and the Finn Shield is usually pretty accurate. Probably, then, the punch would land. On my personal face bone. This, too, met my criteria for a bad outcome.

Alternatives—

I could speak the name Pixel aloud, and Little Nuts would very suddenly acquire a large heavy orange fur hat, anchored firmly in place by ten of Hell's hatpins, in such a way that its removal would necessarily involve the removal of Tony's face, as well. This might distract him long enough for me to have a brainstorm. Or it might just really piss him off.

I could convert to Buddhism and set myself on fire. Keep that one in reserve.

I could ask Tom Hauptmann behind the bar for "a double shot of the twelve-buck stuff," and hold up my hand. We'd rehearsed this—we sell alcohol in south Florida—so I was fairly confident the double-barreled 12-gauge shotgun would arrive positioned so I could grab it out of the air and start firing at once. If I shot Little Nuts enough times at close range, perhaps I could wear down his resolve. But the noise would cause talk in the neighborhood, and the police would probably be curious.

I could page Mike Callahan. I had an emergency number that could theoretically raise him anytime. But I hadn't used it back when we were threatened by the end of the universe, so I was reluctant to use it for one lone human, however formidable. I didn't really know exactly what it was that Mike and his family were doing together, far off somewhere else in space and time—but I'd been given to understand that it was *important*.

There was always, of course, the option that had served me perfectly well for the past half a century. I could split: spin on my heel and run like a scalded son of a bitch. The open gate was only steps behind me; in under two seconds I could be out of the compound. Within which Tony would have my wife and daughter, some of my friends, my bar, and my home on which to vent his irritation. It was actually even a little worse than that, because the version of Erin present today was old enough to qualify as rapeable for someone like Tony. No, bugging out didn't sound like fun.

Perhaps the scattergun was my best option after all. Shoot Tony as many times as it took to kill him, kick his body into the pool, cover it, and when the cops arrived, have everybody blink and say, What noise? I was just settling, most reluctantly, on that option when Erin spoke up.

"How would you like something *better* than money?"

"No such thing," Tony Donuts Junior said automatically. Then he registered who had spoken and turned slowly to regard Erin. She met his gaze without flinching. She was standing with all her weight on her right leg and a hand on her left hip, which was slightly toward him. It was not an explicitly provocative pose . . . but even her father had to admit she looked damned good.

Tony made a horrid sound with both snort and snicker in it, and shook his head. "No such thing," he repeated with assurance.

"Are you sure about that?" she asked.

She didn't put any innuendo into it at all, but of course Tony heard some anyway. "Fuckin'-A. I want that," he said, gesturing with his chin toward her body, "I take the first piece goin' by I like. Money, I gotta wait for some asshole ta hand me."

Erin started to reply—and then seemed to think better of whatever she'd been about to say. He gave her a second or two to come up with something else, then decided he'd won the point, and turned back to me. "And waitin really pisses me off."

He began walking toward me, looking remarkably like a Jack Kirby character. The Incredible Hulk after he'd finally found a competent tailor, perhaps, or Ben Grimm with body hair, or Doctor Doom in mufti. I could feel his footsteps through the soles of my feet.

Oh, I thought, if only Mike were here! Or Mickey Finn

with his starkiller finger. Or Nikky Tesla and his death ray . . . or the Lucky Duck with his paranormal power to pervert probability . . . or even just Long-Drink with his hickory nightstick and Fast Eddie with his wicked little blackjack . . .

None of them being present, the crisis got solved by Tom Hauptman and his brain.

Tom likes to be around conversation, especially good conversation, but he doesn't talk much himself. Which is sort of strange, considering he was a minister for nearly a decade. He lost the habit of talking, along with his wife and then his faith, in a banana republic dungeon where he was held incommunicado for ten years. From the early Sixties to the early Seventies. He managed to completely miss The Beatles—and all that implies. The sexual revolution; civil rights; the murders of JFK, RFK, MLK; Vietnam; protest; pot, acid, mescaline, psilocybin, peyote; counterculture in general; Altamont, Woodstock, Apollo 11, Watergate—Tom missed all of it, busy watching his wife die, and then mourning her. By the time he got out, sprung by the CIA, Reverend Hauptman was so hopelessly out of touch, he would have been finished as a minister even if he'd still wanted to be one. Heaven knows what might have happened to Tom if he hadn't gotten confused and lucky enough to try to stick up Callahan's Place with an unloaded gun.

That was the night his tenure as our backup bartender began . . . and for most of the ensuing twenty-five years or so, Tom has been a quiet mainstay behind the bar, calm, competent, cheerful, and steady. Now, all at once, he became a bona fide official Hero of The Place—by cutting through the Gordian knot that baffled me with a single blow of his voice.

"Here."

That voice was so soft, gentle, and unafraid, it stopped the juggernaut in his tracks, where a bellowed "Freeze, motherfucker!" might have had no effect. Like a tank acquiring a target, Little Nuts swiveled to confront the upstart. What he saw made the corners of his mouth turn up with pleasure—and made me and most of the rest of us gasp.

Tom was holding out the drawer from the cash register in one hand, at enough of a tilt that you could see it was pretty full of cash. (I don't go to the bank very often, because if I do, then I'm in the bank.) In his other hand he held out an unzipped empty orange backpack made of some sort of lightweight space-age polymer. When he was sure he had Tony's attention, he emptied the drawer into the backpack. First the change, then the ones, fives, tens, and twenties.

Pay the man.

I'm not sure I can explain why not, but in a million years I would never have thought of that simple, brilliant ploy. It would buy us twenty four hours of scheming time, and all it would cost us was money. You know that sports stadium maneuver, The Wave? Eyebrows did that all around, as people grasped the elegance of the solution.

Tom set the empty cash drawer down, reached up the bar a ways, snagged the open cigar box from which people take their change on their way out, and added its contents to the backpack. Then he dropped in his own wallet, pocket change, and watch and passed the sack to the nearest patron, Shorty Steinitz. Looking glum but game, Shorty added his own wallet and change and passed it on.

Okay, this was good. Things were looking up. We would fill the backpack with baubles, and the giant would go away, for now at least, and with him would go immediate danger, and we could finally get some furshlugginer thinking done. I was *not* yet beginning to relax, but I was beginning to envision a universe in which relaxation was sometimes permitted to such as me, when I saw a fist break the surface of the pool, holding a beer can, followed at once by Lex's head.

The geometry was such that he was, barely, out of Tony's field of vision. But I knew why he had surfaced, and my heart sank. (Wait, let me just look at that sentence for a minute. Okay, I'm good now.) This had come up once before, and so had Lex. (Sorry. I'll try to get control.) From his point of view, tossing an empty beer can into the pool was like some clown lobbing trash through your living-room window. What he had done the last time it happened was to return the can, at high speed. By then it wasn't empty anymore but three-quarters full of pool water, and its previous owner, a tourist from California, had his back turned, so the impact dropped him like a poleaxed steer, and his friends ended up having to drive him up to the emergency room on Stock Island.

I'd bought Lex a drink, then. But I did not want him to do it again. A beer *barrel*, full of cement, would probably not knock down Tony Donuts Junior. It *would* make him turn around . . . whereupon he would see, treading water there in the pool, something that looked very much as if the Creature from the Black Lagoon's dermatologist was finally beginning to make some headway with his complexion, but only above the waist. This was the kind of sight that might make Little Nuts *big*-time nuts. But there was nothing I could do about it; where I was standing, Tony would see me if I tried to signal Lex to duck out of sight.

Beyond Tony I saw my grown-up daughter, striking in that dress—then all at once I was seeing only the dress, falling empty to the ground. In the pool, Lex's head suddenly disappeared beneath the water, as if he'd been yanked downward from below. A human might have had time to yelp, but Lex had no air in his lungs yet.

Unfortunately, none of this was noticed by Marty, the last customer sitting at my end of the bar. Having put his own valuables into the backpack, he got up to walk it down to the other end of the bar. If he got where he was going, and Tony's eyes followed him, the man-monster was going to notice that Erin wasn't there anymore . . . and then that her dress was.

The whistle was earsplitting, the strident thumb-and-pinkie kind of whistle you use to summon a cab in New York.

The shout that followed it was nearly as loud and just as piercing. "Hey, Goliath—screw you!"

Little Nuts became very still. He did not even look toward the upstart, yet. Only his face moved, slightly, and in a most unaccustomed way: his expression became thoughtful. "Screw me?" he mused.

"Yeah. Screw your mother, too."

Tony snorted. From his expression, you could see that he had run into this sort of thing before—suicides who picked him rather than the cops to assist them—and that he regarded the chore as part of the white ape's burden, tedious but sometimes unavoidable. "Screw my mother, too?" His voice was getting quieter.

The other got even louder. "Why not? Everybody else has."

Tony pursed his lips. Time to swivel round and take a first and last look at this fool. "Everybody else ha-oly *shit!*"

"What are ya, a fuckin' parrot?" Harry shrieked. "Damn right, everybody else has . . . except her husband, of course."

Little Nuts was so startled, he blinked and backed up a half step. "Jesus Christ. A fuckin' parrot . . ."

"What are you, related to Robert De Niro? Are you? Are you related to De Niro? I don't see anybody else here related to De Niro—"

A new, moving shadow appeared suddenly, on the poolside tile behind Tony, and begin sliding across the water toward me. I glanced up quickly. Through a gap in the poinciana canopy above I glimpsed Erin, a tiny figure perhaps half a mile above us, falling. Why was she sky-diving at a time like this? Oh, of course. Air-drying herself. She plummeted down to maybe a hundred feet overhead and winked out of existence. The next moment—no, actually, the same one—she was standing where she had been before, down at the far end of the bar, dressing hastily.

I was afraid Tony would turn and see her—how long could a bird hold his interest? But Harry picked that moment to do his signature piece. It captivated Erin when she first met Harry, at age two, and it did not fail to amuse Tony Donuts Junior now. Behind the bar, on top of The Machine, stands a miniature toilet. It's a scale model of an old-fashioned water closet, the kind with an overhead tank of water you flush by pulling a chain, and it's perfectly functional. Harry hopped up onto it now, put it to its intended use, and yanked the chain with his beak, causing it to flush noisily.

Tony cracked up. The sound was remarkably similar to the noise Lex makes when he surfaces and swaps the water in his lungs for air—if Lex were the size of a killer whale, that is, and lived in a fetid pool at the center of an immense dark dank echoey cave. By the time the ghastly sound was over, Erin was dressed again. I heaved a small sigh of relief. A very small one.

Jim Omar had just finished contributing to the backpack, and there were no other potential donors. Erin took the bag from his big hands before he could stop her and took it to Tony. He heard her sandals slapping the tiles, turned his head, and his grin got wider.

When Erin reached him, she solemnly handed him the backpack. He lifted it up next to his ear, shook it, and listened to the sound. Then he frowned in thought, a process which apparently involved moving his tongue in a slow circle against the inside of his left cheek. "Ya light," he said over his shoulder to me. "Other hand, you an ya friends all showed respect. Okay, what the fuck. I don't hurt nobody taday."

He turned back to my grown daughter. "Like the French guys say, *oh cunt rare*," he told her. He reached out one of his snow shovel hands and took a firm grasp on her right breast.

I moved forward to kill him with my teeth, but Zoey seemed to be in the way. No matter how I moved, somehow she kept being in the way. I stopped trying and watched to see what Erin did.

She acted as if Tony's hand did not exist. She met his gaze squarely, her own expression as serene as that of a meditating monk or a professional poker player. Her voice when she spoke was pitched so low Zoey and I could barely make out her words, and we were the nearest people to her and Tony now. "How would you like something that's better than either sex *or* money?" she asked him.

He blinked at her a few times, and then snorted. "No such t'ing." He kneaded her breast, not gently. Zoey had a firm grip on my weapon arm by then, and her other hand over my mouth.

Erin continued ignoring Tony's molestation, kept looking him square in the eye. "You're wrong," she told him quietly. "I'll see you tomorrow. Not here, in town. If you don't agree that what I show you then is better than sex or money, you can have both of them instead."

Now I had a hand over Zoey's mouth.

This proposal seemed to interest Tony. He stopped kneading while he thought it over. I couldn't see his tongue tip circling on the inside of his cheek, from where I stood, but I could picture it. "Oh yeah?"

Erin nodded once. "Yeah."

I hoped she had him figured right. I'd have assumed, myself, that a guy like Tony would prefer them uncooperative. And would be too childish to defer immediate pleasure for future reward.

But she had appealed successfully to his child's curiosity. "Okay," he said, and let his hands fall and stepped back a pace. "This I gotta see."

She nodded. "Tomorrow, then."

He shrugged his right shoulder to settle the backpack and turned to go, but she held up a hand to stop him. "Tom," she called over her shoulder, "don't you have an indelible Magic Marker under the bar?"

"No, Erin."

"Over by the controls for the pool lights."

"I don't think s—Wait, you're right, here it is."

He gave it to Fifty-Fifty, who brought it to Erin. She offered it to Tony, and when he took it from her left hand, she left the hand out, palm up. "Sign your name here," she said. "Just the way you sign it on a check."

Tony frowned at her, suspecting some sort of put-on. He must have decided what the hell. How many people in his life could possibly have tried to put him on? He uncapped the marker and scribbled on the palm of her hand. When he attempted to keep writing right on up her wrist, she pulled her hand away and plucked the marker from his grasp. "See you tomorrow," she told him.

He was beginning to understand that she was not afraid of him, and it amused the hell out of him. "Yeah," he said. He turned on his heel and headed for the exit, walking right through Zoey and me as if we had been stalks of rye in his path. By the time I had my feet under me and was tracking him again, he was nearly to the gate. Just as he reached it, a woman tried to enter, and they almost collided.

When they both came to a halt, inches apart, the top of her head came up to about the middle of his chest. She stood her ground, glared up at him, and waited for him to back up and get out of her way. Instead he reached out, grabbed both *her* breasts, and honked them. She emitted a hypersonic shriek, her eyes rolled up in her head, and she fainted. Tony chuckled one last time and let go of her; she dropped like a sack of rocks, landed on her back, and lay still. He stepped over her and left. For today.

Do I have to tell you the unconscious woman on my doorstep was Field Inspector Ludnyola Czrjghnczl? It didn't surprise *me* any.

Being nearest, Zoey and I were the first to reach her.

"They just don't make civil servants like they used to," I said, kneeling beside the sleeping bureaucrat. Pulse strong and regular, respiration nominal, color pale but not really much paler than what she had started with.

"They do seem to have skimped on materials," Zoey agreed, staring down at her. "I've got shoes I bet weigh more than she does."

"Her first visit, it took her at least five minutes to become hysterical. Today, she passed out cold in under five seconds. At this rate tomorrow morning she'll wake up thinking of us and die before she can get out of bed."

"You say that like it's a bad thing."

The Field Inspector's eyelashes began fluttering. All at once she sucked in a great volume of air through her mouth, and her eyes snapped open. The first thing she saw was me, and she tried very hard to back away from me, but planet Earth was in the way. Then she caught sight of Zoey, and that was different. A characteristic dull glitter I hadn't realized was missing returned to her eyes, and she stopped wanting to escape. She actually said, "Aha." She got to her feet slowly and methodically, as if it were a new procedure and she was translating the instructions from colloquial Fukienese. She brushed off my attempts to help, and accepted Zoey's, so that when she was on her feet again, they were face-to-face.

"You are Zoey Berkowitz," she charged.

Zoey pleaded guilty with a nod.

"Maternal parent and legal coguardian of the minor child Erin Stonebender-Berkowitz."

Zoey admitted the second count of the indictment.

"Is the said child here now?"

"No," Zoey and I said together, pointedly not looking anywhere near the grown-up Erin.

The Field Inspector's manner grew a degree or two chillier. "I see," she said. It was the middle of the afternoon on a school day. "And where is she, at this point in time? If you know."

"At the library," I said—unfortunately, at the same instant that Zoey said, "At the gym." A perfect train wreck. Needless to say, there is no gym anywhere near Key West's only library. Neither of us even tried to salvage it; we just stood there with egg on our faces and waited for what would come next.

Once more she managed to cool another degree or two without quite freezing solid. "I see," she said again, probably lying this time. "And when will she be back?"

This time neither of us spoke, waiting for the other to go first.

"You don't know when she will return."

"At suppertime," I said, precisely as Zoey said, "Not until late." Then we both sighed.

So did the Field Inspector. "I would like to inspect the child's domicile," she said.

"Now?" Zoey and I squeaked in unison, and then exchanged a glance, as if to say, *See, that wasn't so hard*.

"Is that a problem?"

Zoey and I keep The Place pretty organized—the bar, barbecue, pool, deck, fireplace, grounds, and parking lot are all kept just as clean and together as we can manage to make them. Even the exterior of our own home is at least as well maintained as those of the other four cottages. The inside, however, is customarily a sty. Zoey and I try to be responsible innkeepers, but as far as our own quarters go, we've agreed since we met that if you find you have the energy for housework, you're just not doing enough fucking. I tried to remember when was the last time we'd hosed the place out, and failed.

Field Inspector Czrjghnczl grew impatient. "The bungalow in the center would be yours, I take it," she said, and set off for the house without waiting for an answer. Zoey and I both opened our mouths to call after her, and perhaps Zoey had actually thought of something to say—I know I was bluffing—but then I spotted something and waved my hand to catch her eye, and pointed. Crumpled on the ground between two chairs: Erin's dress.

So we watched the Field Inspector in silence as she strode across the compound to our home, ignoring every one of my customers and giving the widest possible berth to the pool. She marched right up the steps, pushed the screen door open, and went inside without so much as pausing, let alone knocking; the door swung shut behind her with a *clack*.

Zoey and I looked at each other, sighed, took each other's hand, and followed after her. "I hope Erin had time to make a dent," Zoey said.

"I hope she had time to get out of sight bef—"

Earsplitting scream.

My front door did not have time to open again: Field Inspector Ludnyola Czrjghnczl came right back out through it like a cannonball through a condom. She was already moving so fast that her feet never touched the porch, and once she had earth rather than floor under her feet again, she accelerated sharply. Zoey and I could both tell we were in her way, and tried to move apart so she could pass between us, but our reflexes weren't fast enough; she struck our still-joined hands so hard that we spun apart in opposite directions. By the time I got my feet under me and got oriented, she was out the gate and gone, thundering footsteps doppler-ing off toward Duval Street.

Dead silence in The Place. As one, we all turned to stare at my house.

Nothing happened for ten longish seconds. Nobody seemed disposed to go in the house and investigate. Certainly not me, and it was my house. Finally we heard a high-pitched extremely irritated voice inside mutter, "Oh, God damn it. All right, let's get it over with." Another voice, lower in pitch and more resigned in tone, said, "I zuppoze ve may ass vell." I knew both voices—we all did—but we still didn't get it yet.

Alf the Key deer and Ralph Von Wau Wau came out onto my porch together. By which I mean *together*.

"What the hell does a person have to do to get a little friggin' *privacy* around here?" Alf asked us.

In retrospect I figure it must have been the abrasive, pugnacious manner, the tendency to turn conversation to confrontation. I can't think why else I'd have looked at a delicate graceful elfin creature with a high voice and jumped to the conclusion that it was male.

"Doesn't anybody knock anymore?"

"Now, Alafair," Ralph reminded her, "ziss iss not our house."

"It wasn't *hers* either, damn it. She should have knocked." Alf's nose was glowing bright red.

In my defense, I wasn't the only one who'd misjudged Alf's sex; so had pretty much everyone else. You could tell by the wave of laughter that rose up and filled the compound.

Does that make us sound insensitive to Alf and Ralph's discomfiture? We weren't, I promise you. They were our friends, and we were all fond of both of them; the pain of empathy was part of why we had to laugh so loud. Another part was release of tension: we had just, in the space of a few minutes, survived very-near-misses by two different planet-killing asteroids—a sociopathic monster and a civil servant. The first excuse to laugh that came along was a goner. We—no offense to Ralph—howled.

Alf's nose, being where she keeps part of her brains, is normally very large and bright red; now embarrassment made it look like a molten baseball or a radioactive tomato. "Haven't you assholes ever seen two people in love before?" she demanded indignantly. Just then her partner finally managed to achieve separation, with a small popping-cork sound like punctuation by Victor Borge.

This set off a second wave of laughter, louder and more intense than the first.

Divine fire suddenly touched my brow. "Be careful, Ralph," I called out. "If she ever decides the relationship's in the toilet, she's liable—"

Just behind me, an unmistakable foghorn voice joined in. "—to send you a deer john letter," Doc Webster and I finished together.

The laughter redoubled, mixed now with applause. Doc and I exchanged bows, and then a low five. He and his wife,

Mei-Ling, had obviously come from an afternoon at the beach, just in time to steal my punchline.

The infuriated little quadruped stuck her tongue out and gave us a loud Key deer Bronx cheer. The pitch of her voice made it sound like a model airplane doing loops.

Suddenly the Doc's expression changed. "Oh, my God," he murmured.

"Doc, what is it?" Mei-Ling asked, alarmed.

He had a thousand-yard stare. "Don't you know who that is there with Ralph?" he said, gesturing toward the porch.

I braced myself. I didn't know exactly what was coming, but I feared the worst.

Mei-Ling's eyes widened, then closed. She took a deep breath, opened them again, and she and her husband said the awful words together.

"She's rude Alf, the red nose-brain deer."

The group scream of horror and dismay actually caused the poinciana canopy overhead to shiver and shed scarlet leaves; to our neighbors, it must have sounded as if we'd all been suddenly immersed in chilled bat guano. It probably would have frightened them, if they hadn't been our neighbors. A ragged barrage of mixed nuts, used tea bags, swizzle sticks, sugar packets, ice cubes, balled-up napkins, tomatoes, scoops of ice cream, the contents of numerous glasses, and at least one shoe began to rain down on the Websters. And there Zoey and I were, right in the line of fire. . . .

5

PROS AND CONS

I put out the word.

Well, we all did. Cell phones were made to beep and glow, then chittered into. Laptops were booted—G chord—and coaxed into producing the sound of a thousand baby chicks somewhere far away being fried in oil, followed by the "Chi *gong*, chi *gong*" that announces a successful Internet connection (what the Chinese have to do with it, I'll never understand) and the popcorn sounds of e-mail being typed and sent. A fax or two were transmitted. In one or two extreme cases, actual physical messengers were dispatched to summon people so eccentric or so broke they did not use *any* communications technology. Whatever the medium, the message always boiled down to, "Please come to The Place tonight for a Counsel Council." In one case it was compressed all the way down to, "Jake says hey Rube."

By an hour or so after sundown, just about all the hard-core regulars currently in town were present, along with a scattering of newer parishioners including novices and even postulants like Alf and Lexington.

Given the logistics of our layout, there's really only one practical way to hold a large conference in The Place. Everybody who expects to be talking a lot more or less has to get into the pool. Everyone else gathers around it to listen and respond. Fortunately in Key West the weather is *always* perfect for this. I customarily open the bar for the duration of a Council: anybody may help himself, as long as he fetches at least one drink to someone in the pool each time he does. The cash drawer is left open, folks deposit their money without supervision or formalities, and the next day I just figure out how much booze is missing and punch that into the register to humor the IRS.

"Okay," I said, when I judged it was time to call us to order, "all of you know the basics of the situation now, right? We need to defeat a giant homicidal psychopath, in such a way that he doesn't find out. Now it seems—"

"Order of Jake, point," said Walter.

"Yes, Walter?"

"Is really trip this necessary? We offed him pay today; why keep on it not doing? Money's no us for problem."

"Good pinto," Brad agreed.

Walter had a point. There's this cluricaune . . . never mind, it's a long story. What it comes down to is, we all more or less gave up worrying about money a long time ago. There was no reason we couldn't just pay the weekly bite Little Nuts demanded and forget him.

"That's easy for *us* to say," said Double Bill. "Few of our neighbor establishments are as fiscally fortunate."

There were rumbles of agreement. Most of the bars in Key West—like most of the people in Key West—are just barely hanging on.

"You want that guy in here every week, like a recurring yeast infection?" Long-Drink asked Walter and Brad.

They frowned. "Hell, on," Brad muttered. "Ton if we can help it."

Treading water beside me, Willard spoke up. No, I take that back: he wasn't Willard, now. He was the Professor once again, for the first time in many years. "There's another point to consider," he said. "Remember what Little Nuts wants the money *for*. He plans to use it to finance a war with the Russian mob—here on Key West."

There was a collective *rooba rooba* of dismay.

"Sounds like the problem might be self-correcting, then," suggested Marty.

The Professor looked pained. "How's that?"

"Well, there are three possible outcomes. The Russians win, and everything goes back to just the way it was. Or they and Tony Junior take each other out, and we're shut of two nuisances. At worst Tony wins, in which case we're no worse off than we are right now. Better, maybe, because he turns his attention elsewhere."

"That turns out not to be the case, I'm afraid," said the Professor. (I don't believe I know any politer way to say "You're full of shit.") "In the first place, you neglect a fourth possibility: Tony and the Russians might prove so evenly matched that neither can defeat the other. Key West is not a big rock; they could easily destroy it altogether."

A rumble went around that was the vocal equivalent of a shudder.

"But consider this," the Professor said. "No matter which of the four outcomes we get . . . we definitely get a boatload of FBI agents and state cops with it."

"Jesus Christ!" said at least a dozen people. I was one of them. Another dozen or so went for "Holy shit!" "My word,"

"God bless my soul," "Yikes," and "Ouch" also had their adherents, and we're multicultural enough that *"Caramba," "Bojemoi," "Sacre bleu," "Vaffanculo,"* and *"Oy,"* all put in an appearance.

"They'll be all over Key West like ants at a picnic," the Professor went on when the hubbub had subsided somewhat. "They'll talk to everybody they think Tony might have extorted. We're having trouble enough dealing with a state education department inspector—does anybody here think we're ready to persuade the FBI we're normal citizens?"

I thought about it. Suppose Lex stayed at the bottom of the pool, and Ralph and Alf kept their mouths shut, and Erin held off on time-traveling or teleporting anywhere for an hour or so, and none of the Callahans picked that moment to arrive naked from the other end of space and time, and no aliens or gangsters happened to shoot any of us or set off any thermonuclear devices in our midst . . . could we possibly all play normal human beings well enough to convince FBI agents?

Nah.

No way in hell. I wasn't sure exactly what it would be, but *something* would surely go wrong. Pixel, perhaps: I was confident I could get Ralph and Alf to (literally) play dumb, but as one of my favorite songwriters said, you just can't herd cats: there's simply no controlling Pixel. (Well, maybe two of his former servants could manage it, a little—Robert and Virginia Heinlein—but nobody since.) He'd probably take offense at something and walk through a wall and that'd be it. Or Nikola Tesla would show up, juggling balls of fire—and Nikky has been *pissed* at the FBI ever since they stole all his papers and possessions from his hotel safe the day he died. With my luck, he'd demand his stuff back and underline the point with lightning bolts.

One of our newer regulars, Papaya, spoke up. He's got a terrible stutter I won't attempt to reproduce, on the grounds that Papaya would edit it out of his speech if he could do so in life, and I *can* do it for him here, so why not. (What about Walter and Brad, then, you ask? Neither of them has a problem with the way they speak. Why—do you?) I mention it only because he's a classic example of why I contend we need laws to constrain parents in the naming of their children. His people are Cajun Conchs, who came to the Keys generations ago from Nova Scotia by way of Louisiana, and they thought nothing of naming a boy after one of their favorite local fruits. Unfortunately the family name was LaMode. If you tell people your name is Papaya LaMode, they'll naturally conclude you have a stutter, not to mention an odd sense of humor; almost inevitably, you'll develop both. Maybe the sense of humor is compensation enough; I don't know. "So if I'm hearing you right, we seem to have four basic alternatives—none of which is acceptable. Is that the situation?"

The Professor and I exchanged a glance across the pool. "Well," he said, "that *was* the situation . . . until Erin changed the rules. It turns out she has a fifth ace up her sleeve."

"The Ace of Thugs," Erin said.

She was her usual age again, now. Usual for this ficton, I mean. She sat cross-legged at the approximate center of the pool, a few inches above the surface of the water. I've never quite understood how she can do that. It isn't quite Transiting, the form of teleportation Solace and the Callahans taught her—is it? I asked her about it, once. The trouble was, she answered me.

"It has allowed her," the Professor went on, "to devise the first new con I've heard of in a very long while. If we can pull this off, not only will we get left alone to continue our valuable research in defining the maximum human tolerance for bliss, but also everyplace between here and Miami is going to become a slightly nicer place to be."

Papaya frowned. "Parts of Florida becoming *nicer?*" He shuddered. "That just ain't natural."

"Neither is a party," Doc Webster said softly from his chaise longue over on the bar side of the pool. "You have to make it happen."

"Amen," said several voices.

"Hush, Doc—I want to hear about this new con," said Mei-Ling, running fond fingers through the memory of her husband's hair.

Like more than one of my customers, Mei-Ling used to be a player herself once—before her conscience started bothering her, and she retired to respectability as an honest whore. ("Now the marks *ask* me to screw them," she told me once. "And they're *happy* I'm good at it.") By the kind of synchronicity which would be implausible anywhere else, and seems inevitable in The Place, four other patrons of mine happened to follow the same unconventional career path . . . and all five ended up working in the same whorehouse: the one Mike Callahan's wife, Lady Sally, used to run in Brooklyn. At different times, is the kicker—all five met each other for the first time here in Key West, the day I arrived to open up The Place back in 1989. In a further resonance, the other four are two couples, who both met and married while working at Lady Sally's House: Joe and Arethusa Quigley (of whom more anon), and the Professor and Maureen.

(I once ventured to suggest that Mei-Ling's marriage to Doc Webster slightly damaged the perfection of the symmetry. "Not at all," the Doc said. "I did the same jobs as the other five, just more efficiently. A good con man takes your money and sells you first-rate bullshit. A good hooker takes your money and sends you away feeling better. I was a physician: I split the difference." The best I could come back with was, "And the fee.")

Doc murmured something in Fukienese that caused his wife's fingers to slide down the back of his head and begin kneading at the base of his skull. "Yes, Erin dear: tell us—" He interrupted himself to purr briefly. Or maybe it was more Fukienese. "—what exactly is your new game?"

"I just heard of a new one, way up in western Canada someplace," Joe Quigley interrupted. "Second cousin of mine. Some kind of time-travel scam."

"So is mine," Erin admitted, looking interested.

"Huh. I wouldn't put it past my second cousin to claim-jump a new con. Yours involve The Beatles?"

Now Erin was confused. "No."

"Elvis?"

She shook her head. "The biggest celebrity involved in mine is the conqueror of Florida."

"Jesus Christ!" said Long-Drink McGonnigle. "You mean Jeb, the man so accursed by God he has George Bush for both father and brother?"

"I saw that movie," Susie Maser said. "Faye Dunaway. She was his sister *and* his daughter."

Doc Webster nodded. "*Chinatown*. With Nick Jackleson."

In a heroic attempt to regain and focus the attention of the group, Erin raised her volume slightly. "I didn't mean the present governor. I'm talking about the very first European ever to see the place."

"Knack Sickle Gin," said the Doc, trying to get it right.

"Jackson Nickel," Walter riposted, getting into the spirit of the thing.

Erin raised her volume a little more—and herself, too,

another foot or two higher above the water. "And I don't claim that it's a new con—far from it. What I'm talking about is probably the first con that was ever perpetrated on a white man in this state, actually."

"Nixon Jackal," the doc muttered. He shook his head irritably. "Jack's Knuckle In."

I was near enough to pick up mild alarm in his tone, and began to be mildly alarmed myself. Doc was emphatically not a rude man. Almost pathologically not a rude man. And he loved Erin. He seemed to have caught a case of spoonerism as if it were hiccups.

Erin unfolded her legs and stood up on the surface of the pool. "Actually, the only change I'm really making in the scam is to cheat. That will make it much easier. But it will also—"

Smokes spoke up. "Who *was* the conqueror of Florida? Flagler, right?" Smokes is another example of what I was talking about earlier. *Smokes* is actually not a nickname, despite the fact that he is one of maybe ten living humans who enjoy marijuana more than I do, and looks it, and his last name is Pott. In fact he had his first name legally changed, at *considerable* difficulty and expense, largely because he could no longer stand the one his parents had thoughtlessly seen fit to saddle him with. Pete. Well, if your name is Smokes Pott, you're going to end up living in Key West. That's just the way it is. So again we see how careless parental nomenclature can warp destiny. (There's even a tiny pun in there, for smoking pot must start with a peat pot.)

"Jack Sickle Nun . . . Jack Nicholson. Ha!" Doc had finally nailed it.

"No," Shorty Steinitz said. "Jack Nicholson was *mayor*, not governor. Not in Florida, either. California, someplace with a chewy name. . . ."

"I thinking think of you're East Clintwood," Walter said helpfully.

"Actually, Smokes," Erin said, with the kind of infinite patience whose subtext says, If you really make me keep being this patient for infinity, I will kill you all in your beds, "the conqueror and first ruler of Florida was Ponce—"

"A *ponce?*" Shorty Steinitz said loudly, struggling to follow the conversation with his good ear. He glanced across the pool to Smokes. "I'm sorry, young feller, I thought you said Flagler." He bent close to his wife, who hasn't *got* a good ear, and bellowed, "He said *fegeleh.*" Then he looked puzzled and turned back to Erin. "The governor of Florida is a ponce? He doesn't seem good-looking enough to me."

Erin closed her eyes, sighed, visibly counted to five, and let herself begin very slowly sinking into the water.

Fast Eddie couldn't stand it. He hit a crashing discord on his piano and stood up so fast the stool crashed over. It seemed an odd time for a Jerry Lee Lewis impression, but from long association with Eddie, I automatically got ready to supply the vocal. Instead he slammed the cover down on the keyboard.

"Fa Chrissake, don't youse *get* it?" he shouted. "What's de oldest scam in Florida?"

"Real estate," Double Bill said positively.

Eddie made a sound like logging on to the Internet five octaves lower, sucked air, and yelled at the top of his lungs, "Gah dammit, *she's talkin about de Foun'ain a Ute!*"

There was a momentary hush. Erin was in up to where, a few hours ago, her breasts had been, and still sinking. Over behind the bar, The Machine farted and peeped, signaling the end of its automatic self-cleansing ritual.

Ensign Bowman, one of half a dozen swabbies from the

naval base who've become semiregulars in recent years, broke the silence. "What's a Ute?"

Susie Maser shook her head. "That's a different picture. *My Cousin Vinnie.*" Then she suddenly looked dismayed.

The top of Erin's head slipped beneath the surface.

It's my opinion Ensign Bowman was actually asking for information; I don't think he knew the film. Nonetheless it was unfortunate, because it happens that Susie's husband Slippery Joe prides himself on his Joe Pesci imitation, undeservedly, and everyone present knew it. Susie and his other wife Suzy both realized what they had to do, and didn't hesitate, thank heaven—he was already beginning to squint and curl his upper lip when they threw him in the pool. Fortunately he missed Lex by a good yard or two.

Long-Drink McGonnigle happened to be floating nearby; he was pushed into me by the tsunami. "The other bourbon and the draft beer and salt are already in the back," he murmured to me.

I grinned. A fellow Donald Westlake fan. I'd just been thinking the same thing myself. "Thanks, Rollo. How about the vodka and red wine?" I helped him to safe harbor next to me at the side of the pool.

"Oh, he was in earlier. He'll be back tomorrow," said Long-Drink.

(We were referencing a bar in Westlake's immortal Dortmunder series, and I could probably have made everything twice as confused by saying its name aloud, just then.)

Finally Slippery Joe had been hauled out, and his wives had stripped him, dressed him in a beach towel toga and sent him off to my place to put his clothes in the dryer, and Fast Eddie had bellowed "SHADDAP A'READY," and order, insofar as we know that term at The Place, had been restored.

"Go ahead, Erin," said Eddie, "We'll lissen, dis time." He

said the second sentence with special emphasis, and we all noticed that Eddie's right hand was around behind him, where he stores the nasty little blackjack he uses on those rare occasions when a troublemaker wanders in.

"Thank you, Uncle Eddie," said Erin with quiet dignity. By now she had surfaced again, and was sitting zazen on the water, legs crossed beneath her, spine straight, hands joined on her lap with thumbtips touching in the Zen version of the mudra. She looked slowly around at us all, shedding water from her hair that glistened in the poolside lights. "Uncle Eddie guessed correctly a minute ago: I intend to sell Tony Donuts Junior the Fountain of Youth."

Dead silence.

Then, *rooba rooba rooba*, interspersed with giggles.

"How that gonna help us, girl?" Bad Death Wallace asked. He looks like a Rastafarian, and used to be one until, he claims, he started thinking about how weird it was to worship someone named Highly Silly Ass, Eh? After an ugly misunderstanding with the police concerning his own name—actually his father named him, after watching his mother perish in childbirth—he left Montego Bay in a cargo container, hoping to reach America. But like so many apostates, expatriates, and fugitives before him, he settled for Key West instead.

"The hell with how it can help us," said Noah González. "Let's think about how it can *hurt* us."

"He has a point, Erin," Arethusa Quigley said. "Have you figured a way to handle the blowoff without any comeback? Tony doesn't strike me as the kind of mark who'll take his screwing and chalk it up."

"Jesus, no," agreed her husband, Joe. "Every time I think of him I picture a large ugly mountain brought to life by

Claymation. He couldn't actually *kill* any of us, of course. . . . Well, now, wait a minute, that's not strictly—"

"*You miss my point,*" Noah said urgently. "I'm not talking about anything as trivial as grievous personal injury or massive property damage. Am I, Erin?"

She chose not to answer.

"Earlier today you looked, for a time, markedly older than usual. Now you once again look your normal age. And you say you're planning to run some kind of Fountain of Youth sting. *Ergo*—" He sighed, looked down at his sandals, and back up. "—you're going to use time travel. Right?"

My daughter didn't duck it. "That's right, Noah."

He spread his hands and said to the group, "There you are. What she's planning to risk is *everything*."

Rooba rooba rooba rooba.

Nearly all of us read science fiction; the rest have at least seen sci fi; we all had a fair grasp of the scope of catastrophe that becomes possible once you start tampering with the fabric of history—whether it's past or future history. If Erin's monkeying around with Time were to accidentally create a paradox, there was indeed an excellent chance that the universe, all of reality, might go away.

Worse—never have existed.

"Well," Zoey said, "we've played for those kind of stakes before," and the *rooba-rooba*ing dwindled away into silence.

She was correct, of course. Ten years earlier, upon our group's arrival in Key West, circumstances (and Nikola Tesla) had forced us to take action to prevent Mir, the Russian space station, from collapsing into an extremely strange state, one with a much lower energy density than what is hereabouts called "perfect" vacuum. Had we failed, all matter as we know it would promptly have ceased to exist within that pinpoint of supervacuum—no more electrons, protons, neutrons, quarks, ergo no atoms or molecules of any kind—and it would then have expanded spherically to engulf and annihilate the entire universe, at the speed of light. A sort of Big Bang, I guess you could say, if you could say that.

No need to thank us; we weren't doing anything else that day anyway. The point is that dicing with the fate of the universe was something at which we had a little experience—more than most people, anyway. Furthermore, we had *succeeded* that last time. You've probably noticed the universe exists. (It's not *our* fault it sucks.)

And finally, that success had been due in large—no, enormous—part to Erin, who had been a two-year-old at the time. Everyone present had either been here back then or had heard the story since. Zoey's reminder had a calming, reassuring effect on us all.

"You're right, Zoey," Arethusa said. "My apologies, Erin. Of course you're aware of the risks, you probably understand them better than I do, and you're definitely the most responsible person here—obviously you've thought this through. So lay it out for us: What is the plan?"

Erin grimaced. "Well, actually . . . I don't exactly have one, as such. I was kind of hoping you and Joe and Willard and Maureen could come up with something good. You're the professionals."

Dead silence.

It expanded spherically to engulf the universe. At light speed.

Finally the Professor put an arm around his wife and spoke up. "You may always," he said serenely, "leave these little things to us."

Erin relaxed slightly. "Thank you, Uncle Willard. I—I've been kind of counting on you. And Maureen. Oh—and you, too, Joe and Arethusa, and Mei-Ling! I know you're all rated peers by your colleagues. But the Professor and Maureen are the only ones here with relevant experience: they've actually *conned* a Tony Donuts already. And won."

The Professor lowered one eyebrow. "Only with considerable help from Lady Sally, in the form of technology sufficiently advanced that even Eric Drexler would call it magic."

Maureen took her head from his shoulder. "You're too modest, my love. We'd have done just fine on our own, if it hadn't been for rotten bad luck. Who could have imagined that even Tony would be stupid enough to print all his phony bills with the same serial number?"

He patted her hair affectionately. "Thank you, love. But really, who could have imagined him being anything else? I just didn't think of it."

Fast Eddie couldn't contain his agitation. He waved for Erin's attention. "Yo, kiddo—I don't geddit. Youse already started *woikin'* the scam dis aftanoon: I seen youse bein older—old enough ta drink legal. How can youse not know what de scam *is?*"

She shook her head. "That wasn't me you saw, Eddo. That was the me I'm going to become in eight more years. Obviously, *she* knows what the scam is. For her, it's ancient history. But I haven't gotten to that page yet."

"But I—" Eddie began, just as I said, "But then—" and Walter said, "How then but—"

She sighed, held up a hand, and rotated around to look at all of us in turn. She generated no ripples on the water in doing so. "Look," she said, "nobody here knows much at all about time travel. I've always been careful to speak just as little as possible on the subject, because that's what Mike Callahan and Lady Sally McGee made me promise, before they taught me how to do it. I know some of you have been curious, and I appreciate you not pressing me on it. This is one of those rare instances when less said really *is* better."

"I'd rather not know anything about it," Noah said, "and I wish nobody else did. Like I said before, it's just too damned dangerous to be fiddling with. You obviously excepted, Erin; you're a supergenius. But nobody else here is."

Erin shrugged. "I have good days. Well, one basic general principle of time travel that several of you already know, and that it shouldn't endanger the rest of you any to learn about, is the principle I call miscegenation, or Conservation of Surprise. Basically it means you're not allowed to peek ahead. Except in certain strictly limited circumstances, information both must not and may not ever be allowed to travel against the flow. I could write a note to my future self, even tell her something in it that she doesn't know . . . but she can't tell me *anything*, and I can't send any messages back to my younger self."

"Can you cheat?" Long-Drink McGonnigle asked. "Like, say you want to tell yourself at age ten who's going to win the World Series that year. Could you time-travel back to, say, ten months before you were born and leave a sealed note with a lawyer with instructions to deliver it to you on your tenth birthday? Or would the action of handing him the envelope cause the universe to pop like a bubble?"

Erin closed her eyes, took a deep breath, and let it out slowly. "Uncle Phil, the fact that you could ask that question proves the point that people should be told as little as possible about how time travel works. So here's the last little bit you need to know—and it's just about everything I know about the scam we're going to run on Tony." She paused, looking for the right words. "There's . . . there's a *sensation*, that I can't describe to you because you've never felt it in your life, but in order to be able to talk about it, let's say it's a tingling on the top of the head. That's a poor analogy because it isn't localized, but let it go. When I feel that particular kind of tingling, I know it means that one of my future selves wants to travel back to my time. It's like asking permission or requesting clearance."

"But if de older Erin does come back here, *youse* gotta go someplace else."

"That's right, Uncle Eddie. Like the cliché almost says, you can't be at two places in the same time. A very big boom would result—at best! So if you feel that special kind of tingling, you have two basic choices. First, you can do nothing at all . . . and after a while the tingling will go away and that's the end of that. Access denied. Or, you could agree to vacate the ficton, hop to some other place, time where you don't already exist, leaving this one to your future self for a while."

"It's sort of like 'condo-share Time,' isn't it?" Long-Drink marveled, adding "Ow!" when someone kicked him in the shin.

"How do you know when it's safe to come back home to your own ficton?" asked the Professor.

"There's another sensation. Call it a tingling on the soles of your feet."

"So this afternoon . . . ," I said, trying to look as if I understood this well enough to complete the sentence.

"This afternoon just before Tony arrived, I felt my scalp tingle, decided to assume my future self knew what it was doing, and the next thing I knew I was wandering around the year 2007, gawking like a tourist."

Fast Eddie opened his mouth.

"And I can't tell you how proud I am that none of my friends would be silly or inconsiderate enough to ask me about what I learned there. *Then,* I mean."

Eddie closed his mouth.

"I guessed immediately what I must be th—What I must be *going* to be thinking—No, wait, I was in 2007, so it's 'what I must *have thought.*'"

"Give it up, dear," Zoey said. "The language wasn't designed to cope with changing fictons—you'll only break it if you try and stretch it that way. You guessed immediately that your future self was planning some sort of time-travel con—"

Erin threw her a grateful look. "Right. That was really all the hint I needed. A con that involves looking progressively younger . . . in Florida . . . what else can it be but the Fountain of Youth?"

"I ask it before, I ask it again," said Bad Death. "Okay, you make Tony Donuts think this fountain be real. I see that you can. *What good is it?*"

Fast Eddie thought that was self-evident. "We can sell it to him, in exchange for . . . *oh.*"

"We tell him, 'Go 'way, don't bother us no more, we make you forever young.' Okay. Next day he wake up one day older, like always. How come he gonna let us live?"

Eddie shrugged. "How come hair conditioner *always* looks like spoim?"

That stopped the clock for a few seconds. When it became clear that nobody had a theory they were prepared to share, Erin went on.

"I'm not really sure *how* it helps us. That's one of the things I was hoping our five resident former players could help me figure out." She turned to them hopefully.

Joe Quigley and the Professor exchanged a meaningful glance. "The basic outline is clear, I think." Joe said.

Prof nodded. "I agree, Giuseppe. The cry goes up and down the Keys: "Donuts is toast!"

Arethusa shook her head. "I don't get it."

Maureen added, "Me either."

Joe turned to his wife. "We persuade Tony the Fountain is real. Then we offer to sell him the location—for more money than he can possibly come up with, even if he rolled up every Russian gangster in Key West."

Arethusa brightened quickest. She's very empathic, and she used to have two heads once. "I get it, love!"

"Explain it to me, Joe," Maureen asked.

"Follow Tony's elephantine thought process. Where could a guy like him possibly get a really big piece of money?"

"The Mafia." she said at once.

"Right. No place else. And when you borrow Mafia money, whose money is it?"

"Charlie Ponte in Miami."

Arethusa shook her head. "He just hands it to you. Whose money *is* it?"

Maureen blinked. "Oh. Well, ultimately I suppose it belongs to the Fi—*Oh*. I get it now."

"*I* don't," said several of us.

"It belongs to the Five Old Men," the Professor told us. "They whose names are not spoken, and whose location is not speculated upon. The ones who own everything."

"The Five *Old* Men," Maureen stressed. "They have something damned close to half a millennium of experience between them. These guys call Bert the Shirt *sonny*."

Her husband nodded. "As soon as Tony thinks of borrowing the money, he'll think of two things: who he's borrowing it from, and what a hassle it'll be to get it from the old bastards. Even someone as bone stupid as Tony should then think, 'Yo, if I tell them what I want it for, and offer to share, I'll get the money no sweat . . . and once I make them young, overnight I become the sixth richest man in the criminal world.'"

"Not enough to make it into the *Fortune* 500, perhaps," said Joe, "but not bad for a wop without a button. And maybe even enough to buy a button."

Fast Eddie was already grinning like a wolf, and so was I. "And then when the magic water turns out to be bogus—," I said.

"Donuts gets dunked," Eddie finished. Grunts of pain were heard here and there.

"Wired to an anchor," Lexington agreed.

"Is that how they're doing it now?" asked the Professor.

Lex nodded. "For true, man. Them cement shoe, the body come back up when the knees go sometimes. Embarrassing."

"Ah."

"Also, very few boats already got cement on them. *All* boats got anchor and wire."

I started to object . . . then realized that if you're dumping a body at sea, and you're not a moron, you're doing it from a stolen boat. Stealing a boat gets tricky with a struggling victim under one arm and a bag of cement under the other. "Gentlemen, we digress."

The Professor nodded happily. "One of the reasons I come here, dear boy. Try this, for example: Imagine you're an ancient evil lizard, blinking in the sun."

"Huh?"

"One of the Five. It's been decades since you've felt a genuine emotion of any kind, let alone passion. It's been decades since you even wished you could still get an erection, nearly as long since you really enjoyed having an enemy killed. You're determined to live forever, but deep down you know you're going to fail—soon, even. Then somebody promises you youth. Forever. He brings proof that convinces you. He takes your money. Raises your hopes. And then you find out he made a fool out of you. Will you be upset?"

Picturing it, I shuddered. "A tad."

"Enough to affect your judgment, perhaps?"

I felt my eyes widening and the hair on the back of my neck beginning to stand up. "Are you talking about *pinning* Tony's murder on them?"

He spread his hands. "Why not? It's not as if we'd be framing them. They'll be *guilty*."

"Could you pin it on all five?" Jim Omar asked. "Nonslip?"

The Professor grimaced in thought. "Maybe not," he conceded.

"Then I say don't do it."

I got my voice back. "Forget that—don't even *think* about it!" I climbed out of the water and stood at poolside to lend my words more weight. "I'm sorry, Willard, but I'm invoking my authority as den mother, here. I have very few house rules, but this is one of them: *We are not taking on the Mafia.*"

"I have to say that sounds reasonable to me, Prof," said Long-Drink.

"Fuckin'-A," said Fast Eddie. "Ya take out a shot dat big, de shrapnel spreads. A lotta innocent bystanders fall. I don't want dat on my conscience."

The Professor sighed and conceded the point. "You're right, of course. The sheer elegance of it carried me away for a moment there. All right, we settle for driving off the mammoth, and leave the brontosaurs alone, and yes, I *know* they're not called brontosaurs anymore. Would someone please bring me a large beaker of booze? Sparing the lives of gangsters is thirsty work." A flagon of firewater was delivered to him, bucket-brigade style, and he drank deep.

"Okay," said Erin, "we're making great progress. I like the general outline of the scam. But I want to know the specifics. What exactly am I supposed to tell the mammoth when he comes grazing in tomorrow and it's time to Tell the Tale? What is the Tale I'll be Telling him?"

"Yes, Willard," said Maureen. "Where is this silly Fountain of Youth supposed to be, and how do we sell it to Tony?"

"All right," the Professor said, licking his lips. "Let's discuss that."

And for the next hour or so, we did.

6

WHEN SHE WAS SEVENTEEN

When I was seventeen
I drank some very good beer . . .
—H.J. Simpson

The next afternoon found Tony Donuts driving down Duval Street in a topless Jeep, glaring into each T-shirt shop he passed.

Nobody has *ever* driven Duval Street at more than thirty miles an hour, and the only one ever to reach that speed was a drunk attempting a getaway. Generally traffic on Duval moves slower than some of the pedestrians, largely because of them. So for one thing, Tony's glares into storefronts were more than just split-second deals. They usually lasted long enough to constitute at least some real reconnaissance, without much risk of his rear-ending some elderly tourist couple from Wisconsin.

For another thing, he had plenty of time to notice the attractive blonde in a yellow shorts-and-top combo, coming his way on the south side of the street—even enough to recognize her and recall where he'd seen her before, though it took him a while. By the time he worked out *why* it had taken him so long to place her, however, he was already past her.

He jammed on the brakes, put the Jeep in reverse, and stepped on the gas. He just had time to see her wave at him and step into an alley between a bar and a head shop before he was rear-ended by an elderly tourist couple from Wisconsin. He considered ignoring this and turning hard left into the alley, but saw that the alley was too narrow to accommodate his vehicle. He sighed, shut off the Jeep, and got out. The already shaken tourist couple turned to stone. A line of cars was forming behind theirs, but not one honked. Tony tossed the geezer the keys to the Jeep and pointed to it with his thumb. "Meet me here this time tamorra," he said. "Have that fixed."

"Yessir," said the geezer. The keys had bounced off his face and landed somewhere near his feet. He made no attempt to retrieve them, moved no voluntary muscle until Tony turned away to enter the alley.

Nearly at once the man monster found that the alley was barely wide enough to accommodate *him*, and no cleaner than anything else along Duval Street. He cursed under his breath and plunged ahead anyway. In six steps his double-breasted suit needed dry-cleaning. He thought of giving up and going back . . . but behind him he heard the geezer from Wisconsin trying to start up the Jeep and yelling at his geezette to follow him back to the motel, and Tony just didn't feel like dealing with all that crap. So he pressed on, and in six more steps his suit needed reweaving.

The next time his passage was impeded by an air conditioner sticking a few inches out into the alley, he drove it entirely into the building with a single blow from the heel of his fist and kept going. Behind him, a drunk biker stuck his head and a knife out the hole, looked at Tony's back, changed his mind, and withdrew without speaking. "Act of God, man," Tony heard the biker say to someone inside.

At the end of the alley was another alley running parallel to Duval Street, wider than the first but not by much. Not wide enough for most delivery trucks, for example, which is another of the reasons why traffic runs so slow on Duval, and a hint as to how long ago downtown Key West was laid out. Tony reached this mews just in time to catch a good look at the blonde before she entered the back door of some shop or other. But when he reached the door, it was locked.

He was already sweating in his suit. He was *always* sweating in his suit; he just didn't know any gangster costume with short pants or a tank top. He considered giving up the chase. It was, after all, just a broad.

But he'd had two pretty good looks at her now, and he was pretty sure. Having lived in a few states with different statutory ages of consent, Tony had become almost as good as a barkeeper at judging ages, especially female ages . . . and he was just about positive what he was following now was the sassy broad whose boob he'd honked the day before—only today she was a good three or four years younger. It was the boob that nailed it down for him, actually. Broads could make themselves look younger, and God knew they could make their boobs look bigger, even be bigger . . . but in Tony's experience they did not make boobs *smaller*.

It's her kid sister, he told himself. *Her kid sister, that's all it is. Sisters look a lot alike sometimes.* But he kept remembering her waving good-bye as she'd entered the alley. Something had been written on the palm of her hand, in Magic Marker. Too far away to see clearly, but it *could* have been his signature. . . .

And if it *was* her, she was not only an interesting mystery, but a mystery who had promised that today she was going to show him something better than money or sex.

So Tony mopped at his soaking forehead with a handkerchief so expensive it was almost useless, sighed again, punched the door once, and then walked over it.

He found himself in an everything shoppe, one of those dimly lit, mildewy-smelling, overstuffed junkyards in which the only thing you *can't* find is the way out. It looked like where all the yard sales live during the week. He tried to spot the broad, but the place stunned the eye somehow. A coot (the stage right after geezer, when you aren't even trying to fake it anymore) stood nearby, gaping at Tony where a door should be; Tony grabbed him by the shoulder and said, "Blonde come in just now? Yellow playsuit?"

The coot nodded so rapidly the vertebrae of his neck sounded like castanets and dust flew out of his beard.

Tony lifted him clear off the floor with the one hand, straight-arm, with no apparent effort. "Where?"

The coot gestured with the arm that still functioned, toward the front of the shop, toward Duval Street and its crowds.

"Out?"

More frantic nodding.

Tony brought the coot so close their eyes were inches apart. "Where to?" But when the coot pissed himself Tony knew he didn't know, so he just let him drop and stepped over him.

The front of the store was deserted, which figured. As he looked around to see if she was hiding somewhere, a photocopy machine he hadn't noticed suddenly wheezed noisily into life a foot away, surprising him. Tony didn't like surprises, so he punched the machine to teach it a lesson, and the piece of paper it had just extruded as its dying act went fluttering to the floor. He would have ignored anything white with print on it . . . but this sheet was dark. It stirred his memory, catapulted him back to carefree days of youth spent documenting the crack of his own and others' buttocks in the school library. It was a photocopy of an open human hand, in such high contrast that the skin didn't look as poorly mummified as usual, and it was quite easy to make out Tony's own signature across the palm.

He still couldn't see the way out of the dump, so he made one of his own. Soon he was outside in sunshine again, surrounded by rubble, broken glass, and an expanding ring of tourists, fugitives, weirdos, and college students on break. The majority of them were either stoned or drunk, and nearly all of them had come there for the specific purpose of exhibiting bad judgment—but nobody jostled Tony or criticized him for blocking traffic or even raised an eyebrow. Nobody ever did. He looked east, failed to spot the blonde in the crowd, looked west just as she blew past him on a bicycle, barely missing him. As she went by she lifted her hand, displaying his autograph again, and when he raised his own hands to deflect a possible slap, she darted under his guard . . . and pinched his left nipple.

He gaped after her. He was a man not often astonished. There were other bicyclists too nearby to escape; he could have had his pick of bikes. It was just too frigging hot for a bike race in a business suit. Instead he found himself staring, mesmerized, at the teenage buttocks and thighs that were pedaling her away from him.

It was only after she'd turned north a few blocks down and disappeared from view that he realized he could have jacked a moped just as easily as a one-speed clunker bike, and maybe caught her. Tony had not been in Key West long enough yet to think of mopeds as serious transportation.

Screw it, he decided. Key West was a speed bump; she wasn't going anywhere. Put her on the to-do list and get back to work. He began looking around for the donor of his next car. This time something with air-conditioning.

The hooker he rented that night earned every penny.

As for us, there really wasn't much worth reporting for us to *do*, that day. Tony came by at his usual time for his daily bite, refraining from robbing my customers individually now that we had established a business relationship. Instead he tried to pump me about the mysterious blonde broad. Bolstered by the company and telepathic support of my friends, I found the courage to look him in his fearsome eye and convince him I knew nothing about her, had never seen her before yesterday, couldn't tell him where she was. (It helped that technically I wasn't, quite, lying. I'd never met either the twenty-one- or the seventeen-year old Erin, had never seen either before yesterday . . . and didn't have a clue where either was now. Only *when* they were.) Tony believed me and left, and that was that day as far as our con was concerned.

Nevertheless, it was the most memorable day of the entire affair for me—all because of what started out that night seeming to be the sort of absolutely generic, standard issue, garden-variety philosophical conversation for which bars are notorious.

It was late, getting on toward closing time. Few remained, Eddie had packed it in for the night, and people were keeping their voices down in consideration of those who might be asleep in the five cottages. I had left my post behind the bar, and gone around back of it—*behind* behind the bar, if you follow me—to empty the used-grounds hopper of The Machine into a trash can. The area back there behind the big wall of booze bottles is relatively secluded, and not heavily used due to the nature of trash cans in Florida sunshine; if the breeze fails, the smell can be something you could raise houseplants in. But we aren't becalmed much at The Place, and some folks like privacy, so I keep a few tables back there. I came upon Doc Webster sitting alone at one now. That was odd; the Doc may not be the most gregarious man I know, but he's definitely in the top three. We've had a firm no-prying policy in force for decades, but it's pretty much always been blatant hypocrisy.

Rather than simply stepping over there and asking him why he was by himself, however, I began singing a new song parody I was working up, softly, as if to myself. The tune was Sir Paul's title song for the James Bond film *Live and Let Die*.

When we were young, with our heads in an open book
We used to read Niven/Pournelle
(you know you did, you know you did, you know you did)
And in this ever-changing world, Pournelle and Niven
hope the fans will still buy . . .

I paused and waited hopefully. And was pleased when, as I'd hoped, the Doc was unable to prevent himself from singing, *"The Mote in God's Eye—"* He was willing to accept company.

"Let me guess," I said, strolling over to his table. "You're sitting by yourself because some Cuban-Irish guy persuaded you to try a taco scone."

He was off his game. It took him a whole second to identify the straightline, see the punchline I planned, and improve on it. "The famous 'scone with the wind,' yes, it was Tara-ble."

I took a seat downwind of him and fired up a doobie. Slimmer than a soda straw, but it was Texada Timewarp from

British Columbia; two or three hits would be plenty. And again the Doc surprised me. I'd sat downwind out of courtesy, because I knew he wasn't a head, but he reached out and took the joint out of my fingers, and shortened it an inch with a single toke. Which he held so long, the exhalation was barely visible, long enough for me to have two more tokes of my own. Our eyes met, and we beamed at each other like twin Buddhas, one chubby and one skinny, while the night began to sparkle in our peripheral vision.

I offered him a second hit, but he waved it away, so I set the joint down in an ashtray. After a few minutes of shared silent stone, he suddenly asked, "Do you think we'll ever see Mike again, Jake?" That toke had hoarsened his voice a little.

The question took me by surprise. "Why, sure. I guess. One of these days."

"It's been ten years now."

He was right. The question had been bothering me, too. I didn't often let it rise up to conscious level. "I guess he figured we were ready to solo. You know?"

"Well, I wish he'd asked first."

"Doc, are you pissed off about something? At Mike Callahan?"

"At myself. At all of us idiots. For *years* we had him around all the time. We didn't really know for sure that he was *literally* superhuman until right near the end, there, but it was pretty much always clear that he knew stuff nobody else knew. Am I right?"

I hear that question a lot. The answer is always, "Yeah, you're right." This time it happened to be accurate.

"Every fucking night of the week we had him. And then he buggered off to the ass end of space or the far end of time or some damn thing—but he came back to visit at fairly frequent intervals, partied with us for days at a time, helped us save the world once, am I right?" After the first one, a nod suffices. "And then when we all moved down here, he showed up for Opening Day, spent one whole night with us, and we haven't seen hide nor hair of the wonderful son of a bitch since, not him nor his whole fam damily, am I right?"

Nod. "What's your point, Doc?"

"We blew it. That's my point. All of us. How could we be so goddamn stupid?"

"Blew what?"

"How could we have had unfettered access, for so long, to a man who clearly knew some of the final answers—and never once have asked him any of the questions?"

I knew what he meant, and didn't want to admit it. "What questions?"

"Don't play dumb, Jake. The important questions."

I was too stoned *not* to admit it. "Oh. Those."

"How did all this—" He gestured at the universe around us. "—get here? How did I come to be stuck here in it? Will I end, when I cool? If not, then what?" He relit the joint, took a second great hit.

So I continued for him. "Does it matter what I do in the meantime? If so, why? Is it all *going* somewhere? Is there some kind of point? Or is virtue its own *only* reward? Is there a God?"

Doc exhaled and took up the litany. "And if so, is anyone mounting an assault on Heaven? That's the thing I never grokked about religious belief, you know? All that time I spent watching people die for a living . . . watching their loved ones buckle with grief and loss . . . seeing that all human lives begin with agony, and most of them end with it . . . that no more than five or ten percent of real-life stories, if that, get anything you could possibly call a happy ending—" Deep breath. "—that a good half of even those of us lucky enough to die in a hospital bed die in unbearable pain, which God allegedly forbids us to shorten . . . that when we *beg* Him on our knees for ten thousand years straight to explain why this torture must happen, to as many souls as procreatively possible, all we get back is 'Trust me.'" Deep breath. He reached across the table, took my hand, squeezed. "I can understand people who believe in God, Jacob. I just can't understand why they aren't trying their best to kill the motherfucker."

"Jesus Christ, Sam!"

He let go of my hand, picked up what was left of the joint, and squinted at it. It had gone out again. "This is ditty pood grope," he said, and then he sighed and his shoulders slumped. "Shit."

"Sam, what's wrong?"

He dropped the roach on the table. "I was about to say it seemed to help suppress the spoonerisms. I brant seem to latch a cake. Oh, bin of a *such!*" Without warning he slapped the ashtray into a nearby ficus.

Shocked, I took his hand back and held it in both of mine. "What's the matter? Something with Mei-Ling?" It was a natural conclusion to leap to. Doc's wife, at age forty-mumble, was the only one of the five Lady Sally's alumnae who was still working—and that profession is a lot more dangerous these days than it used to be.

He leaned closer, added his free hand to the pile, and lowered his voice. "Jake . . . I have a humor in my ted."

Suddenly I was too stupid to untangle a spoonerism. "What?"

"I have a tomb brainer. Damn it, a train boomer. *Shit.*" He lowered his head, took a deep breath, and said slowly and carefully, "There is an evil spider growing in my skull. It will sill . . . will kill me soon."

I could feel my eyeballs trying to bulge out of my head. "Oh, my God. Oh, Sam!"

In my head I was thinking, No, there's been a mistake, the script editor has fucked up, this is wrong, wrong! Doc Webster isn't one of the ones who *die*, for Chrissakes. He's not a spear-carrier; he's one of the heroes. Like me.

"Spoonerism is one of the symptoms," he explained. "It'll get progressively worse. After a while I won't even know for sure if I'm newing . . . if I'm doing it or not."

"How long?" I heard myself ask. He would say a year, and I would tell him about my cousin in Canada who'd been told he had a brain tumor that would kill him in a year, and was still alive and well three years later—

He shrugged. "Maybe a week. Maybe a month. Not two."

I felt a wave of dizziness. "Who else knows?"

"Aside from professionals, only Mei-Ling, until just now. I was hoping to keep it that way, for as pong as lossable. But she can't wake the late atone."

So that was why the doc had been sitting alone.

"She's home, crying?"

He nodded. "I certainly hope so. I left to give her the chance."

I've read that in the Old West, if you really pissed off the Comanche, they used to cut open your chest and pour in hot coals while you were still alive. I felt like that now, only with ice cubes. I couldn't seem to get enough air, felt my stomach clench like a fist, and wondered briefly if I were having a heart attack. This news was more than I could encompass, way more than I was prepared to accept. "I can't carry this alone, either, Sam," I said. "I gotta tell everybody. I'm sorry."

"I know." He nodded. "I know, Jake. I've known that since you sat down. Shared pain is lessened." He shuddered slightly. "But you tell them for me, okay? I've been dying all trey, and I just can't deem to suet."

I said nothing. I was trying to decide whether I had it in me to tell all my friends that my oldest friend—just about everybody's oldest friend—was on his way out. Doc Webster had been responsible for bringing many of us to Callahan's in the first place. (Pun intended.)

And just then a strange and wonderfully dopey thing happened. More to relieve the tension in our necks than anything else, he and I both happened to lift our gazes skyward—just as a meteor flared overhead. Automatically we sucked a little air through our teeth. And then the doc said, with quiet wonder, "Wow— a starting shoe."

For some reason, I broke up. It started as a giggle, and before I knew it, I was laughing so hard I literally fell off my ass, ended up curled up on the ground, pounding it and whooping.

Well, you know. Maybe Ebola is as contagious as laughter . . . but I doubt it. Doc lost it seconds after I did, and remained seated only because his center of gravity is lower; that's my story, anyway. When we might have stopped laughing, he said, "Trust me to find a ridiculous death," and we were off again.

After a while I helped him to his feet and walked him home. It didn't take long: Doc and Mei-Ling live right next door to me and Zoey, no more than a hundred yards from the bar. He barely had time to tell me the one about the lion who enters a clearing and sees two men, one reading a book and the other typing away on a laptop, and knows at once which man to eat first (readers digest, and writers cramp), and then we were there. We stood at his door, looking at each other for a long moment, as awkward and self-conscious as teenage first-daters trying to decide whether to go for a good-night kiss or just agree what a terrific time we'd had. Two unusually articulate men, completely at a loss for words. Finally he sighed and said, "Well, thanks, Timmy—I really had a terrific time," so I pulled him into my arms and hugged him as hard as I could and kissed the side of his neck and he stroked my hair and hugged back, and it was quite some time before we remembered to be embarrassed again and let go.

He flashed me the crooked smile I knew so well and went inside, and I stood there a moment. I hadn't quite finished all my closing rituals yet, and distant murmurs told me there were still a few customers in the house. But none of the undone chores was mission-critical, and I don't have any regulars I don't trust to close The Place. To hell with it. I left the compound by the parking lot entrance, where I'd be less likely to be seen leaving, and walked west to Mallory Square.

Packed and bustling though it is at sunset, the square is almost always completely deserted late at night: the area is too open and exposed and just a bit too well lit to constitute a good place to neck. As always, there was no slightest trace of evidence that dozens of vendors and street performers had been doing lucrative business here only hours earlier, not even an empty film container to mark the passage of thousands of stunned, stoned, or stained tourists and their children. As usual, the only one present was John the Fisherman, fishing alone off the south end of the pier just as he has every night of his life, as far as anyone can remember; we exchanged nods as I passed. I sat on concrete right at the edge of the dock, at the spot where Will Soto always sets up his tightrope for the sunset celebration, lit the stub of my Texada Timewarp, and stared across a few hundred yards of dark slow water at what the Chamber of Commerce would like you to call Sunset Key, and every Conch calls Tank Island. It was an absolutely textbook Key West night: air the temperature and the approximate humidity of a spit-take, coming from the west in a gentle, steady breeze against my face. It kept away the fried-food-and-beer smells of Duval a few blocks behind me; I smelled only brine, iodine, my roach, and a faint hint of petroleum product spills from that day's cruise ships. In the far distance a huge dark cloud loomed over the Gulf of Mexico, heading this way, but it would be hours before it arrived. It seemed a perfect metaphor. Darkness coming for my oldest friend, still a ways off but unstoppable.

I sat there for maybe an hour. I tried to wrap my mind around the news, and failed. I tried to imagine a world without Doc Webster in it, finding the funny parts for us, and failed. I tried to cry for him, and failed.

Finally I made up my mind, found a pay phone, dialed from memory a number I'd once solemnly promised myself I would never use again, and failed at that, too. I couldn't raise so much as voice mail. I counted twenty-five rings, then gave up. Did you know that with the proper wrist action, you can get the handset of a pay phone to skip seven times? (Try it yourself.) When I got back to The Place I found that as expected someone had done an imperfect but adequate job of closing up for me. I just set out food for Pixel and Harry, dropped a pair of hard-boiled eggs into the pool for Lex's breakfast, and went straight to bed. Okay, went stoned to bed.

Zoey got in about half an hour later, dragging her bass and her ass. She'd had a jazz gig that night, and the way it works for her is, the better the music she plays, the more exhausted she is when she comes home. I thought I was doing a fair job of feigning sleep until she said, "Jesus, Jake, what's the matter? Is Erin okay?"

I rolled over. "What do you, read shoulder blades? Erin's fine, sound asleep. Come to bed."

"Are *you* okay?"

"Hey, my wife says I'm a lot better than okay."

"To you, maybe. What's wrong?"

"Can we talk about it in the morning?"

"Of course we can. We can talk about it whenever we like. Right now, for instance."

She wasn't going to let it go, so I decided to just get it over with, tell her the news as calmly and dispassionately as I could and then try to comfort her. "You know how I'm always saying Doc's puns are brain damaged?" I began, and then I lost it, started crying as hard as I ever have in my life, in great racking sobs that threatened to tear my diaphragm, might have if not for the strength in my Zoey's arms. After a while I was able to squeeze out words between shuddering intakes of breath, "Tumor," and, "Inoperable," and, "Mindkiller," and, "Week. Month, tops." Somewhere in there, Erin joined the hug, and even in my pain I was impressed because I've personally seen her sleep through both a hurricane and a riot.

A long time later I came to the awareness that I was cried out, hollow. It was like vomiting: you don't exactly feel good afterwards, just a tiny bit less rotten—but that tiny bit makes the difference between intolerable and endurable. I realized there seemed to be only one pair of arms around me now, opened my eyes and learned they were my daughter's. I started to ask where her mother was, and then I knew. Zoey was next door, with Mei-Ling. I closed my eyes, and when I opened them again it was morning, and the arms holding me were once again my wife's, and we were both crying.

I usually keep bartender's hours. That day, I was awake at the crack of dawn.

Even so, leaving my bed took everything I had; leaving my house seemed out of the question. I knew there was a perfect sunny day outside, because there nearly always was, and I wanted no part of it. An insoluble dilemma lay out there. The moment I stepped out onto my porch I would start seeing and being seen by my friends, some of them anyway. I knew I could not look even one of my friends in the eye even momentarily without telling them that Doc was dying, and yet for the life of me I could not imagine myself doing so, could not think of the right words to use. So I dithered around in the house as long as possible, and then some more. I made what even for me was a special omelette, so large and complicated that it really should have been considered a full-scale omel, and wolfed the whole thing down. Zoey and Pixel stared at me. I frequently cook omelettes—for supper; it may have been the first time either of them had ever seen me eat a bite less than five hours after awakening. I did all the dirty dishes, by hand, and dried them all with a towel. Zoey and Pixel stared even harder. I made the bed—well, I always do that, being almost always the last one out of it, but this day I decided it was not only time to change the sheets, but also to rotate *and* flip the mattress. Then I collected the trash that would not be put out for another three days, and began coaxing the old newspapers into a more orderly stack. Erin and Pixel were staring at each other now.

When I started alphabetizing the spice rack, Zoey came over and put a firm hand on my shoulder. "The bad times, too," she said enigmatically, and slipped her arm through mine. "Come on, Slim. Let's go open the store."

I closed my eyes and sighed. Three times in a row, each longer and deeper than the last. And finally nodded.

By the time we got as far as the porch, my nose and ears had already given me a pretty accurate head count and roster. Roughly three dozen folks, nearly all hard-core long-timers. Unusually large crowd for so early in the day. Had the news about Doc leaked already? No, I realized; the faithful had begun to gather in anticipation and support of the imminent scamming of Tony Donuts Junior. I'd forgotten I also had that to look forward to. I'd have balked there in the doorway if it were possible to balk while arm in arm with a moving Zoey.

After ten years in Key West I had become enough of a connoisseur to discern the differences between a garden-variety perfect day and a Platonic ideal; that day was one of the latter. The blue of the sky looked like about six coats, hand rubbed. Sunlight danced on the surface of the pool like Tinkerbell's gym class. A gentle breeze carried scents of Key lime, coral dust, sunblock, sulfur, seashore, and the competing but compatible lunch smells of several culinary schools, chiefly Cuban, Creole, and Islands cooking from Bahama Village to the south of us. Somewhere nearby, children and a small dog hooted with joy and did something that made rhythmic crunching gravel sounds like castanets. In the fifty-yard walk to the bar, I was smiled at, nodded at, or waved to by just about everyone present. They all seemed to accept my answering grimace as a smile.

Tom Hauptman was at the stick, selling as much cola and lemonade as beer, and he'd just started making somebody a Cuban sandwich; the gloriously layered fragrances of ham, roast pork, cheese, pickle, and press-toasted bread were already beginning to circulate. I left Zoey at her usual stool and joined Tom behind the bar. But instead of pitching in with the sandwiches, I squatted down, opened a cabinet, and took out a grey cylinder the approximate size of a can of baseballs, if there is such a thing. Some seated at the bar fell silent as they recognized it, and they sat up straighter. A very kind person named Colin MacDonald once fetched it back from Ireland for me. Its simple greyscale label reads, in part,

The World's Oldest Whiskey Distillery

BUSHMILLS
DISTILLERY RESERVE
SINGLE IRISH
MALT WHISKEY

This Premium Irish Whiskey is exclusive
to Visitors at the Old Bushmills
Distillery originally granted its
Licence to distil in 1608.

Aged 12 Years

THIS BOTTLE WAS SPECIALLY
LABELED FOR
Jake Stonebender
AT THE DISTILLERY

I cracked the lid, eased out the amber bottle, and set it reverently on the bar. Its front label mirrored the one on the can; the one on the back said,

Bushmills Distillery Reserve
is a Single Malt Whiskey
aged in oak casks for 12–14 years.
We have selected this whiskey for its
exceptional quality and
smoothness.

*This fine whiskey has a soft, sherried
nose giving way to a full-bodied,
malty taste with overtones
of almond and marzipan.*

The bottle was within an inch or two of being full. I went
to the dishwasher, took out a full rack of shot glasses, and
began setting them up on the bar top next to the Bushmills
Distillery Reserve, in rows. Silence broke out along the bar,
and slowly metastasized to the nearby tables, the pool and
lounge chairs, and the croquet pitch someone had set up just
beyond the fireplace. Those who were free to do so started
drifting toward the bar; the rest began arranging things so as
to be able to do the same, if they could. It was way too early
in the day to be drinking whiskey, especially that whiskey, but
they all knew I knew that.

I counted heads, skipping those I knew would not drink
whiskey for one reason and another, and set out that many
shot glasses. When I was done filling them all, the bottle had
only two or three shots left in it. I poured assorted soft drinks
for the nondrinkers.

"Fill your hands," I said, and soon the bar top was empty
except for the bottle. I picked it up and took it with me to the
chalk line before the fireplace. People made way for me, then
waited for me to make my toast.

Whoever had closed up for me the night before had not
only shoveled out the ashes, but had also taken the trouble to
set up the next evening's fire for me: a pyramid of wood on a
base of kindling and crumpled newsprint. I thought about
lighting it, or having it lit; either seemed too much trouble,
too theatrical. A fire in the morning in Key West is ridiculous,
like a cold shower outdoors in Nunavut. I'd been trying to
think of the right words since the night before. It seemed

time to give up, and just say whatever the hell came into my head. Only nothing came into my head.

I turned and looked around at my friends. They could all see I was in pain. Not telling them what it was was impolite, keeping them in suspense. I lifted the bottle, as one lifts a glass to propose a toast, and everybody lifted theirs. "Empty your glasses," I said, and upended the bottle and drank until nothing came out.

Nobody argued or questioned or mentioned the early hour; as one they drank with me.

I tossed the bottle a few inches in the air, changed my grip on it to its neck, and flung it into the fireplace, so hard that it managed to destroy the fire setup before exploding against the back wall.

"I planned for that bottle to last a lifetime," I said, and then shook my head. "I just didn't know whose."

I could see faces begin to change, and I understood that keeping them all in the dark any longer now would be unforgivable—and still, forcing out the few simple words was harder than fingertip push-ups.

"Doc's dying. Maybe one week, maybe four. Not eight. Brain tumor."

Five seconds of pindrop silence crawled by, and then something happened for which I can find no other adjective than that most overused of words, *awesome*. Maybe you were in a crowd when you heard about 9/11, or about the Nameless One backshooting Johnny Lennon, and you know what I mean; if you don't, I hope you never find out. When two or three dozen adults all suddenly burst loudly into tears at once, it goes beyond sad or tragic or even terrible; it's all three of those, certainly, but most of all it's just . . . awesome.

Groans, sobs, wails, wordless outcries of all kinds. Loudest was Long-Drink McGonnigle, who fell to his knees, bellowing like a speared bull. Lex made a gargling sound, cut the water in a running dive, and disappeared. Every couple there turned to each other and embraced, their empty glasses still in hand. So did many singles; multiperson hugs formed simultaneously in several locations. Some people just sat down as if their strings had been cut, on the ground if necessary. Fast Eddie's head was on his keyboard, his hands clasped on the back of his head. Noah González turned on his heel and walked away as if rejecting the whole business, then stopped and came back—then left again, then came back—I remember thinking it must be hard for him to keep pivoting that way with only the one leg. Tommy Janssen dropped his empty glass, beat his temples with the heels of his hands three times, then held his skull in them as if to keep it from bursting. I found myself in a group embrace with Double Bill, Josie Bauer, Arethusa, either Suzy or Susie Maser, and my wife. A group embrace with everybody sobbing in a different rhythm is really weird, but there was some comfort in it just the same.

An empty glass burst in the fireplace. I didn't see who started it. Suzy Maser was second. Then Omar. A few seconds later, three more glasses arrived together, then a scattering, and finally the barrage began in earnest. The hug I was in broke up in order to participate. That fireplace is designed specifically to retain broken glass under just such conditions, but shards sprayed from it now, and so did brick chips.

Finally it dwindled away as we all ran out of ammo—except for Long-Drink. When his glass was gone, he threw his hat after it . . . and then his sunglasses, and then his cigarettes, and then his beeper, and then his watch . . . he was reaching behind him for his wallet when Omar and Tommy put hands on his shoulders and made him stop. Gently but firmly they got him to his feet and led him away like James

Brown, to the cottage he shares with Tommy. I was vaguely glad it lies to the north of my own, between mine and Eddie's, so they didn't have to pass Doc and Mei-Ling's place to get there. Maureen hurried ahead of them and got the door, then followed them in.

Eventually people started talking, of course. But you know, even in my grief I noticed then that not once did one person ask me a single stupid question. Nobody said, "Are they sure?" or, "Can't they do something?" or, "Why don't they operate?" or, "How's Mei-Ling taking it?" or any of the useless things people always say in such situations, because they feel they have to say something and there *is* nothing sensible. I was asked only one question, and it was a pretty good one; I only wished I had a happy answer. Fast Eddie called out, "Yo Jake. Mike don't answer?"

People stopped talking to hear my reply. I found that I could not trust my voice, even with a single syllable, so I just shook my head. And that made everyone slump a bit more, but nobody felt a need to follow up with, "Not even his machine?" or, "Did you let it ring ten times?" or, "Are you sure you got the number right?" or any other intelligence-insulting question. *Okay, we can't order up a miracle, it was worth a try, let's move on,* was the general attitude. Do you see why I've devoted my life to hanging out with those people? Within the next couple of minutes, we had sorted ourselves out, quite automatically, without direction or conscious decision. Each one of us needed help, to one degree or another—some more, some less. Each one of us had some kind of help to give—some more, some less. We'd known each other a long time, and been mutually telepathic more than once. So we triaged ourselves, without needing to think much about it. We mixed and matched and remixed and improvised until those in need got some and those with surplus gave some, and everyone found at least some measure of solace. With the help of alcohol, cannabis, tobacco, coffee, chocolate, and food—but most of all with the help of each other—we got through that morning together.

All of us except the Professor and Erin, who spent most of it way over on the other side of town, with nobody but Tony Donuts Junior for company.

7

TELLING THE TALE

No conditions are permanent;
No conditions are reliable;
Nothing is self.
—the Buddha

Of Antonio Donnazzio Junior his own mother had once said, "You know how some people don't know shit? Little Tony don't *suspect* shit." (To which his maternal grandfather had replied, "Fuckin-A. Little prick makes his old man look like that Lord Stevie Hawkins. Whaddya mean, who? You know who I mean. Rain Man in a wheelchair.") There had never been the slightest danger of Tony Junior suddenly needing a tuxedo because he'd been invited to Stockholm, and no one had ever, at least not with sincerity, asked his advice on anything.

Nevertheless, he'd had an entire night to integrate in his mind both brand-new information—*I know somebody who can get younger*—with some of the oldest information his brain retained—*the world is owned by five very very old men*.

Everything he had been doing for the past few weeks, ever since he'd arrived in Key West, had the single purpose of impressing one or more of those very very old men. For although he was not bright enough to have figured it out for himself, he had finally terrorized someone knowledgeable into explaining to him that this was what it would take for him to become a made guy—that no mere capo or even don would or even could make that decision. Pressed, hard, his informant had explained that it wasn't, at least not entirely, because Tony wasn't Sicilian, and it wasn't, at least not entirely, because he was, let's face it, a potential discipline problem, and it wasn't even that most people found him a little intimidating on a one-to-one basis, or even a one-to-six-heavily-armed basis. What it mostly was, really, was that he was the son of Tony Donuts Senior, who in his own gaudy passage through life had made few even temporary allies and no friends, and not for nothin', but it didn't help he even had the same friggin' *name* fachrissake. This was monstrously, manifestly unfair, of course, but there was nothing Tony Junior could do about it except strangle his informant, which was small satisfaction.

Mulling it over for months, he'd seen that the Five Old Men could not be either frightened or reasoned with. They would have to be bribed. But they were used to being bribed by the best, with the most, so it was going to take a pretty big piece of money.

That was what had led to his southward migration. The only plan he'd come up with himself for raising serious money was to double the tax he imposed on each of his personal stable of extortion victims. It was not a great plan. His standard rates had not been merciful, even by protection racket standards; doubled, they became a burden so crushing that a few of the goats actually dared to balk. During one such renegotiation Tony found himself distracted, and digressed to ask the other party where in the *hell* he'd ever found such a stupid T-shirt. The shop owner had acquired the memorably obscene garment in question on Duval Street during a recent vacation in Key West, had noticed the obvious signs of Russian mob incursion there, and was well aware of Tony's only frustrated ambition; in desperate hope of shortening his hospital stay, he invented the whole scam on the spot and gave it to Tony. Go down there, roll up the Commies, give their balls and their loot to the old men, and they'll give you a button. It took two or three repetitions, each faster and more concise than the last, for Tony to grasp the nub of the scheme, but when he did, he liked it so much that he generously put its inventor out of his misery at once.

On arrival in Key West, he quickly learned that Einstein had screwed him. The Russians were well dug in, in numbers that even he had to respect, and their principal racket appeared to be money laundering, about which Tony understood slightly less than nothing. They'd be hard to take, and once taken would constitute a prize he wasn't even sure how to pick up, much less present to the old men.

So he had stalled. First he would lock up the rest of Key West, which anyone could see was a boat race for a man of his talents, and then from that power base he would take on the Russians. So far, the strategy was not working a hell of a lot better than it had for Napoleon or Hitler.

It was just as much aggravation and legwork to lock up Key West as any other city, but once you had it, there was far less than usual to steal. Tony slowly learned that Key West was where all the losers in North America ended up, sooner or later. A few days after he had that epiphany, it occurred to him that Key West was where *he* had ended up, and from that time on, he tended to be even more impatient and irritable than his nature would have dictated. Not good.

And then along came his lucky break, the unexpected

answer to all his problems. Not just a miracle, but *the* miracle: the only thing that the Five Old Men wanted more than money. In the possession of a girl. Who got littler and more defenseless—and more infuriatingly insolent—every time he saw her.

Tony's impatience escalated to a state not far short of frenzy.

So when he went to Duval Street to get his Jeep back the next morning, he was in no mood to waste any time on the transaction. He had a broad to hunt. And was aware that almost every other male on Duval Street was also hunting a broad, which was bound to obscure his view, and also that there were *thousands* of broads around, maybe half of them blond, at least this week.

Fortunately for the peace of the commonweal, the staff of the emergency room at the hospital on Stock Island, and himself, the elderly tourist from Wisconsin was punctual. When Tony got out of the cab, which departed without waiting for payment, there the geezer was, and there parked beside him was Tony's Jeep.

Tony walked around the vehicle with a critical eye. From the front bumper to the new rear one, it was visibly in far better condition than it had been yesterday. He grunted in satisfaction. Even the interior looked good: the floors had been swept, the ashtray had been emptied, and a crack in the driver's seat upholstery that had been starting to annoy him was repaired. He turned, leaned back against the vehicle, and said, "Ahright," holding out his hand for the keys.

"Had to pay double to have it ready this fast," the geezer said, greatly relieved by Tony's approval. In a wild spasm of optimism, he passed over the receipt along with the keys. "Come to thirteen hundred."

"You got fucked," Tony told him. He climbed into the Jeep, started it up, and drove away without looking, confident that the stream of traffic would let him in.

His plan was to drive a few blocks farther, park, and go up to the observation deck of the Holiday Inn LaConcha. It is one of the tallest structures in Key West (the tallest with an elevator), and centrally located. The only way to get a better view of the entire island at once is to rent a helicopter, and helicopters are noisy and don't serve booze. But before he'd driven even half a block, Tony's attention was distracted by something irritatingly not-right about the brake pedal.

He stopped to examine the problem. (Fortunately the driver behind him today was more alert than the geezer had been yesterday, and stopped so far short of rear-ending Tony that even when his own car got rear-ended and punted forward a foot, he was still okay.) The problem turned out to be just what it had seemed to be: a piece of paper, ridiculously taped to the brake. With difficulty he bent and picked it up. (Another collision occurred, several vehicles back; croquet effect pushed the first car in line to within a few inches of Tony's brand-new rear bumper, and the driver began having an anxiety attack.)

It was a photocopy of a delicate hand with Tony's own inimitable signature on it, and its middle finger was extended.

Tony had just ten seconds ago inspected the interior of the Jeep, and there had been no paper taped to its brake pedal then. Therefore, the little miracle broad was no more than a couple of hundred yards behind him, laughing at him.

He climbed out of the Jeep just before it was jolted forward a foot by the car immediately behind it, amid a blaring of horns that fell silent when he appeared. Automatically he started to tell the other driver to have the Jeep back here, fixed, by tomorrow, but the man seemed to have fainted.

Tony had no time to screw around; he gave the responsibility and keys to the second driver in line—an elderly nun from Fresno—and forgot the Jeep's existence for now.

He could see the geezer from where he stood, sitting now in the front seat of his own car, being berated by his geezette. He had begun to drive away from there, but then the traffic had halted, stopping him halfway out of his parking space. Apparently he was farsighted; before Tony had taken more than a few steps in that direction, the old bird saw him, paled, spun the wheel hard left, and stomped on the gas. His car slammed into a gap between two of the vehicles blocking it, and burst through them; the impact helped it complete its U-turn on the narrow street, and then it was dwindling into the distance, bound directly for Wisconsin. The hectoring geezette seemed to be pinned in place by her personal safety device, now: an airbag supporting a gasbag.

Tony Donuts Junior didn't do running. He walked rapidly to the spot where his Jeep had been parked only moments before, planted himself in the empty parking space, and began turning in a slow clockwise circle. He was sure the girl he was looking for would appear.

It didn't turn out well for him.

The first pedestrian he saw was another geezer—no, a coot—this one solidly built, heavily tanned, balding on top, and possessed of a splendid round grey-and-white beard.

Tony's gaze continued moving clockwise, and five degrees later encountered another stocky coot with a tan and a Kris Kringle beard.

A little to the right of him, a third sanguine Santa in khaki shorts and sandals was gesturing with his pipe at a fourth bronzed Geppetto in a Hawaiian shirt. Tony's gaze slowed but kept moving.

A few people to the right of them, a pair of Japanese

tourists were excitedly photographing yet another florid white-bearded senior, this one in slacks and a jacket with lots of pockets and epaulets.

Tony and his gaze stopped rotating, and his pulse climbed. Almost nothing frightened him, and hardly anything made him uneasy—but he had heard terrified drunks in bars read aloud from the *Post* or the *Enquirer* on this very subject more than once, and had seen numerous movies about it, all nearly identical (ironically), and all of them creepy.

Jesus, he thought, *they're all the same fuckin guy—they're whaddyacallit, clunes!*

He tried to recall what it was about clunes that was so creepy—were they from space?—but could remember for sure only that there were scientists involved. Tony regarded scientists the same way Conan the Barbarian did wizards. Even strength and balls were no use against them.

Still, these clunes were doing nothing overtly threatening, and nobody else on the street seemed alarmed by them, plus which anyway how much trouble could even half a dozen Xerox copies of an overweight Obi-Wan Kenobi be for a guy like Tony?

The word "copies" reminded him of his *other* science project. Miracle Girl. Who, come to think of it, had been using photocopies to taunt him—was this more of her work? Tony really hated it when people were subtle. More determined than ever to wring the secret of youth from her, so he could then wring her neck in good conscience, he was just about to resume his clockwise scan when something belatedly registered on him. He backed up dubiously, but no shit. There between Geppetto and Santa, holding Geppetto's hand in fact, was a woman his eye had subtracted the first time because she was the wrong age, race, and shape to be Miracle Girl, an Asian in her thirties (he estimated) with no hips and a pleasant smile. Tony was well aware that standards in Key West differed greatly from those of Brooklyn, particularly at the beaches, but he was sure this was the first woman he had seen stark naked on Duval Street in broad daylight.

No, not naked—she was wearing paint. Some talented artist had painted fishnet stockings, a frilly white garter belt, a lacy white cupless bra and tiny white crotchless panties on her tanned skin. And the high heels had to be real.

By now a certain sense of unreality was beginning to grow upon Tony. He'd seen at once on arrival that nearly everyone in Key West was fucked up somehow, but this was getting excessive. Since he didn't read, tuned out most of what people said to him, and changed the channel if he didn't hear at least small arms fire, there was no way he could have heard of Key West's legendary weeklong Fantasy Fest—Mardi Gras without the ugly parts, Carnevale without the dark side— which was about to start that evening, and probably no hope of his understanding that in another few hours, and for the next few nights, the woman he was staring at might seem overdressed for the party. No more could he be expected to have heard of Ernest Hemingway, fathomed the Hemingway Lookalike Contest held in Key West every April, or appreciated that he was looking at several of that year's finalists, gathered together informally to boggle the Fantasy Fest tourists and promote their own festival. Tony's policy when faced with the weird was to think about something else, so he was just about to return his attention, again, to the search for Miracle Girl when a car horn went off a couple of feet from his ear.

It was not, oddly, the first time in his adult life that someone had honked at Tony Donuts Junior, but he was the only living person who knew that. Doesn't matter how tough you are, a car honks right next to you, you're gonna flinch, and

Tony *hated* flinching. Plus which he was busy now. He turned to confront the offending vehicle, a van with a heavily tinted windshield that had pulled halfway into the parking space and clearly wanted him to move so it could finish the job. Tony glared at the unseen driver and gave him the finger. The horn sounded again, longer this time. Tony swelled himself until his clothes threatened to split like Bruce Banner's when he turned into the Incredible Hulk (*"Eat me!"*), and tried to recall just where you punched a van of that particular make to kill it.

The engine shut down, doors opened, and four people got out. Tony swelled another increment . . . then slowly began to deflate. (*"Drink me!"*)

He had been in Key West long enough to know it was *the* mecca for East Coast drag queens, the place where people from Provincetown and Fire Island went to see something really exotic. Tony had never had a problem with queers in his life, any more than with muggers. He even grasped that drag queens weren't necessarily queers, having raped some of both. But these four were striking. For a start, they were *gorgeous,* even by the standards of Key West. In face, body, dress, carriage, makeup, and style, they would have passed in daylight not just for women, but bombshells.

If they had not each been very close to Tony's size.

He had seen guys almost his size before—admittedly, not often—and was confident he could take all four at once if it came to it. He'd taken guys *bigger* than him; viciousness was what counted in the end, and viciousness was his best thing. He also knew that dropping these clowns could take a good half hour of hard work in the hot Florida sun, and that to have that long to work, here on the main drag, he'd have to put down at least one or two cops, too. And none of this would help him find Miracle Girl. Without a word he turned his back on the quartet and stepped back up onto the sidewalk, deleting clunes and clowns alike from his universe.

Only as the driver was pulling the van into the parking space did it occur to Tony that an outside observer might have misunderstood, and believed that he'd been made to back down. By *broads* . . . and not even real broads. Miracle Girl had probably observed it, and was laughing at him right now. His shirt split in the back, not vertically but the hard way. He heard the van door slam behind him as the driver got out to rejoin his sisters, and when the inevitable tittering began, he turned around again. Of course they weren't looking anywhere near him, and could not stop murmuring and giggling.

The van was parked sloppily, angled in and nearly a yard (Tony believed the only use for the metric system was to confuse juries as to how much drugs you'd been caught holding) from the sidewalk. He walked to the front of the van, studied it, and put his fist through the windshield at its lower right corner. This let him get a good grip on the window post. His right arm swelled, his shirt split all the way from cuff to shoulder under his suit, the van's tires all made sounds like a moron imitating a motorboat, and the van moved a couple of feet deeper into the parking space and a foot closer to the curb. The drag queens all hit the mute button. Duval Street itself became comparatively quiet for a main, uh, drag.

Tony studied his work and frowned. The van was closer to the curb, but its angle was even worse now. He walked to the rear quarter, transvestites scattering out of his way, and saw that to get as good a grip at this end he would have to punch through the wall of the van. He frowned up at the sun, sighed . . . walked around behind the van, and put it flush against the curb with a single kick. A complexly layered sound issued from inside it, mostly treble but with some bottom, as well. "All my goddamn *makeup!*" wailed the stricken driver. One of his friends put a hand over his mouth, and all three led him hastily away. Aside from his dwindling sobs, the only sound to be heard on that part of Duval Street was the clashing music from the nearest dozen establishments, the composite murmur of a dozen air conditioners, and an elderly nun half a block away, swearing colorfully as she tried to pry a crumpled bumper away from the rear wheels of a Jeep with a short tire iron.

Satisfaction carried Tony for several seconds, before it dawned on him that by now his chances of spotting Miracle Girl had plummeted to lower than the neckline on the van's driver. Prioritizing had always been a problem of Tony's; it was why he liked shotguns. There just never seemed to be enough hours in the day to terrorize all the pains in the ass who had it coming; someone was bound to slip through the cracks, and it always seemed to be the biggest pain in the ass.

But Tony Donuts Junior was not the sort of man who gave up on something just because he knew it wasn't going to work. He doggedly resumed his by-now-hopeless clockwise scanning rotation, and got a whole two seconds' look right at her before he felt a sharp tug at his nipple, the right one this time, and realized she had blown past him on a bicycle *again*.

He'd failed to recognize her for those two seconds because he'd been looking for a seventeen-year-old. Today she was no more than thirteen, tops, boobs like apples, hair short like a boy.

Since he had worked out in some detail exactly what he would do if this ever happened again, and reminded himself to remember not to forget, it only took him five or six seconds to work out what to do. No time to hot-wire the van, no point jacking other wheels with traffic at a standstill, too hot to run, the key to eternal power and wealth was disappearing down

Duval Street as he watched. Briefly he pictured himself in a bicycle race with a kid . . . and that finally brought his train of thought back to Shining Time Station. He located the nearest moped—he thought of it as a baby motorcycle—and by the time he reached it, nobody was driving it anymore. *Now watch, Witch Bitch*, thought Tony (noticing nothing about the sentence), and he bestrode the moped, and while he was figuring out how to make it go, both tires quit. There was no bang, they simply farted themselves dead in harmony.

There was no time for rage; Miracle Girl's lead was increasing with every second. Tony spotted a slightly bigger moped, presumably stronger, driven by an obvious rich guy who proved his superior intelligence by bringing it to Tony without being told, as soon as he saw Tony's gaze lock on it. As the rich guy handed it over, he gave a very quick little pantomime lesson in moped driving and stepped back. Tony sat cautiously, lifted both feet from the ground. The tires accepted the load, and he kept his balance, but he looked profoundly ridiculous, his knees sticking out to the sides like the booms of a swordfish boat. No matter. Tony would not learn to mind being laughed at until someone tried it. Several bystanders struggled with that very impulse, seeing him now, but they all mastered it. He stared up Duval Street, acquired his target—that was definitely a thirteen-year-old ass, tops—hunched forward over the handlebars of his moped as he'd seen bikers do before laying rubber, and twisted the accelerator grip like a knife, as far as it would rotate. The moped whined like a neurotic chain saw, and in under five seconds went from zero to ten, where it topped out.

Even the fear of death and the love of life itself could not prevent giggles from breaking out on Duval Street then. One oblivious child frankly whooped, and every third adult seemed to be coughing, rubbing his upper lip, or smoking an imaginary cigarette. Tony glowered down at the moped, already learning to mind this, and decided to treat the accelerator like a neck—if you can't twist it any farther, twist *hard*. The result was exactly the same: it snapped, spun freely, and the patient stopped screaming, coughed, and died.

Everyone lost it now. Even a monster like Tony couldn't kill *everybody*. The Hemingway clones tried hard to laugh loudest, but one of the drag queens topped them.

Tony climbed off the body—it was already leaking and starting to cool—flung it through the windshield of the van, and considered his options. Miracle Girl was still visible in the middle distance, but only just; heavy pedestrian traffic had her stopped, but not for long. Under this remarkable confluence of pressures, serial traumas, provocations, and incompossible yearnings, Tony Donuts Junior accomplished something painful and for him almost unprecedented. He reasoned.

Miss Thirteen was heading west on Duval. If she kept going straight for too much longer, she would pedal off a dock and into the Gulf of Mexico. If she hung a left at any point, she could go one whole block to Whitehead, where traffic was almost as slow, and then pedal off a dock into the Florida Strait. Those little side streets south of Duval were the heart of Tony's new manor, the barnyard of his victim-farm. If she did go that way, he would find her spoor easily.

But if she hung a right, she could go anywhere in Old Town, over fifty square blocks, pass all the nicest houses and scenery, and encounter far fewer moving cars—or keep going past Old Town to anywhere in Key West—or leave the rock altogether and start pedaling for America, a hundred gorgeous miles north.

Tony shrugged off the ruins of his suit jacket—double-breasted, yes; double-backed, no—and shirt, and he started running west after her as fast as he could; the first chance he got, he hung a right. Behind him, the laughter faltered for a moment, then resumed. Yeah, he definitely minded being laughed at, now that he'd tried it.

Among the other pedestrians Tony pushed out of his way as he ran were two spacemen, a Chinese Tarzan, Lady Godiva riding on a pig, and a Bahamian butterfly with really gorgeous wings—more Fantasy Fest people jumping the gun, trying out or drying out their costumes in advance. He ignored them, except as impediments in the obstacle course he was running, but they contributed to his growing sense of unreality.

He decided to turn left one block north, onto Simonton. It paralleled Duval for its entire length, and had vastly less traffic, pedestrian or auto; he would be able to run at nearly full speed without hurting anybody. No matter where Miracle Girl made her own right off Duval, Tony would see her cross Simonton from left to right, and adjust his own course. He was fairly confident he could run down a little girl on a bike who didn't know she was being chased.

Despite his concentration, weird pedestrians he passed kept threatening to distract him as he ran—a topless nun, a six-foot white rabbit writing something on a business card with a pen, a midget witch, a little girl who gave him the finger as she rode by on a blue moped, a famous movie star whose name he could almost remember, some idiot walking a live kangaroo on a leash—but hey, that was just life in Key West, and Tony was focused now, concentrating, eye on the prize, so determined to not miss his quarry crossing the street up ahead that it took him a good half a block to think, *A little girl who gave me the finger as she rode by?* He slammed to a

halt in a spray of sidewalk-chips and spun around in time to
see the tail end of a blue moped that had just turned right.

It ain't her, he thought. *No way. She just couldn'ta got back
here that fast, not even on a fuckin' Moped. Forget about it—
it would take a miracle for that girl there to be—*

—Miracle Girl . . .

He began to run again, back the way he had just come.

Halfway back to Duval, he saw a blue moped chained to a
parking meter in front of one of the rare shops with a closed
door. The place had no windows, no Muzak, and apparently
no name, unless ADULT XXXXX 21+ ONLY was a name. The
air above the moped's tailpipe shimmered. Tony thundered to
a halt, caught his breath, planed sweat from his forehead with
the edge of his hand and flung it on the sidewalk, and went
inside.

It was *dark* in there. After having been out in the sunshine,
Tony found it only slightly less dark when he remembered to
take off his sunglasses. He stood with his back to the door,
blocking the exit, while he waited for his eyes to adjust. It was
also massively air-conditioned in there, which Tony hated,
especially after exercise; already he could feel a charley horse
threatening in his left calf. The more he made out of his sur-
roundings, the bigger his pupils got, and soon he could see
just fine. Tony had been involved in the distribution end of
the porn business once or twice, until amateur video killed
it—and some of the stuff offered for sale in this chilly little
hole in the wall startled him, even shocked him in one or two
cases. He made himself ignore it and looked around for the
girl. No sign of her, and nowhere she could be hiding unless
she could fit into a video box or hide behind a magazine. The
whole place was about the size of a New York kitchen. There
was a counter on the right, with an aging hippie behind it, but

it didn't look like he had enough room back there even to take advantage of the merchandise without barking his knuckles.

Still, there was nowhere else to go. Tony approached the counter—racks of videotape boxes slid aside to make way for him—and confronted the clerk. Long curly hair, lots of mustache, and a silly little tuft of beard hanging off his chin. He reminded Tony of Buffalo Bill—or was it General Custer he was thinking of?—only with mostly grey hair. He was dressed conservatively for a hippie, by Key West standards, but he didn't look scared of Tony, so he must be very stoned. Tony put enough menace and volume in his voice to get the guy's attention. "I'm lookin for a blonde, about thirteen, short hair."

"Aisle three," said the hippie. "Second row from the top."

Tony closed his eyes, took a deep breath, and began counting to ten. At five, he forgot he was counting and said, "Not in a movie. For real."

The hippie shook his head. "We don't do live," he said. "Take a left on Duval, go about five blocks—but you better have a lot of money, and be prepared to settle for a pretty good fake."

Tony started over from three, having lost his place, and this time got to seven before deciding screw it. Softly, slowly, he said, "About a minute ago. A real live little teenybopper. Blond hair, yellow outfit. Got off a blue bike and came in here."

The hippie opened his mouth.

"If you're ready to die, right now, keep on bullshittin me."

The hippie closed his mouth.

"Or keep me waitin five more seconds," Tony suggested.

The hippie again opened his mouth, and of course Tony could see he was getting ready to lie, so Tony naturally got ready to hit him, and of course the hippie could see that so he started to duck behind the counter, where of course there would be some sort of lame weapon, so naturally Tony decided to pound him on the top of his head so hard he'd lose interest in weapons for a while, and he made his hand into a fist and his arm into a club and raised it high, but before he could bring it down, a soft high voice behind him, back there in the space where Tony had just personally made certain there were no people and no ways for one to enter or leave, said, "Let it go. I'm afraid he's not going to take no for an answer."

Tony stopped and turned around and stared at the thirteen-year-old girl until even he realized that he looked like a parody of the Statue of Liberty and put his arm down at his side.

She wore what looked like the same sunsuit, a lemon yellow sleeveless one-piece affair that ended in shorts, only it looked a lot bigger on her today. The outfit had a belt—no, two belts, only one of which went through the belt loops— what was that about?

"Thank you for your loyalty, Willard," she went on, "but I won't have your blood spilled in my behalf. I fear I have far too much of that against my account already."

"Your call, Ida," said the hippie. "I think you're making a mistake."

"If so, it won't be the first, will it? I'm *tired*, Willard. Tired of hiding and running and being afraid. Perhaps a . . . a really strong, brutal man is what I've needed all along."

Tony was not a subtle man; nuance usually pissed him off. But it was dawning on him that, in some way he was not equipped to parse, this kid did *not* sound like a thirteen-year-old trying to sound like a grown-up. What she sounded like was a very old lady trying to sound like a kid. Physically she was perfect, looked just like a little kid on the verge of puberty. Verbally, though, she was completely unconvincing.

"You ain't no little kid," he accused.

"And you are no fool," she said. Behind him, Willard the hippie smothered a sneeze and excused himself.

Tony ignored him. "How old are you? Really?"

She sighed, looked up to the ceiling—then squared her shoulders and looked him in the eye as she answered. "I was born in 1848."

Tony knew how to solve arithmetic problems: frighten the nearest person into giving you the answer. He frowned ferociously, swelled his shoulders, and asked, "How old does that make you?"

"She's a hundred and fifty-one," Willard said behind him.

Tony turned and looked at him. He was pretty good at telling when people were bullshitting him—they tended to be pale and sweaty, and tremble noticeably—and this Willard seemed no more frightened than people usually were when confined in an enclosed space with Tony Donuts Junior. He didn't even look as if he expected Tony to believe him—that more than anything else made Tony think that the old hippie was telling the truth.

He turned back to Miracle Girl, took a long second look at her eyes, and mentally promoted her to Miracle Woman. No, Miracle Hag.

Ambiguity and Tony were barely nodding acquaintances, but now he experienced a rare mixed reaction. This was certainly good news. The little bitch was even more valuable than he'd realized. Tony had a sudden mental image of one of the Five Old Men, just after Tony explained to him that he would soon be screwing like a teenager again, and picturing that smile made even Tony want to flinch just a bit—he was about to be richer than a CEO. Hell, richer than a CEO's lawyer.

On the other hand, the only kinds of humans Tony had

ever had the slightest difficulty in controlling had been hags and little girls. He could dimly sense that a combination of both was not going to be good for him.

But this little Miracle Hag seemed, at least for the moment, to have surrendered. "Willard is correct," she said. "I was born Ida Alice Shourds in 1848." She waited, seeming to expect him to react to the name, then continued. "If you look me up in the public records, you'll be told that I died nearly seventy years ago, at the age of eighty-two. I died in a little sanitarium in upstate New York, where I had been locked away for thirty-three years. Can you imagine, sir, what passed for a mental hospital in Central Valley, New York, in the early part of this century? What it was like to be confined in such a place?"

Tony felt his shoulders tighten. "My old man died in a hatch," he said. "Federal prisoner. They had him on drugs so bad, he was takin' guff from janitors."

Ida's face showed empathy that even he knew should have been impossible for a thirteen-year-old. "Then perhaps you can appreciate that decades ago, before your father was born, they kept patients docile with methods that would one day make Thorazine seem an enlightened breakthrough."

"Doctors," said Tony.

"Indeed."

"So you faked bein' dead somehow an busted out."

She nodded. "With Willard's help. He was a janitor at the sanitarium then."

Tony glanced over his shoulder at the hippie. "How old are *you*?" he asked.

"Almost ninety," Willard admitted.

"Ya don't look a day over sixty."

Willard thanked him solemnly. Tony returned his attention to Ida. "Okay. So you died seventy years ago. Continue the story."

"My death may have been faked, but that most certainly did not make it painless," she said. "You see, at the time of my death my name was Ida Alice Flagler, and I was worth thirteen million dollars."

"That's 1930 dollars," Willard put in.

"Of which I never got to spend a penny," she said bitterly.

An encyclopedia compiled by Tony Donuts Junior would have been a very slim paperback, but he had been in the state of Florida for several weeks now. If he'd spent as much time in Salt Lake City, the name Brigham Young would by now have begun to ring a bell. "Flagler, Flagler . . . guy that invented Florida?"

She grimaced. "In the same sense that Edison invented the lightbulb, that's right. Pretty much everything from Saint Augustine to Key West, Henry Flagler built from nothing. The day a little settlement called Fort Dallas incorporated and changed its name to Miami, a century ago, Henry owned six hundred acres of what is now downtown, and the railroad that was the only way to get there. Before he was done, he drove that railroad to the end of the state and a hundred miles out to sea, to this very pile of coral we're standing on— boarded his personal car in Saint Augustine and stepped down off it here in Key West."

"He musta had dough."

Behind him Willard began, "He was one—"

Tony interrupted him. "Getcher ass out here, Moonbeam. I'm gettin a stiff neck lookin' atcha." He allowed two seconds' grace, then turned his whole body around. "I *said*—"

"Okay, okay." Willard turned to his right, and in two strides reached the wall at the far end of the counter. He did something behind the counter, and the wall opened on concealed hinges, became a doorway. He stepped through it, closed it behind him—*snick!*—and in a few seconds a rack of video boxes against the back wall swung away to reveal another secret doorway, from which Willard emerged. He closed that behind him, too, and came over to stand beside little Ida Flagler. He did not quite touch her, but Tony read his body language and knew he would die for her if necessary. Tough shit for him.

Tony had gotten a good close look as the hippie squeezed past. "That's a good rug," he stated. "So's the beard."

"Not many people can tell," said Ida.

"So?" Willard said belligerently.

"So nuttin. Finish yah story."

Willard glared but continued. "I was saying, Henry Flagler, Samuel Andrews, and John D. Rockefeller were the three founders of Standard Oil, one of the greatest monopolies in history. The first antitrust laws were invented specifically to stop *them*. In today's money, Flagler paid something like a billion dollars for his ticket to ride that train from Saint Gus to Key West. Yeah, he had dough."

"He warehoused me in a hellhole for thirty-three years," Ida said, "and left me a thirteen-million-dollar estate, like a tip, so that none of my heirs would raise any inconvenient questions about my competence—the bastard."

Tony admired his technique. "Well, you got your revenge. I heard he croaked a long time ago."

"In 1913," Ida agreed. "But I'm afraid his death was no more real than my own. The only difference was, he *did* take it with him. Henry is still alive. He simply decided to duck out on the Great War—the First World War, they call it now—and he never found a reason to come back up from underground. He spent the first eighty years of his life piling up money, *doing* things . . . and he's passed the last eighty spending it all, invisible to the world, accomplishing nothing whatsoever except to enjoy life."

"That's the way I'd do it," said Tony. "Now tell the part about how come you guys don't lie down an shut up when ya die."

She hesitated, looked down at her feet. It was stupid, she'd come this far, there was no way she was gonna not tell him, all three of them knew that, and still she hesitated—that was how reluctant she was to say it. Finally Willard put a gentle hand on her shoulder. Somehow that enabled her to look up and answer. "The first time Henry came to Florida, in 1878, he *hated* it. His first wife, Mary Harkness, was dying of tuberculosis, and the doctors said she needed to be warm in winter, so he brought her to Jacksonville. He loathed it there so much that after a few weeks he went back to New York, even though he knew she wouldn't stay without him. She died in New York in 1881."

Tony made a growling noise. "I'm gettin bored."

"I was one of her nurses. Henry and I were married in the summer of 1883. But by the time he could get away from business it was midwinter. So I persuaded him we should honeymoon in Florida—only this time we went to Saint Augustine. It was there that everything changed."

"He liked it dis time," Tony suggested, in a let's-make-this-move voice.

"That's what it says in the history books," she agreed. "He'd looked at Jacksonville and seen a backwater; now he looked at Saint Augustine and saw infinite potential, saw an entire state waiting to be carved out of the swamp and sold to gullible northerners. They never explain what the difference was, why Saint Augustine was so much more inspiring."

"But you will," said Tony. "Very soon."

Willard spoke up. "Columbus never saw America, spent all his time island-hopping around the Caribbean. Saint Augustine is the spot where the very first European stepped ashore onto the continent of North America, and because it was Palm Sunday, and the Spanish for that is *Pascua Florida*, the 'Feast of the Flowers,' he named the place Florida. Same guy that discovered Puerto Rico, as it happens. Ask me his name."

"Am I not makin it plain," asked Tony, "that I'm gettin pissed off?"

"His name was Don Juan Ponce de León," Ida said quickly, and waited.

For a couple of seconds Tony coasted in neutral, staring out the windshield, and then the fog lifted. He had read that name once, on a restaurant place mat. "Wait a minute—wait a minute, you mean Pounce Dee *Lee*-on?"

Willard had a brief coughing fit. When it was done, Ida said, "That's right, Tony. Pounce Dee Lee On. When my rotten husband, Henry, brought me to Saint Augustine, three hundred and seventy years later, he rediscovered what Pounce had found there long before—"

"Holy shit," murmured Tony. "Da Fount'n A Ute!"

8

BURYING THE HOOK

When you are fooled by something else, the damage will not be
so big. But when you are fooled by yourself, it is fatal.
No more medicine.
—Shunryu Suzuki Roshi

That is correct, the Fountain of Youth, Mr.—What *is* your
name?"

Tony was so bemused, he answered truthfully. "Donnazzio,
Tony Donnazzio."

"He found the secret of eternal youth, Mr. Donnazzio,
rediscovered what, uh, Pounce had found four centuries earlier. We stumbled on it together, on our belated honeymoon,
while looking for a discreet place to—to be alone in Nature. I
don't think anyone else but Henry would ever even have
thought to try such an unlikely, uninviting spot, much less
persist as long as he did. He was a man of remarkable stub-
bornness. I was becoming quite put out with him. And then
suddenly there it was. A natural spring, whose water happens
to have passed through just the right rare mineral deposits in
just the right amounts in just the right sequence while underground. The effect was immediate and unmistakable; we
never did get around to . . . what we had come there for that

day. We had to find ways to hide from the servants and staff for the next day or two, until we learned how to convincingly make ourselves look as old as we were supposed to be again. Henry said we mustn't let the secret of the spring slip out until we'd had time to think through how to handle it properly.

"When I finally understood he meant us to keep the secret *forever*, so that forever we could be not merely immortal but the *only* immortals, I realized what a monster I had married. I resolved to break with him and reveal the secret to the world. But I had underestimated Henry's power and ruthlessness. Like a fool, I allowed him to guess my intentions. The next thing I knew I was officially a hopeless lunatic, and Henry had forced the Florida legislature to make lunacy grounds for divorce just long enough to end our marriage, and he was remarried to Mary Kenan, a tramp who'd been his mistress for the past decade. My only consolation is that he never breathed a word about the Fount to Mary, never let her suspect his own aging was only cosmetic, and skipped out on her when he was ready to fake his own death. Three years later, she married a fellow named Bingham; and I think he may have murdered her; in any case, she died mysteriously within a year."

Tony had seen people wrinkle their foreheads when they thought; he tried it now, and it didn't seem to help any. But the little thinking he did get done made him wrinkle up his forehead even more. "Where's he now, this Henry?"

The teenybopper hag shrugged and gestured toward the door. "Out there, somewhere. Invisible. Transparent to most radar. He's had more than a century in which to insulate himself from the official world. He has no address, no phone number, no e-mail address. He has no legal identity, and as many phony ones as he likes. He pays no taxes. His fingerprints aren't on file anywhere. He probably doesn't have a reflection in the mirror anymore, or show up on satellite photos. And he has more money than the *Fortune* 500, nearly as much as the United States of America, all of it off the books."

The fundamental absurdities and contradictions of the story troubled Tony not at all. He admired this Fagola's technique. That was the way Tony woulda done it, in his shoes. The guy was as mean as Tony, as tough as Tony, richer than Tony had ever fantasized being—richer than the Five Old Men put together!—and he'd had something like a century and a half to get himself dug in, to erase his tracks from anywhere cops could see. He was way too dangerous to live, and one day would have to be hunted—*carefully*—and exterminated. The sole flaw in his program, so far as Tony could see, had been sentimentally allowing his wife to remain alive as a mental patient. Well, correcting other people's mistakes was one of Tony's best things. Just as soon as little Mrs. Ida Alice Shourds Flagler had told him the only useful thing she seemed to know, admittedly a very useful thing—

"Where's it at, this Fount'n A Ute? Exackly."

She squared her shoulders and looked him in the eye. She had obviously been expecting this. "I will—"

"Ida, *no*," Willard groaned.

She shrugged him off. "I will sell you that information for ten million dollars. Cash. No more than half of it in hundreds."

Tony stared at her.

"Yes, I know," she said. "It is worth incalculably more than that. The sum is ludicrously small. But my back is to the wall. I will settle for ten million—with one condition."

"Yeah?"

"You agree that once you have taken possession of the

Fount, you will supply Willard and me with five gallons apiece of its water. We will take that and the money and go away, and that'll be the last you'll see or hear of either of us for at least a thousand years. We're quiet people, Mr. Donnazzio; there should be plenty of room on the planet for all of us."

Tony chose not to debate the point at that time. "Ten mil is a big piece of money."

"It is the absolute minimum I will consider, for two reasons."

"Gimme the first one first."

"You travel in different circles than Willard and I, Mr. Donnazzio. Just from what I've seen of you in the last few days, I'm sure you have a quite considerable reputation locally, and perhaps in more distant quarters, as well. But we have no way to evaluate that—and we *must* be absolutely sure you're the right man for this job. The Fount is so hard to stumble across by accident that only one man seems to manage it every four or five hundred years. If you come for the Fount, Henry will know someone must have told you about it. There is no one but me who could have told you. So he will know that I'm alive."

This was getting complicated for Tony. "So?"

"Mr. Donaz—"

"Call me Tony."

"Tony, my former husband is probably the richest, most powerful, most dangerous man alive. First he will try to destroy you. If he succeeds, eventually he will come for me, and Willard. If I'm to send you up against Henry, I must be confident that you have a reasonable chance of defeating him. You understand?"

He was following the individual sentences, but didn't quite see how they added up to ten mil. "Maybe."

"Willard?"

Willard interpreted, using extravagant hand gestures. "If you fuck up, it's our ass, Tony. Flagler has so much juice, if you're not the kind of guy who can come up with ten mil in a day or two, if you're just muscle, then you're just not in his league, and we'd be crazy to tell you dick. Plus which if he takes you out, we'll need ten mil just to stay out of his way. Capisce?"

Much better. "Gotcha," Tony said. "Okay, how about this? How about I start snappin parts offa ya, start out wit little bits, and keep snappin stuff until you tell me dick no matter *how* crazy it is?"

Willard turned pale, but Ida stood her ground. "Do you think I'm more afraid of you than I am of Henry Flagler, Tony?"

"You oughta be."

"Perhaps so, but I'm not. I made up my mind seventy years ago: I will *never* permit Henry to lock me away again. The tools they have for mind control these days are just too good. So I took steps to see that the means of painless suicide are always with me. You can't frighten me with torture or with death. And Willard honestly doesn't know just where the Fountain is."

Tony believed her on both counts. She'd have been crazy to trust Willard. He could kill her, but he couldn't scare her. And if he killed her, he had no fountain. "What's the *second* reason you want ten mil?"

"The only reason Willard and I are both still young," Ida told him, "is that once—once—in the past, we were able to arrange secret access to the Fount, for just long enough to spirit away a few precious quarts undetected. Once you and Henry tangle, that will become infinitely more difficult, for decades to come, whichever of you wins . . . and vastly more expensive, when a chance finally does arrive. Ten million dollars is cutting it very close, I think."

Privately Tony saw her point. "That ain't *my* problem, kid. I still like snappin stuff. Maybe I can't frighten you, but I bet I can frighten Willard."

"You lose," said Willard at once.

"No, Tony," said Ida, very firmly, and Tony was quite surprised to notice himself move about half an inch farther away from Willard. "Willard is the only person on this planet I care a damn about. I owe him everything. My life, my sanity, my dignity—he gave me all those back, when I was dead and worse than dead. He has more courage than anyone I know. You could 'snap things,' as you put it, all afternoon and he would tell you nothing. But we're not going to prove that, because if you lay a hand on him, I'll be out of here faster than you can stop me, and I'll run straight to the Naval Air Station and tell them all about the Fount. Or maybe I'll run over to Greene Street and discuss the matter with Mel Fisher, the world-famous treasure hunter."

"Bullshit. They'd laugh you out the door. You'd end up right back in the hatch."

"Not if I proved my story," said Ida.

Tony was starting to understand why she had begun to bug him: she reminded him of nuns. He hated nuns. You *had* to argue with them, but it was almost always a waste of energy that ended in humiliation. "What, you got a sample a the Ute Water on ya right now?"

She nodded and turned around. Now Tony understood the second belt at her waist. It wasn't part of her outfit, after all, but of a fanny pack she wore at the small of her back. A little one, just big enough to hold, say, a wallet and a bottle of spring water. The pack looked full. She turned around to face him again. "And I have a bit more of it hidden elsewhere. A very little bit more."

He held out his hand. "Lemme try some."

"Out of the question."

"Ten mil, I don't get a taste? You never sold drugs before, have ya?"

"What's the point? You *know* it works; you've seen me get younger."

He shook his head. "Not yet, I ain't. All I know, maybe you got older sisters look like you, an' you're all runnin' some kinda game on me. Lemme try some."

Her turn to shake her head. "No. I need you to remain just as strong, mature, potent, and wise as you are right now, Tony. The more immature your body and judgment become, the greater the risk that Henry will crush you."

Well, that was hard to argue with. He had to agree that he was at this moment a perfect specimen of manhood in his prime. Still. "Ten mil and no sample. I dunno, lady."

"Oh, for Heaven's sake!" With quick impatient movements she pulled the fanny pack around in front of herself, unzipped it, took out what looked like a standard clear plastic one-liter bottle of distilled or spring water. It was nearly empty, only an inch or two of water left at the bottom. Before Tony could frame a question, she twisted off the cap and drank half the bottle's contents. Then she capped it again, put it back into the pack, held her hand up and slightly to the side of her face, and Tony could see his own familiar signature on the palm of her hand—the one he had written (or so he believed) on a considerably older girl yesterday. As he recognized it, she *changed,* right in front of his eyes—

Tony had once made a guy eat a grenade, and had not

flinched even when one of the guy's eyeballs ended up in Tony's own shirt pocket, staring up at him. He flinched now.

Just as an earthquake is outrageous because the ground is simply not supposed to move like that, what he saw happen to her was outrageous because bone and flesh are not supposed to *flow* that way, to *shimmer* so confusingly, to *sparkle* in such a manner. What it was incredibly like, Tony thought, was somebody beaming down from the *Enterprise*, except that the somebody was already there to start with, and the sound was different. Less of a *mzzzzzzzzzhaou*—and more of a *whuff!* Weirdest of all, it was only the girl herself who sparkled and shifted: her clothing was unaffected.

When it was over, Ida Alice Shourds was, tops, seven years old. The yellow outfit was no longer snug on her; the shorts were halfway to her knees now. The autograph on her palm was smaller, like the palm itself, but still legible.

The Miracle Brat was saying something to him.

Tony was busy. There was no other way—he was thinking. Doing his best, anyway.

For ten mil in a hurry, he would have to go to Charlie Ponte. Was there any chance in hell he could get ten huge off of Charlie without stating a reason? Even with maximum vig?

No way. *Two* huge, Charlie might just have gone for—because Tony was known to be a serious man whose word was good (save when given to a civilian or a cop), and because he was way too noticeable and memorable to hide anywhere in the world, and mostly because Charlie almost certainly *had* two huge of his own lying around in cash, convenient for disbursement. Also Tony knew that Charlie hated his guts, behind him being his father's son, and would have relished the constant hope that Tony might fuck up, miss a payment, and provide Charlie with an excuse to raise up the full power of his authority for executive action against Tony.

But *ten* million in cash was more than Carlo Pontevecchio aka Charlie Ponte would have around—of his own money. To come up with that much, he would have to lay it off on the Five Old Men. Two mil each, probably. That meant he would have to be given a reason. A real good one.

Tony had a reason. He just wasn't sure it would do him any good. He laboriously assembled a mental picture of himself about to tell Charlie Ponte about the Fountain a Ute, pushed the PLAY button, and watched it unfold in his mind's eye. The results did not please him. Then he created another movie, in which Charlie passed along Tony's explanation, five times, to the most skeptical humans in the solar system. An even more emphatic thumbs-down this time.

Was there a fake reason that *would* persuade the old men to cough up a couple mil apiece? If so, was there a chance in hell that Tony Donuts Junior could think of it?

Like computers, some chimpanzees and nearly all politicians, Tony lacked true intelligence, or even the hardware to run it on, but was often able to mask this by relying on certain painfully learned algorithms—or as he called them, Rules a Tums. One of the oldest such subroutines in his repertoire stated that if he really wanted something but the price was too high, threatening to maim or kill the vendor might prove effective—and if not, actually doing so would at least be soothing. Tony had developed a mild distaste for beating up seven-year-old girls, back about the time he'd been graduating from juvie to adult court, so he decided to work on Willard instead, to start with, and see how she felt about that—

Ida must have read his intention on his face. As he was bunching his shoulders, before he had even begun to turn

toward Willard, she yelled, "Run, Prof!" and pulled over a
rack of videotapes to block Tony's path. Willard sprang for
the same hidden door by which he'd entered and slammed it
behind him before Tony could kick his way through the smut-
slide. A second, distant slamming sound a few seconds later
confirmed that Willard was not going to reappear behind the
counter this time. Without pausing for thought, or even an
algorithm, Tony snatched the kid up—grabbed her at the
waist with both hands, lifted her clear off the floor, and *shook*
her, while growling, "Bad girl!" He kept shaking until he
could tell she was either unconscious or so dizzy as to amount
to the same thing, and then he slung her over his shoulder
and headed for the street. For all he knew, Willard might
return in a matter of moments with cops, or a gun. Tony did
not exactly have a plan yet—but he did know that if you have
a treasure in your hands, and you don't know how to use it,
you at least make sure it'll stay in your hands until you figure
it out.

Chasing down the nun who had his Jeep, while carrying an
unconscious child, sounded too aggravating to even think
about. So Tony curbed his impatience and himself. He stood
there on the sidewalk outside the porn shop, ignoring the
stares of pedestrians, browsing passing cars with his eyes.
Key West is a favorite destination for owners of convertibles;
one came along nearly at once, an ancient and hence sturdy
Dodge, slowing for its turn onto Duval Street. It contained
two college students dressed as morons and drunk enough to
pass. The nearer one had a long ponytail, so that was what
Tony yanked him out of the car by as it glided past. The
driver *stood* on the brake, turned his head, saw a creature out
of nightmare clutching his buddy and another victim, and
stalled the convertible. Tony dropped the unconscious Ida

Alice into the empty passenger seat, casually tossed the student over his shoulder into the porn shop, and walked around to the driver's side. By the time he got there, the driver, ice-cold sober now, had scrambled over the windshield, crawled across the hood, and disappeared. Tony took his place, restarted the Dodge, and drove away from there.

He drove to his rental cottage on William Street, pulled the Dodge into the Jeep's garage around back, and went in to get a few items for the road. He was able to carry the brat inside without being seen by any nosy neighbors, largely because he never had any. By the time he carried her back out to the car and dropped her back in the passenger seat, she was beginning to come around—and her ankles were locked together by a pair of standard-issue handcuffs. Nobody outside the car was going to see them, but there was no chance of her jumping out and running away on him.

"Where's the Profes . . . Where's Willard?" she asked as he was fastening her seat belt.

"Still runnin', I bet. Forget him. Listen up: If you want that ten mil, I gotta convince a guy, okay? You're gonna drink some more a the Ute Water in fronta this guy, show him what's what, just like you did for me. Then he gives me the ten mil, and you tell me where the Ute Water comes from—*me* you tell, not this guy—and then I give you the ten mil an everybody has a nice day."

Her expression was skeptical—even for a seven-year-old—but she made no reply.

He left Key West, took US 1 across Cow Key Channel to Stock Island, entering the long straight pipeline that led east and north back up the chain of Keys to America. With good traffic he could reach Charlie Ponte's place in Miami in three or four hours.

———

Key West is so laid back, and its street layout so eccentric, that it is often possible to tail a car through town on a bicycle. The Professor was able to keep up with Tony's stolen convertible, right up until it was clear it was going to leave the island. Then he gave up the chase and found a pay phone. (He told me later it was the first and only time in his life he'd ever even briefly wished he owned a cell phone.)

I'd have thought that on the day I spoke the words, "Doc Webster is dying," to my friends, no other declarative statement could possibly qualify as important. But I changed my mind fast when the Professor said, "Jake, I think Erin may be in trouble."

Zoey, a good twenty yards away, saw my expression and came running. *What?*

I held up a hand—*I'm trying to find out*—put the Professor on speakerphone, and said, "What kind of trouble is she in, Prof?" People fell silent and listened.

"Everything went just as planned, right up to where my character bugged out to save his neck. But when Tony came outside with her, she was unconscious."

"What?" I was incredulous. "How the hell can somebody knock out a teleport? Especially one as alert as Erin?"

He sighed. "My theory is, he literally did it without thinking. She never had a chance to see it coming, because even he didn't. Probably picked her up and shook her until she passed out. I didn't see any signs he'd actually hit her."

"She was just unconscious? You're *sure?*" Zoey said urgently.

"Absolutely," he said at once. "I saw her awake and talking a little later on, at Tony's place."

She slumped slightly, and so did I. "Thank you, Willard."

I was confused. "So why isn't everything okay now? She's conscious—and now she knows enough to watch out for further impulse-decisions of Tony's. If anything else happens she doesn't like, worst case, she just teleports back here and we all have dinner." No response. "Right?"

Willard spoke with obvious reluctance. "He stopped at his place before he left town, to change clothes and I suspect to collect his gun and some ammo. Whatever—he carried her inside with him, unconscious. When they came back out, she was awake . . . but he'd hobbled her with a pair of handcuffs."

"Oh, *shit*," Zoey and I both said together, and several people around us groaned or gasped.

One teleports naked or not at all. Why this is so, Erin has explained to me several times, and I still don't get it, any more than I can grasp how she teleports in the first place, but the bottom line is, for whatever reasons, organic and inorganic matter can't travel together in the same load. You can teleport your clothing ahead of you, and dress on arrival if you like— or you can simply rob a clothesline at your destination. Or, as Erin had earlier, you can teleport into existing clothing if you happen to know where a set the right size has just been vacated. But not with metal touching your skin. If you're wearing so much as a class ring, you can't teleport at all. As long as Erin wore those cuffs on her ankles, she was at the mercy of Tony Donuts Junior.

Zoey and I embraced. Friends moved in from all sides and it became a group hug. "Oh Jake," she groaned in my ear, *"she's only seven years old."*

"She saved the universe when she was two," I reminded her.

"Twice, really," said Long-Drink McGonnigle, from somewhere to my left.

"With you and Nikola Tesla and Jim Omar and half a dozen other people. She's *alone* with that gorilla," Zoey continued. Her voice was rising in pitch and speed.

"So better she's seven than a teenager," I said, tightening

my embrace. "The day she came out of your belly she was a thousand times smarter than Tony——"

"Sure—that's how she ended up in chains in his car—most of the people he's killed were smarter than him, nearly everyone is——"

I didn't have a comeback for that one, and I could feel her working up toward hysterics. Now that I thought about it, so was I. Screw logic. My irreplaceable daughter was in the murderous hands of a moronic mastodon, her secret weapon disabled, and *she was only seven—*

Tanya Latimer's speaking voice is a lot like Pearl Bailey's singing voice: low, liquid and soothing, absolutely unhurried and unworried. From somewhere behind me she purred, "Zoey, honey, did you read comic books when you were a little girl?"

"Sure, what the hell has——"

"Did you ever read *Superboy* comics?"

"For a while, but——"

"But you stopped after a while, didn't you?"

"Well——" The onslaught of questions was confusing.

"I'll tell you why you stopped. No suspense. Whenever Lex Luthor or somebody tried to kill that boy, you *knew* they were going to fail, didn't you? How did you know that?"

"Well, obviously, you knew he was going to grow up to be Superm—Oh. *Oh.*"

We had seen **Er**in at ages above seven. We had lived with a more-than-seven-year-old Erin daily for more than five years now. Ergo, she was positively not going to die at age seven. In fact, we knew for certain she would live to *at least* age twenty-one, because we'd already met her at that age.

Come to think of it, she was not even going to sustain any noticeable injuries—or we'd have noticed them, back when she was seven and she returned from this time-hop caper.

Zoey and I pulled apart just enough to look into each other's eyes, and I could see we were in complete agreement. No logic chain, however compelling, can be strong enough or solid enough when the fate of your child is at stake. Thanks to Tanya, we could now *prove* there was nothing for us to worry about . . . so now we were only worried *half* to death.

But that was clearly better than panic, which was where we'd been heading. *Keep thinking, Butch—that's what you're good at.* . . . "Thank you, Tanya. Okay, I'm going to assume Erin is gonna get through this okay because we all broke our asses saving her. That way I got something to do besides go berserk. Anybody got a problem with that?" No. "Okay, she's on her way north with the Creature from the Black Lagoon. Prof, how good is his car?"

The split-second hesitation cued me that the answer would not be comforting. *Can't help you, Sundance.* "Pretty good, Jake. An old Dodge ragtop, kept up. It moved pretty good."

And I could guess what kind of driver Tony would be. *Rules? In a knife fight?* Few humans could find Tony in their rearview mirror and continue to block his path for long. "Shit. What have we got?" I didn't own wheels myself, hadn't since I sold the ancient school bus in which I'd brought my family down to Key West, ten years before. But some of the gang kept up the hobby.

"I got a Lada," Shorty Steinitz said. Nobody laughed.

"I got a Vincent," said Marty Pignatelli.

It didn't register for me, but several people murmured "Holy shit!" or some equivalent.

"A what, Marty?"

"A Vincent Black Shadow," he said.

Now it did register . . . and I said, "Holy shit!" Even I've heard of the Black Shadow. It's sort of the Stradivarius of high-performance motorcycles. It eats Harleys and shits Yamahas. "I didn't even realize you had a bike, Fifty."

He shrugged. "I was a statie."

"Huh." Well, I was impressed . . . but on the other hand, the last time I'd ridden a bike, the ancient Irish blessing had come entirely too true: the road rose up to meet me. Not stopping when it reached my ass. I was starting to feel a little trapped. *You damn fool—the* fall*'ll probably kill you*. . . .

Double Bill diagnosed my expression. "I have something better, Jacob."

"Hard to believe, but go ahead."

"I have a little twenty-two-foot Grady White semi-V over at Houseboat Row, with a new pair of two-twenty-five Johnsons on her and full cans."

I blinked at him. "Moderate your language, suh—there are ladies present."

"He means a fast boat," Tanya said. "Fueled up."

Jim Omar was somewhere nearby in the hug. "He means a floating rocket, Jake. Traffic's lighter on the Atlantic Ocean than on US 1. You'll probably be in Miami before Tony clears the Keys."

Bolivia, huh, Butch? Falling off a rocket and onto water did sound better than falling off a Vincent onto asphalt. And not only was Omar right about traffic, Florida boaters are slightly less likely than Florida motorists to assert the right of way with small arms fire. "Okay. Zoey, would you please call Bert and get an address for where Charlie Ponte does meets in Miami, while I get ready to go? Bill, you'll drive this boat, okay? Tom, pack us a few of your Cuban sandwiches and a couple of beers, and dial up a thermos of Atherton Tablelands with cream and sugar." The group hug began to break up. "I don't suppose anybody's got high explosives lying around handy?"

"Sure ting," said Fast Eddie. "Grenades. How many ya want?"

Eddie lives next door to me. "Two should do it."

Zoey stopped poking at the phone. "Jake, what the *hell* do you plan to do with a pair of grenades?"

"Just before we knock on Charlie's door, I'm gonna have Bill duct-tape them into my hands and then pull the pins. I don't care how tough a guy is—you do that, and even Tony Donuts or Charlie Ponte is gonna go right to Plan B. And you and I and Erin are all bombproof."

"I'm not," Double Bill reminded me.

"Stand behind me and you'll be fine."

"Bull-*grunty*. You provide as much blast-shadow as a hat rack, you skinny bastard."

Zoey got my attention by rapping the top of my skull with the phone. "Jake. Listen to me. *No grenades.*"

I don't get it. She likes the Three Stooges. "Aw . . . you're no fun." Whack! "*Ow.* Okay, I promise. How about a nice little Uzi? Nobody'll notice that in Miami." I went to our cottage and changed into clothes a Mafia capo would find less contemptible than sandals, baggy shorts, and a Hawaiian shirt emitting as many energetic photons as Duval Street. It was stuff 1 hadn't worn since I'd left Long Island, high in polyester content. The hair and beard undid a lot of the effect, of course, but it always had.

As I was tying the last shoelace, Zoey came in and handed me a notepad sheet on which was written Charlie Ponte's meeting-place address and his private phone number. She, too, was dressed as a tourist, and it looked a hell of a lot better on her. "Tell me this is going to be all right, Spice," she said.

"It's a pipe," I said at once, straightening up and taking her by the shoulders. "You know the logic as well as I do. If anything were to happen to her, it'd be a paradox, and the universe abhors a paradox. We could probably stay here all night singing Beatles songs, and everything would still work out just fine—it *has* to."

She closed her eyes. "Really? You're sure?" Her shoulder muscles felt like rattan under my fingers.

"Absolutely." I closed my own eyes and confessed. "That's why it's taking all my strength to keep myself from digging the Meddler's Belt out of storage and using it to peek ahead to the back of the book."

Barring Mike Callahan himself, the Meddler was the first time traveler I ever met. He was a freelancer who'd come back from the not-too-distant future to the year 1975, to try to spare someone he loved great pain.* He hadn't had access to the deluxe *far*-future no-moving-parts method of time travel the Callahans and Erin employed; instead he employed a time machine of his own invention, a belt roughly as bulky and cumbersome as the one heavyweight champions wear. Most people who were there that night, including the Meddler himself, believed they saw that belt destroyed with their own eyes, tossed into the fireplace by Mike Callahan. Only a handful of us knew that Mike had used sleight of hand, and the real Meddler's Belt still existed . . . gathering mildew in my storage closet.

"Ah." Now her shoulders were made of steel cable. "' . . . but that would be wrong,'" she quoted, using a comedy Nixon voice that quavered too much. (First presidency to die of a staff infection.)

*See "The Law of Conservation of Pain," in *Callahan's Crosstime Saloon*—ed.

"Cheating," I agreed.

Our eyes opened and found each other. "You got some kind of problem with cheating?" she asked softly.

I *was* tempted. Quite. But—"It'd be stupid. For several excellent reasons . . . but primarily because an unfamiliar method of time travel is way more risk than we need to take," I said. "You don't gamble with the universe to calm your nerves."

Her shoulders relaxed slightly. "You're right. I'm sorry, Slim."

"Gimme a kiss, we got a boat to catch."

She did that, thoroughly. "You watch my ass and I'll watch yours."

"Deal."

We left the cottage, saw Bill just past the bar at poolside with a small ice chest and an underseat bag he was just zipping shut. "We're ready," Zoey called. "Let's *go*."

He straightened and looked embarrassed. You'd think a man who wears shirts that make mine look drab, a sarong, a Popeye cap, and a gold ring on his bare big toe would look embarrassed more often, but he doesn't. "Uh—," he said. "I have expressed myself poorly. I humbly apologize."

"What are you talking about?"

He hesitated only a second, but that was long enough; Zoey and I had both guessed by the time he explained. "It's a two-man boat."

She stopped in her tracks. "I'll squeeze in," she insisted in a dangerous tone of voice.

We said nothing. Zoey masses only a little less than Bill and me put together. I'm scrawny and he's short. She's neither.

"I will fucking water-ski!"

Another good place for a silence.

"God damn it, Jake, I am *not* going to sit here, chewing my nails and loading the rifles, while the menfolk form a posse and go rescue my little girl from the Comanches, end of story. Forget it—I'd go completely out of my mind. If there's only two seats, Bill's gonna have to teach one of us to drive."

"," Bill and I said in unison.

She drew in the sort of vast chest-filling breath one might use to bellow or scream at someone hard of hearing on the far side of Mars, held it, held it . . . then she let it out so gently, it didn't make a noise, and in a good imitation of her normal conversational voice she said, "I love you, Jake. Bring our daughter home safe to me." She looked around vaguely, not tracking. "Somebody give him a damn cell phone, okay?" Men don't know shit about bravery.

"He can have mine," a voice I almost recognized said.

Field Inspector Czrjghnczl stood just inside the open gate, holding her briefcase in front of her with both hands. Men don't know shit about bravery. She was dressed just as she had been ever since I first saw her, but her face displayed human feeling. "If I heard right," she said to me, "your daughter is in danger. I can see you don't have time to explain it." She took one hand from the briefcase, found her phone, and tossed it to me underhand; I caught it automatically. "Go with God."

I was speechless.

"She's right, Jake," Doc Webster said.

Now I was breathless, and so was everybody else. I spun—and there he was, coming around from behind the bar, moving slow, arm in arm with his wife. He looked like he had a rotten headache, but that was as bad as he looked. His color was okay. "You can stay with us, Zoey. We'll make a bucket of coffee and stay up and fret together, the three of us. Jake knows my number."

He was right: if you converted Doc's phone number's

numbers to their corresponding letters on the keypad (I'm so old I still think, "dial"), they formed a word I won't repeat here, which was unforgettably obscene.

Mei-Ling held out a hand. "Come on, Zo."

"Everybody else is welcome to hang out, too," the Doc added.

Zoey hesitated. She looked over at Field Inspector Czrjgh-nczl and sighed. "Want to join us?" she asked. "I'll try to explain what's going on."

The bureaucrat blinked. "I'd love to."

What comes after speechless and breathless? Beliefless?

I filed it all to be dealt with later, squeezed Zoey's hand, and went to get the thermos Tom Hauptman had just finished filling.

9

BA-DA-STING!

Our lives are based on what is reasonable and common sense;
truth is apt to be neither.
—Christmas Humphreys

A minute later, Double Bill and I were pedaling like madmen. Duval to South ("Where do all the hippies meet?") to Reynolds to Atlantic Boulevard, past Higgs Beach and Smathers Beach, to the beleaguered but so far unbeaten remnants of Houseboat Row—practically every step of the way was a visual LSD trip, thanks to the Fantasy Fest madness I had forgotten was due to begin that evening. The great lungfuls of air I sucked in as we pedaled tasted not only of the usual sulphur, iodine, frangipani, lime, sunblock, rotting seaweed, and coral, but also of an astonishing potpourri of many different varieties of pot, hash, beer, wine, rum, perfume, perspiration, flatulence, and (least noticeable by far) tobacco. I welcomed the panoply. Whenever I'm frightened enough to retract my own testicles, I like all the distractions I can get. Few places on earth could have provided so many, of such high caliber.

Double Bill's floating rocket, the *Flat Rock,* was moored

between a lavish three-story penthouseboat with three satellite dishes and an elaborately trellised gangplank, and a half-sunken century-old derelict tub, in such a way that it was hard to see from the land but easy to get to. I don't know anything at all about boats or sailing or seamanship or navigation, but I'll tell you this: The *Flat Rock* was well named. Once we cast off and Bill gunned it, it behaved much like a skipped stone, touching the water only occasionally. It was like the backwards of a spacecraft reentering earth's atmosphere: every time the ship glanced off the water, its speed *increased*. God be thanked, I don't get seasick, so once I accepted that all my vertebrae would be fused into a single bone and I would never walk again, I started to almost enjoy myself a little. Then all at once it began to rain so hard the name *Flat Rock* took on a whole different meaning, involving aerial bovine urination.

Nonetheless, I had not quite cut my throat by the time we began to smell Miami, so I'd have to agree the voyage was less aggravation than driving would have been. No traffic lights, no accidents, no potholes, no seniors with the left-turn signal permanently on doing thirty in the passing lane, no endless reshuffling of the same five gas stations and six fast-food brands, no billboards, speed traps, or gunplay, neither oblivious idiots ahead nor homicidal maniacs behind.

By the same token, of course, no Jeeps full of bronzed twenty-somethings in dental-floss bikinis. Life is imperfect.

In the movies or on TV, a meet between a Tony Donuts Junior and a Charlie Ponte would have taken place in a black stretch limo, or in the back room of an espresso joint nobody but mobsters ever went into, or in an abandoned warehouse, or at poolside in Charlie's opulent mansion fortress. Charlie hated cars, coffee, and cobwebs, and nobody he didn't own body and soul ever set foot on his personal home turf. His meets, therefore, took place in an anonymous cheesy two-bedroom house on an eighth-acre in a suburban development so vast it had its own ZIP code. It was called Bay Vista Estates, although it was nowhere near a bay and the longest unobstructed sight line anywhere in it was less than fifty yards unless you looked up.

The "estate" itself was the cheapest possible dwelling that white people with all their teeth or brown people who aspired to become citizens would live in. Its house number had six digits in it, and it was on 851st Lane, and there were also an 851st Street, 851st Way, and 851st Road—all identical to each other and to all their hundreds of companion byways—and then there were also West, East, North, South, NE, SE, SW, and NW variants for each of all of them, and none of these ribbons of tar heavy asphalt ever went even momentarily in a straight line. So although in theory any place can be located by GPS, in practice no SWAT team on earth could have located a given address in that tract in under an hour, much less stormed it. It took me and Double Bill every damn minute of the lead we had gained in taking the *Flat Rock* just to find the right furshlugginer house.

And when we did, there was no good way to surveil it. The whole development had been designed by the same people who do airliner interiors. Everything was not only made of the cheapest possible materials, but shrunk to the absolute minimum possible dimensions, as well. There was nowhere to park that wasn't in front of a hydrant or somebody's house, and most families were already parked in front of their houses because the driveways were precisely long enough to accommodate a single Accord and there were no garages.

The car we'd rented at the marina where we'd left the *Flat Rock* was convincingly crummy, so once we were sure we had the right place this time—the car sloppily parked in front of it was a Dodge convertible—Bill faked engine trouble and stalled out there. As I fiddled around under the hood, mourning the long-gone days when I recognized anything at all under the hood of a car, I studied the layout of Charlie Ponte's meet place out of the corner of my eye.

It didn't look promising. You almost had to turn sideways to walk between houses. The tallest tree I saw anywhere was shorter and skinnier than me. There seemed to be a brief mocking sketch of a fenced yard around back, mate to the band of lawn that separated the front of the house from the single-file sidewalk, but although I could see only a corner of it, I could tell that "backyard" was barely big enough to contain a few deck chairs, a frosted-glass-top table, and a gas grill, none of which would provide very effective cover for a ninja bartender or commando realtor. I don't know what they call that kind of roof, but if you took a thousand short pipes made of brick and sawed them all in half lengthwise, you'd have the materials; assuming a man could somehow get up there unnoticed, his every step would sound like a horse on cobblestones. I decided we were screwed.

Then I noticed something about the high backyard fence. Only a short stretch of it was visible, but I could see that it was made of some opaque space-age composite I didn't know, and that it was about the first thing I'd seen in the whole damn Bay Vista development that ran in a straight line.

I closed my eyes and tried to point my ears like a bat. Sure enough, I picked up a distant rhythmic sound, a sort of pulsing hiss, like wind or seashore but the wrong tempo. I opened my nostrils, and even over the open-hood smells right in my face, I was able to detect an evocative soupçon of diesel in the breeze.

We were right at the perimeter of the tract, mere yards

from the outside world despite all our meandering. Just beyond that backyard fence was a real road, a state road, a road that went in a straight line for miles during which there were no speed bumps at all, and on which it was not only possible but necessary to exceed twenty-five miles per hour.

"Slip me a beer," I murmured to Double Bill, and came round to the side of the engine compartment farthest from the house. He started to pass a bottle out the window. "No, a can," I said. He shrugged and complied, and I took it around to the front of the car. I poked around in there with my free hand awhile, cursing freely and with increasing volume. Finally I cried, "This stupid thing is *fucked*," spun to my left and flung the beer can as high and far as I could.

As I did, a front window of the house came up two inches and a rifle barrel appeared in the opening. I was expecting it—and even so, it was eerie. But the gunman was a pro: he saw that what I'd thrown was not a Molotov cocktail, and that in any case it would easily overshoot the house, and that I was not a hitman but a dork, and he chose not to shoot me. That was good. It would have upset him when the bullet bounced off. And the ricochet might have hurt Double Bill, who is not bulletproof.

Unfired on, I watched a perfectly good beer soar high in the air, cross the property, and come down like a mortar round on the far side of that fence. I listened hard. Several muffled horns, faint sounds of shrieking brakes—but no *crunch* of impact or tinkle of broken glass. That was a relief. I stuck my head under that hood one more time, touched something that looked like it wouldn't kill me and didn't, emerged with a huge smile of triumph and slammed the hood with a flourish. "We can go now," I said to Double Bill, and we did.

Locating the spot out in the real world that lay just beyond that particular section of anonymous backyard fence was a nontrivial problem. Simply finding the nearest exit from the tract was a spaghetti-bowl nightmare, and it turned out that *six* different roads ran past the place at various points, and since they were state roads in a Miami suburb, traffic on all of them sucked. But finally we spotted the skid marks and stains where the can of beer had come down, burst, and been run over one or more times. Bill put his emergency flashers on and slowed to a stop in the right lane just past the spot . . . then backed up until we were twenty yards short of it, and put her in park. Horns blared, and two lanes began merging to get past us.

"Shit," he said, and I didn't disagree.

There was no sidewalk. There wasn't even any shoulder. What lay on this side of the fence was about eight inches of curb, and then the lane we were stopped in. We could balance on that spit of curb, pressed up against the fence, and peer through a hole if we could find or make one—but we were going to be pretty conspicuous doing it. The car wasn't tall enough to provide effective visual cover from oncoming traffic, and the curb was too narrow to squat, crouch, or kneel. In the greater Miami area (and I'd hate to see the lesser), if you stand around, openly committing felonies in plain sight in the middle of a heavily traveled road for too many hours in a row, the theoretical possibility arises that you might just be seen by a cop, on his way off-duty perhaps.

I glanced at the traffic fuming past us. Nearly every driver that went by gave me the finger.

"Got it," Bill said. He studied his sideview mirror carefully, and when a hole in the traffic came along, he was out the door and in front of the car in a jiffy. I squeezed out my side and joined him.

His plan was simple and elegant. We *sat* on that silly curb, with our backs against the wall. The car now shielded us very effectively from the view of traffic coming along our way, and motorists going in the other direction would see only two hapless chumps waiting for the tow truck. If we could find or make a hole in the wall at the right height, either of us could put an eye or an ear to it simply by turning to speak to the other. The only downside was the constant nagging awareness that it was only a matter of time before some drunk decided our flashers were Christmas lights and plowed into the back of our car; in that case we would either stand up *very* quickly and carefully or, more likely, lose our legs.

Still, we felt pretty proud of ourselves. We were within pistol-shot of a Mafia *caporegime,* absolutely unsuspected, and our biggest immediate worry was a hypothetical drunk driver. For parrot-heads without a plan, we weren't doing too shabby. Bill flashed me his pirate's grin and adjusted himself under his sarong for more comfortable sitting. "Cool," he said.

I grinned back at him and nodded. "Now how do we make a small hole in this fence?"

"Tire iron," Bill suggested.

I shook my head. "Rental. Useless, I saw it. The only thing in the world you can do with it is loosen or tighten nuts that happen to be the right size."

"Screwdriver."

"Got one?"

"Uh . . . break off the gearshift lever; use it like an awl."

"How do we make our getaway?"

"The turn signal, then."

I was losing my good cheer. Something infinitely more important than a man monster or a Mafia kingpin was on the other side of that fucking fence: Erin. To be so near her, and screwed by the want of a screwdriver, was—

—screwed? I'm a bartender. *I keep a corkscrew on my key ring.*

I got it out, picked a spot, braced it with my left hand, and put my shoulder into it. In well under a minute it was clear I was wasting my time, but I kept trying.

"Jake, Jake, wait—listen!" said Bill.

I did hear something, which might have been voices raised in anger. Bill and I looked at each other and pressed our ears to the wall, hoping to pick up something by conduction. His face was no more than two feet from mine, so close I was able to notice he'd plucked his nostrils lately. "Hear that?" he whispered.

"What?" I whispered back, and pressed my ear even harder against the wall, and prayed to a God I didn't believe in to please send a beam out of the sky and punch a hole through this miserable stinking sonofabitching wall—

WHANG! My head exploded, and I fell over into the road, saw Bill land beside me.

I couldn't seem to work out what had happened. Then I glanced up at the wall and it was self-evident.

Picture Double Bill and me pressed up against that wall. Our two heads are so close together there's just enough room between them for a third man's head. If one were there, and he were looking straight at you, the bridge of his nose would be at the exact spot where the bullet came through the wall.

Tony solved the problem of finding the meet in typical Alexandrian fashion. He made one attempt at finding it himself and got it wrong—748317 851st Way NE—but the homeowner there was more than happy to leave a hot dinner on the table, shush his crying children, get behind the wheel of his own Corolla, and personally lead Tony and Ida to the *right* address. No problem at all. Once they were there and the guide had been dismissed, Tony got out, slung little Ida Alice over one shoulder, and headed for the door. But there was a small kerfluffle over admission.

"No kids," said the guy on the door, a stocky dour-looking thug in a black long-sleeve shirt, black slacks, and black loafers.

"This ain't no kid," Tony said. "This here is the deal."

"No kids," the man in black repeated. "Mr. Ponte hates kids."

Tony started to get pissed. "This is ten million bucks walkin'—happens to be short and warm; that don't make it a kid."

The door guy knew as well as Tony that Tony could tear him in half any time he felt like it. But he also knew there were worse fates than being torn in half; he stood his ground, kept one hand under his skirt, and looked adamant.

Tony hated to start a meet by murdering the door guy, but he couldn't see an alternative.

"Now I understand why the Roman Empire fell," Ida said.

The thug blinked down at her.

"Listen to me, you road-company butler," she went on, "Mr. Pontevecchio left his extremely comfortable home and came to this godforsaken rabbit warren to discuss a matter involving ten million dollars. I'm not going to bother asking you your name, because when he asks us who wasted his time and lost him that opportunity, I'll only need to say the guinea Johnny Cash. *Vaf fanculo*. Let's go, Antonio."

The thug opened his mouth to reply—

"Let 'em in, Vinnie," said a voice from inside the house.

Vinnie closed his mouth, stepped back, and they went inside.

There was another goon to the left, in front of the hallway that led off to the bedrooms, also with a hand near his waist, but Tony paid no attention to him. He knew there would be at least one more guy somewhere, with his gun already out, but didn't bother looking for him.

Charlie Ponte stood in the mini-living-room, his back to his guests, looking out a closed sliding glass door at the yardlet behind the house. He was balder than Tony remembered, but didn't look at if he'd gained a pound; in fact, he looked surprisingly fit for a man of his years and position. His green silk shirt with pearl buttons would have won a respectful nod from Bert the Shirt; his grey beltless slacks looked as if he had only moments ago taken them out of the dry cleaner's plastic and put them on; the species of lizard from which his boots were made was no longer endangered, because there were the last two of them, right there. Even from behind, he looked dangerous, even to Tony Donuts Junior. Tony set the kid down on her feet and put a proprietary hand on her shoulder. "Yo, Chollie," he said. "Thanks fa seein' me."

Charlie turned around like a gun turret. From the front, he radiated menace the way some women radiate sex appeal. Part of it was that you didn't often see a face *that* ugly that was so absolutely confident you weren't going to laugh at it. Another part was the eyes, doll's eyes, unblinking reptile eyes without a trace of mercy or pity. And some of it was simple knowledge of the awesome invisible power he wielded, as a senior executive of an organization that killed presidents when it felt like it. Strong men had died for annoying him. "Tony," he said. "Ten mil fa what?"

Tony relaxed slightly. For Charlie that was a respectful welcome. "I got somethin' you're gonna like."

"Yeah?"

Tony groped for a way to express it. "I got somethin' the old men are gonna want more than money."

Charlie did not snort, snicker, smirk, or grimace. He had

heard of humor, but didn't see the point. The only thing he said, and that with absolute lack of expression, was, "Uh-huh."

"No shit, Charlie. I—"

"Ex*cuse* me, gentlemen!"

Both men looked down.

Ida was glaring up at Tony Donuts. "Have you no social graces at all, Mr. Donnazzio?"

"S'cuse me," Tony heard himself say. "Chollie, this is Ida. Ida, Chollie."

Charlie regarded her dubiously. "I hate kids."

"I hate bald ugly gangsters with no manners, so we're even."

Charlie looked at Tony. "What the fuck izzis?"

Tony spread his hands. "An old lady."

Charlie stared. "Yeah?"

"An old lady I'm gonna give ten mil to."

"Yeah?"

"Once you give itta me. This is why I'm here."

"Uh-huh." Charlie looked down at Ida, then back up to Tony. "I give you ten huge. Then what? You come back the next day with twelve five? The next day with fifteen? The day after that with twenty?"

Tony shook his big head. "I come back in a few hours with somethin' way better."

"Better than ten mil."

"Somethin' that, when you bring it to the old men, and they hear they paid only ten huge for it, they're gonna say, Chollie, this is the bargain a the century."

Charlie studied him and frowned. "Not a atom bomb."

Tony blinked. "Nah."

"Good, we got them. Okay, what?"

Tony couldn't keep himself from smiling. He dropped a massive hand back onto Ida's shoulder and answered, "Ute."

Charlie Ponte studied him poker-faced for more than fifteen seconds. He knew perfectly well that Tony Donuts Junior did not make jokes, any more than he did himself, and he could see that Tony was not under the influence of any drug Charlie had ever sold, or foaming at the mouth, or addressing people who were not present.

Then he took an equally long silent look at Ida. He had bought and sold thousands of females, most of whom had tried to lie about their age. Her face and body were those of a seven-year-old, no question. But everything else about her—behavior, carriage, diction, vocabulary, stance, above all those striking eyes looking fearlessly into his—said that she was much more than seven years old. He found it disturbing.

He looked back to Tony. "Tell me about it."

Tony smiled again. "Two days ago I seen her the first time. She was in her twenties. Since then, every time I see her, she's younger. Today I catch up to her and find out the story. See, the guy—"

Charlie held up a hand. "You tell the story," he said to the little girl. "What's ya name again?"

"Ida Alice Shourds."

Charlie frowned. "Where do I know that name?"

"You're clearly better educated and more widely read in Florida history than Mr. Donnazzio. You have, I take it, studied the life of Henry Morrison Flagler?"

"Sure. Hero a mine, guy stole Florida."

"Well put. I was his second wife."

Charlie's poker face spread to his entire upper body.

"No shit, Chollie," Tony put in. "She looks like a little kid, but she's over a hunnert years old, this Ida. Her old man found the Fountain a Ute. He ain't dead, this Fagola. On paper, he's dead—really he's out there livin' off the books, havin' a ball. He screwed Ida here, had 'em put her inna hatch and threw away the key, only she got sprung, so naturally she wantsa screw him back. See? So you give me the ten mil like I said, an' I give it to her, an' she takes me ta this Fountain, an then I tell you where it is, an' you tell the Old Men." It had been a long time since Tony had spoken so many words in a row, and he found it tiring thinking of them all. But he knew he needed a big finish, here, and he'd been working on it since he left Key West. "Chollie, lissena me. How'd ya like ta be the guy that can make the Old Men young?"

It was absolutely impossible to guess what was going through Charlie Ponte's head. He might as well have been a statue. All three of his goons became fractionally more alert, and made sure their silencers were affixed. When Mr. Ponte got like this, you had to shoot guys sometimes.

"Why do you come back?" he asked finally.

"Huh?"

"I give you ten mil. You give it to the kid, she brings ya ta the Fountain a Ute. Now you got ten huge in your hand and eternal life. Why do I ever see you again?"

Tony grimaced. "Charlie, come on," he said, and pointed to himself with both hands. "Looka me. Where the fuck am I gonna hide? That Russian spaceship *Mirror*?"

"This Flagler's hidin' pretty good, what you're tellin' me."

"Cause nobody's lookin' for him. After all this shakes out, I might go look him up."

Charlie shook his head. "What's your end a this? You find out where the Fountain is, I gotta pay you *another* ten huge to find out, maybe?"

Tony shook *his* head. "Nah. It's my gift ta you an' the Old Men."

"So what's in it fa—? Ah."

"I wanna get made, Chollie. I get a button, it makes up for all the shit happened to my old man. Hey, tell me I don't deserve it. I'm givin each one a the old men a teenager's balls again. That's gotta be worth a button."

Charlie thought some more. "Not for nothin', Tony, but what do I need you for?"

"Huh?"

"Ida, you care who hands ya this ten mil?"

"Not in the least," she said.

Charlie looked at Tony and raised an eyebrow. "See?"

Tony frowned. "Chollie," he said, "you make me real sad, talkin this shit." His voice began to rise in volume and lower in pitch. "I come to ya like a man, wit respect, I give ya somethin better than any guy ever worked for ya in ya mizzable life, somethin the Old Men'll kiss your ass for, and ya wanna screw me?" He was shouting by now. "Me?"

"Who else is here?"

"God *damn* it," Tony said. "This ain't right, an you know it, Chollie. This is bullshit."

"You don't know what I know," Charlie Ponte said, and the way he said it made even Tony Donuts in a rage take notice.

"Okay, fine," Tony said. "Play it like that. Tell Vinnie behind me ta shoot me."

Charlie said nothing.

Tony turned around to face Vinnie. Vinnie's pistol was out, but pointed at the ceiling. "If you shoot me with that," Tony told him, "I won't kill you."

"You won't?" Vinnie couldn't stop himself from asking.

"Nah." Tony shook his head. "I'll nail both your feet ta the floor. Then I'll go kill your wife, your kids, your parents, an your girlfriend."

The blood drained from Vinnie's face.

"Shoot him, Vinnie," Charlie Ponte said.

Vinnie closed his eyes, took a deep breath, opened them again, took his stance, and fired. The shot sounded like a smoker spitting out a tobacco flake.

The round missed Tony by five inches. It drilled a fairly neat hole through the glass door, which failed to explode into a million shards, because it had not been made by a prop department, and then another hole through the backyard fence.

"Vinnie," Charlie said.

Vinnie sighed. "Sorry, Boss," he said. "I really like my mom." He put the barrel of his gun in his mouth. But before he could pull the trigger, his eyes rolled up in his head and he fainted.

Tony, Charlie, and one of the other goons all said "Whoa!" at once. The second goon said, "Fuck me runnin'." Ida said nothing. Then there was a pause of five seconds, silent except for the sounds of Vinnie falling down, before Tony Donuts said, "Ya see? People start breakin bad, who knows what's gonna happen? Why don't we just do the right thing, here? Have we got a deal, or not?"

"Look at it from where I'm sittin' a minute," said Charlie. "You want ten huge. I say why. You say I got the Fountain a Ute. I say how do I know that? You say, look at this kid, I swear she was older yesterday. You see my problem here, Tony? Due respect, how do I know your head isn't up your ass? No offense."

Tony snorted and regained his grip on Ida's shoulder. "You talked with this bitch. Look at her. You think she's a kid?"

Charlie considered this. Ida looked him square in the eye.

"Come on, you think a midget actor is gonna be that cool after somebody gets shot next to her?"

Charlie shook his head like a horse shaking off flies. "I gotta have more."

"Fine," said Ida. She bent and fiddled with her socks, making sure the cuffs around her ankles didn't touch her skin; they must chafe. Then she turned to the goon she could see and said, loudly and clearly, "I'm going to take a bottle of water from my fanny pack." She moved with slow deliberation, took the bottle out with a thumb and two fingers.

Tony smiled broadly. "There you go. *Now* we'll get this show on the road. Watch her close, Chollie. You, too, pal."

She held up the bottle and sloshed it, showing Charlie the inch or so of water it had left in it. "Point that thing away from me. You're going to flinch in a second," she said to the goon, and waited until he complied.

"Save a little taste for Chollie," Tony suggested.

"No," Ida said. Then she drank the bottle dry.

Tony had to give it up for Charlie—he kept his poker face. *He must have seen some amazing shit in his life*. But the capo's swarthy complexion did lighten by a half shade.

"Fuck me on a pogo stick," said the visible goon, and the one who was supposed to be hidden in the dining room said, *"Basta."*

Ida was about two years old. The yellow shorts and top combination looked like a ludicrously overlarge bell-bottomed jumpsuit now.

"What I tell ya?" Tony said triumphantly.

Ida cinched her belt tighter and rolled up her pant legs. It helped considerably. She still looked a little silly, but no longer looked hilarious. She stepped carefully out of the socks and handcuffs that were now way too big for her ankles, looked up at Charlie Ponte, took a deep breath, and did a cartwheel—beautifully. Then she struck a ballet pose, stood on one leg, and did six quick turns. "The body is a baby's," she said—her voice was several tones higher now, but recognizable. "But as you can see, the brain running it already *knows* how to walk. And think."

"I get it, I get it," said Charlie.

She nodded. "I'll leave you gentlemen to finalize your business, then. Which way are the facilities?"

The men all looked at each other.

"I have to pee."

The goon blocking the hallway entrance stepped aside. "Second onna right," he mumbled.

"There a window in that crapper?" Charlie asked.

"Nah."

"Okay. Make sure she comes back."

After Ida and her elephantine baby-sitter had left the room, nobody said anything for a while. Finally Tony said, "Well, Chollie? Whaddya say? We doin this or what?"

Charlie filled his chest and emptied it. "Sure."

"Ahright," Tony said happily. "So how do I get it? You don't got it here witcha."

It was phrased as a statement, not a question, so Charlie did not allow himself to be insulted by the implication that he might be stupid enough to place himself in the same room as ten million dollars he could not account for and some asshole who wasn't even a made guy. "Ya get outa here, ya get on One, goin nort'. First McDonald's you can see the arches from the highway, you get off an go tru the drivetru. Tell 'em ya want the special order a donuts for Mr. Bridges."

Tony frowned. "They don't sell donuts at McDonald's."

Charlie's face remained expressionless, but his nostrils flared slightly. "That's right. So prolly nobody else is gonna order any tonight."

"Yeah?"

"So they'll be pretty sure you're the right guy ta give the ten million bucks to."

Comprehension washed over Tony's features. "Ah! I getcha. That's slick."

"It's in hundreds, so what's gonna get put in your trunk will be the size a ten packages a typin paper."

"Fine. Okay, as soon as the kid is done peein, I'm outa here. This time tomorrow, I'll call ya an give ya directions ta the Fountain."

"Tony," Charlie said, "don't take this wrong, ahright? I know you're a serious man. But when things get up to ten huge, I gotta say some shit, regardless if you was Einstein. It's like ya get onna plane, an the stewardess *knows* ya know how ta buckle a fuckin seat belt, cause you prolly didn't walk ta the airport, but she's gotta show ya anyway, just so her ass is covered."

Tony shrugged. "Do what ya gotta do."

Charlie nodded. "Thank you. Here it is: If you fuck me on this, Tony, you better not stop runnin' till ya get ta Venus. It ain't just me. This is the Old Men's dough I'm givin' ya. You take their money and come back wit nothin' but your dick in your hand, they'll have ya dyin' for the next year. Dogs in China are gonna hear ya scream, okay?"

Tony nodded nonchalantly. "Whatever. Hey, *Ida*. Wring it 'n' bring it, will ya? We got a lotta drivin ta do."

"How long ya think it'll take ya, this time a day?" Charlie asked.

"Nice try," said Ida, coming back from the bathroom just as Tony was about to answer.

"It was worth a shot," said Charlie.

"Yes, it was," she agreed.

"What the hell are you guys *talkin'* about?" Tony asked.

"I'll explain it to you sometime," she said. "Let's go." And the two-year-old led the man-mountain back out to the car.

"Ya want me ta tail him, Boss?" asked the formerly hidden goon.

"Nah."

"You think when all this shakes out, I could get me some a that Ute Water, Boss? I make my old lady ten years younger, she might start puttin' out again. For me, I mean."

Charlie glowered at him. "What are you, *stunatz?* There's no fuckin' Fountain a Ute, ya moron."

The goon gaped, groped for words that would express his confusion without getting him killed. "But, Boss—I just seen that little girl turn into a baby, wit my own eyes. Din I?"

Withering glare. "Hello? Ever hear a this F/X shit? Nowadays they can make ya see anything. Fuhgeddabout your own eyes, Aldo—lissena what your *brain* tells ya." He snorted and shook his large head. "Fountain a Ute. Come *on*, fachrissake."

Aldo thought he saw daylight. "Ah. So you *ain't* givin' him no ten huge. He get ta McDonald's, he goes inna meat locker."

Charlie shook his head. "I'm givin' him the money, a'right. What the fuck? It ain't *my* money."

Aldo gave up. "Then I don't get it."

"Tony's gettin' stung. By real pros. So I'm just gonna sit back an' watch." He went to the kitchen sink, turned on the cold water, and let it run. "I hated that bastard's father so bad I had him hit, an' I'm *still* pissed off. The son's as big a prick as his papa, he even looks an' sounds like him. I don't just want him dead. I want him runnin' from the Old Men."

"Ahhhhh," said Aldo, and then, "But boss? Ain't they gonna be pissed you gave their ten huge ta Tony for the Fountain a Ute?"

The Mafia chieftain poured himself a glass of cold water and shut the tap. "First place, what fountain? I never heard a no fountain. Tony wanted ten huge, he didn't say why, I thought it over an' I give it ta him. How did I know he was dumb enough ta get stung for it, on somethin' so ridiculous?" He drank some water. "Second place, they're gonna get back their money."

"How?"

Charlie took another long drink, poured out the rest, and set the empty glass down upside down on the Formica countertop. "Jesus, Aldo, think about it. Whoever's connin' him with those little kids, how far you think they're gonna get spendin' hundred-dollar bills wit serial numbers we got onna list? We got a *lotta* friends in banks. If those clowns spend five grand before we roll 'em up, I'll be fuckin' amazed."

Aldo was lost in admiration. "Jesus Christ, that's beautiful, boss."

"Uh-huh. Wake up Vinnie and clean up. We're out of here."

10

WHO KNOWS WHERE OR WHEN?

If it ain't one thing, it's two things.
—Grandfather Stonebender

Oh, I'll probably have a lump for a while. But you can't hurt an Irishman by hitting him in the head."

"You look great for your age, Daddy."

I winced and thanked my naked two-year-old daughter gravely. "And how are you feeling, princess?"

She grinned hugely. "Aw, you know me. I just hope adults enjoy adultery as much as I've enjoyed my infancy."

We were back in the car and moving with traffic, headed for the marina where the *Flat Rock* lay waiting for another chance to telescope my spinal column. The sun was low in the sky, but would probably last long enough for us to get under way, at least. Bill was driving, so that Erin and I could hug.

"So what's up with Tony?" I asked.

Her grin got even bigger. "He's driving north to Saint Augustine. He couldn't get his handcuffs to close tight enough to work on me, and he's one of those guys that hates to drive with the top up, so he solved the problem by tossing me in the trunk."

"Jesus, what an idiot!"

"Oh, you noticed? I wish I could see his face five hours from now, when he gets to the outskirts of Saint Gus and opens that trunk. I left him my clothes and a note that says, *I had another sip hidden in the fanny pack.*"

Bill and I roared with laughter.

"I really enjoyed you at this age," I told her. "It's nice to see it again. You're a cuddly little armful."

"How am I at twenty-one?" she asked.

"The second most beautiful woman on the planet."

"How *is* Mom? Freaking out, right?"

"Roger that."

"You'd think she would have got it out of her system by now."

"If she was ever going to, she would have when you rode the Shuttle to orbit—"

"I'm gonna ride the Shuttle? *Cool.*"

Oh. From her point of view, that hadn't happened yet. This was tricky stuff. "Yeah. Uh, maybe you better not ask why."

"Course not."

"I'm just saying you're right: it's always been irrational for your mother and me to worry about you. You came out of her womb more competent than the two of us put together. But two million years of hard wiring doesn't give a damn about reason. I'm going to have to call her soon and let her know you're okay."

"I know, Daddy. It's flattering. And really sweet. If it makes you guys feel better to worry, you go right ahead. How are you and your friend getting home to Key West? How did you two get here so fast?"

It suddenly dawned on me and Bill that this Erin had not

met him yet. For her, *home* was still Long Island. But she knew about Key West. She must have come from a point after we'd decided to move, but before we got there—because we'd all met Bill the hour we arrived. "I'm sorry—Erin, let me present my good friend and yours-to-be, William B. Williams. Bill, this is my daughter, Erin Stonebender-Berkowitz."

She was delighted. "What a great name! 'Double Bill' . . . pleased to meet you. Do people call you Bbiillll?"

He flashed his pirate grin and took his hand off the gearshift long enough to pat the top of her head. "Only you, sugarbush—nobody else can say it."

"Cool sarong."

"Thanks. I can't understand why anybody in Florida wears pants."

"Me either. So did you guys fly here or what?"

I explained about the *Flat Rock*. "I don't intend to push her on the way home, if that's all right," Bill said. "We really strained her on the way up here."

"And ourselves," I agreed. "I'm gonna need a week of chiropracty to put some space between my ass and my shoulder blades again. It's all right with me if we just let the damn boat *drift* south. Once I call your mother from the marina and let her know you're okay and we're on our way home, I'm not in a hurry anymore." I'd tried to call her already on the borrowed cell phone; unfortunately, when that bullet had smacked into the fence and croquet-balled my head into the street, I'd landed on the phone.

"It's a two-man boat?" Erin asked.

"The only reason your Mom isn't here. But hell, you don't take up any more room than the beer we drank."

She grimaced. "Thanks, but I'm not crazy about open boats. Especially cramped ones, especially for hours and hours. Especially in the dark." The sun was indeed just about to set. "You guys go ahead: I'm just gonna hop home, okay, Daddy?"

"Sure, why not?" I said. "Wish I could do it myself. We'll see you there, pumpkin."

Pop. She was gone.

"Man," said Bill, shaking his head. "Once in a while I think I can imagine what it must be like to teleport. But I can't picture myself attempting it from a moving car."

"She's done it from a moving Space Shuttle. Uh—she will real soon, anyway."

We reached the marina just after the last trace of light left the sky. While Bill prepared the boat for departure, I wandered off to find a pay phone. When I came back, Bill read my expression. "No luck?"

I shook my head. "Two pay phones in this place, both vandalized. And the little putz behind the counter is a redneck who hates all men with beards; he wouldn't let me use the house phone even when I offered him cash. I think he saw our boat and pegged us for dope runners."

"I'll go reason with him," said Bill. He happened to have a heavy wrench in his hand.

"No, forget it," I said, and stepped aboard. "It doesn't matter. By now Erin's long since home, and Zoey knows she's safe. Let's just gas up and go—I'm tired of Miami, and darkness doesn't improve it."

I'm not a boat guy. The trip back home was more pleasant than the mad race north had been. But not a hell of a lot more pleasant. Apparently a boat designed for ultrahigh speed handles poorly at low speed—I believe the technical phrase is, "wallows like a pig"—and the compromise speed Bill settled on was not enough help. I'm always scared on a small boat, and adding in darkness and great distance from shore didn't help a bit. At one point a dolphin broke the surface nearby, for all I know just to say hello, and nearly gave me a heart attack. I never actually became officially seasick, quite, but I was very glad when the lights of Key West came into view, and gladder still when Houseboat Row loomed up out of the darkness.

By the time we approached the gate of The Place, I was damn near euphoric. The warrior returneth home to his lady, triumphant after a successful campaign. Tony Donuts Junior would not be back anytime soon: he had a lifetime of running to begin, and even he wasn't stupid enough to return to a cul-de-sac that was his last known address, where he would stand out like a target, and where any number of people would be happy to rat him out. As for Charlie Ponte and his friends, they had never heard of us and had no reason to. Even if they ever caught up with Tony, and even if they paid attention to a word he babbled, Tony himself wasn't aware of any connection between The Place and the person he thought of as Ida Alice Shourds except that she'd had a drink in there once. He would be more likely to associate her with the porno store whore he'd seen her most recently—and that store had been closed, bankrupted by the Internet, for months. (The owner, an acquaintance of the Professor's, had simply tossed the porn tapes themselves into the Dumpster and left town, the empty boxes still on the shelves.)

On top of everything else, in order to get from Houseboat Row back to The Place, it had been necessary to pass through the first night of Fantasy Fest. Can you picture a party in Paradise, crashed by every benign weirdo in the world? Or have you ever been to the masquerade of a World Science Fiction Convention, and if so can you picture that event with everyone present loaded on mescaline? That's as far as I'm going to go in describing Fantasy Fest here; the job has been done too well too many times before, and you can find lengthy discussion, including streaming video and stills, with two minutes on any search engine. The point is that by the time I was close enough to read the small familiar sign above the gate that discreetly proclaims, THE PLACE ... BECAUSE IT'S TIME, I had been grinning like an idiot for so long my face hurt, and I didn't mind a bit. I can still remember that cotton candy feeling.

Things went sour real fast then.

First of all, just as I reached the open gateway, I remembered for the first time in hours that my friend Doc was dying. The knowledge just dropped unwanted back into my consciousness, and a large fraction of my good cheer got lopped off the top right there.

Then I stepped through the gate and found, instead of the hero's welcome I'd been imagining, a dead house. Even though it wasn't quite midnight yet, The Place was dark, the bar closed, the pool empty; the only action I could detect was lights and murmurs indicating a small quiet gathering on the patio around behind Doc's cottage.

I realized I should have been expecting it. Tom had only done what I'd have done if I'd been paying attention to my business—it was silly to stay open nights during Fantasy Fest, since nearly all my clientele would be out there participating every night. Doubtless that was where most of them were now. Nonetheless, I felt a letdown: nobody was around to slap some fatted calf on the barbie for me.

"I guess I'm just going to head home," Double Bill said. "I'm wiped."

"I hear that," I told him. "But just come in for a cuppa, okay? Zoey's going to want to thank you."

My house was dark. I assumed Zoey would be with the

group behind Doc's place, and I headed there. On the way I found myself thinking that people gathered to comfort a dying man weren't going to be a receptive audience for witty complaints about my boat-battered butt, and caught myself resenting Doc. *Sumbitch has been upstaging me since the day I met him.* At my age you finally start to cut yourself a little slack when you notice your own monstrous selfishness emerging—it's *not* monstrous, it's hardwired, and the only thing that's really your fault is how much you *indulge* it—but it's still never fun to confront. By now my good mood was still in place—but constructed of cornflakes and library paste.

And then I rounded the corner into Doc's backyard, and the people facing my way saw me, and the people facing away from me saw their faces and spun around, and everybody started talking at once. At first all I could glean was that everybody was upset with me for some reason, so there went the last of my good mood. But then I began to pick individual voices out of the wash of sound, and to sort out the questions they were asking me, and in a matter of seconds I went from being officially in a bad mood to being terrified.

The Doc's stentorian "Dammit Jake, whoa didn't you fine?" came through first, followed by Field Inspector Czr-jghnczl's "Is your daughter all right, Mr. Stonebender?" and Long-Drink's, "Jesus, where's Zoey?" and Tom Hauptman's, "Oh, dear, aren't they with you?" and finally Fast Eddie's miserable, shamed, "I'm sorry, boss. I tried ta stop her, but she wouldn't lissena me." As the combined meaning began to come through, I screamed an unspellable syllable, spun on my heel and sprinted as fast as I could to my own cottage next door, kicked the back door open, and raced inside.

The house was empty. Just as I'd feared, the storage closet door stood open. The Meddler's Belt was not in the closet. I stumbled back outside, reeling as if I'd just been punched hard in the face, and headed for Doc's yard again, trying to make it all make sense. Halfway there, I heard my watch give its little hourly chirp and knew it was midnight. I saw something out of the corner of my eye and looked over toward the distant pool in time to see naked two-year-old Erin materialize at the end of the diving board and cry, "HI, EVERYB—! Gee, where *is* everybody?"

"Here," I croaked, and kept going, and she and I arrived together.

Everyone in Doc's yard was on their feet, all still talking at once, and their volume rose sharply when they saw Erin pop into view. It took several more minutes of talking at cross purposes before everyone understood the misunderstandings that had occurred, and their terrible consequences.

I had believed that Erin was going to zip home from Miami to Key West immediately—that is, as straight teleportation, with no time-hopping involved—so I'd concluded that there was no need to find a working pay phone and call Zoey collect: Erin would give her mom the good news faster than I could dial my phone number. Erin, on the other hand, hadn't known I'd ruined the cell phone, and believed I was going to phone home at once—so she had decided to time-shift forward a little on the way and arrive at the same instant I did, so we could all share the joy.

So nobody had phoned, for longer than was reasonable, and then nobody would answer Doc's phone, because I'd broken it, and finally Zoey had just snapped. She had strapped on the Meddler's Belt, set the time dial for some near-future time by which she figured the situation would have to have resolved itself one way or another, and pushed the GO button.

When the mutual explanations had gotten that far, my vision blurred, and I'd have gone down if Jim Omar hadn't caught me.

"She doesn't know, does she, Daddy?" Erin asked me.

"No, honey, I don't think she does. We never discussed it. It never came up."

"Oh . . . my . . . *God.*"

The man who called himself the Meddler had stumbled (will stumble) upon the historically first of three different methods of time travel, and used it only twice, and his discovery had died with him. Then later, I'd heard, there had been an interim method developed, about which I knew nothing except that it had seen limited use for a few centuries after its discovery, and involved much more esoteric technology than the Meddler's Belt. And finally, the *far*-distant-future ficton from which the Callahans hailed had developed the ultimate, no-moving-parts kind.

Only the second and third methods automatically compensated for the inconvenient nature of the universe.

"What's wrong, Erin?" Mei-Ling asked. "Why are you so upset? Your mom got her arrival time off by a little, that's—"

"No," Erin interrupted. "I don't think so. There are *two* dials on that belt, and I'll bet Mom used only one of them. Isn't that right, Uncle Eddie?"

Eddie thought hard. "I seen her twist one ting, an' push a button. I didn't see her do nuttin' else."

Erin groaned.

"That tears it, then," I heard my own voice say from a long way off.

"What's the second file door?" Doc Webster asked with gentle patience. "Excuse me. What is the . . . dial . . . for?"

"Space," Erin told him. "The first dial is for time, and the second is for space. You use it to compensate for the fact that everything in the universe is always in motion."

"Oh, my God," Doc said, turning pale. "Oh, no."

"Jesus Christ!" Omar shouted.

"Hell," the Professor said.

"Oh, dear," Mei-Ling murmured.

I could not get enough air into my chest to make a squeak.

"I don't geddit," Fast Eddie said mournfully.

"Everything moves, Uncle Eddie. Always. The earth rotates at nine hundred miles an hour. It revolves around the sun at nineteen miles a second—which is itself moving through space, revolving around the center of the galaxy. The galaxy is rotating at half a million miles an hour, and it's in motion itself, presently on a collision course with the Andromeda nebula at about six million miles a day. Meanwhile the whole universe is expanding. Everything moves relative to everything else, and nothing stands still—*ever.*"

"Okay—so?"

Erin closed her eyes, and Mei-Ling took up the stick. "So let's say Zoey decided to set the time dial on that belt to this very second now, Eddie. She pushes the button, and *zip*, she's now. But she's not *here* and now . . . because she didn't make any compensating settings to the space dial. Instead, she's . . . well, she's at the point in space where this particular portion of the earth's surface happened to be when she pushed the button. And we're . . . well, not. We've moved. A *long* way."

"Hully Christ," Eddie whispered. "You're tellin' me right this minute she might be somewhere in outer fuckin' space?"

"Without a pressure suit," Omar said dully.

"Ah, geeze," Eddie said, and fainted dead away.

I was terribly afraid I might do the same thing, and I didn't have the time. Usually when you can't seem to inhale it's because you failed to exhale enough. I put both hands on my ribs and pushed hard, emptying my lungs, while trying to blow out an imaginary candle. Automatically they took a deep breath to refill. I did it again, and it worked even better. Blood reoxygenated, I found the nearest lawn chair, sat down, and put my head down between my knees. The dizzy feeling and greying vision receded. By the time I straightened up again. I was only nauseous with terror.

There's a trick about nausea many people don't know. If you can't get medicine, or the medicine isn't working, it can sometimes help to holler at a bunch of innocent bystanders. The less they deserve it, the more it seems to help. It's a derivative of what Valentine Michael Smith learned in the monkey house, I think. Everyone was obliging me by all talking at once, so it was at the top of my lungs that I bellowed, "SHADDAP!"

Silence. Sure enough, the nausea receded one step.

A hundred things to think about at once—which one was *first?* Already a dozen people were opening their mouths to start talking again.

Erin had already managed to bring Eddie around; he was sitting up and shaking his head. "Uncle Eddie," Erin said, "Exactly what time did Mom leave?" She was using the same voice her mother uses to end arguments with me, half an octave higher in pitch, and recognizing that brought the nausea back a half step closer again. But I knew she had asked the right question.

"Just after sunset is da closest I can tell youse," Eddie said. "It was de dark got to her."

"Nobody felt like putting the house lights on," Long-Drink said. "I guess we shoulda."

"Assign blame later, Phil," Erin snapped. "Can anyone else pin the time down any closer? Anybody remember what was on the radio?"

"I wuz playin'," Eddie mourned.

Pixel the cat was suddenly in my face. He materialized on my lap without warning, sublimely confident that I would instinctively cup my hands under him and make a lap in time to keep him from falling, like I always do—but then, most unusually, he leaned forward and poked his face right up against mine. The item he had in his mouth shielded me from tuna breath—and made me draw in a deep breath of my own. Back when I first opened The Place, if I had to leave during business hours for some reason, I'd leave a sign telling potential customers when we would reopen. Almost at once I came to realize that my clientele were perfectly capable of running The Place without me, for limited periods of time, at least, and put the sign in storage. Here it was after all these years—the words WE'LL BE BACK AT: and a yellow clockface with two movable hands.

Pixel actually poked me in the nose with it twice. "I get it, I get it," I said, and he backed off and turned it so Erin could see, too. It read 7:03.

"That's it *exactly*?" Erin said. "You're *sure*, Pixel?"

He turned his massive head back, dropped the thing on my chest, and held it there with one paw, moved the other with exquisite care. When he was done the minute hand was, by my estimation, just over a third of the way between the three and the four. "*Bwrrrrtt!*" he said.

"Thank God!" Erin took in a deep breath and let it out. Her exhale was a little shivery. "Okay," she said, "that's a good start. That's a very good start. That helps a lot. Next question . . . Wait—" She closed her eyes tight for a few moments, then opened them again. "Okay, I presume Mom did not tell any of you how far ahead she intended to hop, or you'd have spoken up by now. No—don't tell me your guess, Phil. Nobody speak—especially you, Daddy!" I shut up. "I want everybody to *write down* their guess. People tend to agree with whoever sounds the most positive, but that doesn't mean he's right. I want your subjective impressions." Eddie and Omar were passing out bar napkins, and just about everybody turned out to have a writing implement on them. "You all know my Mom pretty well, you had a sense of her mood, just how frightened and impatient she was, maybe you got a look at her just before she disappeared. How far forward do you think she would have gone? Don't say it; write it down."

Everybody did, and all the napkins were collected by Pixel and brought to Erin. She riffled through them quickly and lifted her eyes. "Most of you agree she would have hopped to the same time tomorrow night."

"She'd want to go far forward enough to be *sure* of getting an answer, one way or another," Long-Drink said.

Omar, the only other one of us present who had studied the Meddler's Belt at any length, said, "And twenty-four hours is an especially easy setting to make on that dingus."

"I think she would have picked midnight," said Mei-Ling, sounding fairly sure about it.

"I hope to God you're wrong," Erin said. "Why do you think so?"

"We were talking, about ten minutes before she did it . . . and I said to her, 'Don't worry, I guarantee by midnight you'll know the good news.' I'm pretty sure she heard me."

Erin groaned. "Doc, check me: *What's the maximum amount of time she could survive in hard vacuum?*"

"I'm not sure. Twenty seconds, would be my guess. Thirty at the outside."

She slumped and sat down hard on the grass, just like an ordinary two-year-old would. For her, the effect was comical . . . until she pooched out her lower lips just like an ordinary two-year-old who was thinking of bursting into tears.

"If Mom picked midnight," she said, "she's dead." Just about everybody gasped or groaned or said *no* or spoke some sort of obscenity. "*I* picked midnight—and I've been here for at least five minutes, nearly six." She has an excellent sense of time, and we knew it; still I checked, and so did others. My watch, an uncommonly accurate one, said it was 12:05:47.

"So ya time-hop back a few minutes—what'sa problem?" Fast Eddie said.

"I *can't,* Uncle Eddie!" she cried, and did burst into tears. "Don't you get it? There was a me here in the universe from midnight on. *There can't be two-hoo-hoo—*" She was crying too hard to form words now.

I had never seen my daughter cry as a baby—not once. Maybe she made it a point of pride, I don't know. I *had* seen her cry, twice by that point, but only after age seven. Seeing my superbaby, theoretically the most competent of us to deal with this emergency, sobbing like an ordinary infant now— well, it came close to unhinging me.

So I got out my mental power-screwdriver and tightened those fucking hinges down machine-tight, and I got up from my chair and I picked my baby up in my arms and I held her as tight as I could. And said in her perfect little ear, with my very best imitation of serene confidence, "So we will assume that Mom did *not* pick midnight, since that assumption gives us things we can do besides go apeshit. Okay, princess?"

She hugged me back, harder than I would have believed possible, and in five or ten long seconds she had stopped crying. "Okay, Daddy."

"Attagirl. What are the other possible times she could have picked?"

She squirmed in my arms, and Mei-Ling handed her a tissue just before she would have wiped her face on my shirt. "Well, like I said, most of us voted for twenty-four hours."

"Who didn't? Besides Mei-Ling."

"You and me, Daddy. We both guessed one hour."

"Huh!" I said. "Why did you?"

"I don't know," she said. "Just everything I know about Mom. She takes small steps until she's sure it's safe. *Then* she takes a big stride. Why did you pick an hour?"

"Because I was the moron who put the whole idea in her head," I said bitterly. "Just before I left to come after you, as we were getting ready to go, half-kidding I said I was tempted to use the Meddler's Belt to cheat, and peak ahead to the back of the book. And Zoey said something about what's so bad about cheating, not kidding at all. I talked her out of it—I thought I had, anyway, damn it. I pointed out what she already knew: every act of time travel threatens paradox, imperils the whole universe. I said that was just too much risk to take for a case of nerves, and she agreed, God damn it, she *agreed* it was— oh, shit." I sat back down heavily in my chair.

"What, Daddy?"

"I just realized—that was just before she found out she wasn't coming with me and Bill. Before she realized she was going to be sitting here by herself with nothing to do but go out of her mind with worry for an unknown number of hours."

"She wasn't by herself, Jake," Mei-Ling said.

"Whatever. The point I was making was, Zoey had recently had it impressed on her what a dangerous thing using that belt would be. I think even if she got worried enough to use it anyway, she would have tried a short hop, first, and if that didn't k—If that was successful, *then* maybe she'd have leaped ahead as far as midnight, or even tomorrow."

"Why an hour?" the Professor said. "Why not a minute? Or even a few seconds?"

I thought hard. Why was I sure of an hour? "Because," I said, thinking the words as I heard myself speak them, "if she jumped forward one minute, or two, or five, then she'd have taken all the risk, with virtually no chance of reward. If she'd believed the news she wanted would be available within minutes, she'd have just waited for it. One hour feels to me like the compromise she would have picked: the largest increment she would think of as *small* . . . but that might actually be enough to learn something."

Doc Webster the diagnostician was shaking his head gently. "Jesus, Jake . . . that's awful thin."

"It sounds right to me," Erin said. "We were talking once, about how terrible it must be to be clairvoyant, and never have a surprise in your life. And she said, 'Yes, but sometimes I think it'd be nice if every now and then you could peek ahead for just an hour or so, just to get your bearings.' I remember I agreed with her."

"An hour *or so*," Long-Drink repeated thoughtfully.

"You can't dial an 'or so,' Drink," Omar argued. "She'd probably have picked one hour. The two people who know her best both share that intuition—that's good enough for me."

My heart was hammering so loud I could barely follow the discussion, much less contribute any more. It was dawning on me that, under the scenario I was proposing, my beloved had been dead for hours by now—boiled and burst and terribly cold. . . .

Unless we did something about that.

"Okay, Erin," I said, loud enough to get the floor. "Let's start with those two assumptions. Zoey left at 7:03 and—" I glanced at Pixel's clock again to confirm my memory. "—and twenty-two seconds. And her intent was to hop forward exactly one hour. Is that enough information for you to figure out exactly where she ended up, and rescue her?"

Her face twisted up so bad that for a moment I thought she was going to cry again. I guess she wanted to. "Oh, God, Daddy, *I don't know*. Let me think—" She closed her eyes, bit down hard on her left thumbtip, and with her right hand tugged rhythmically at the hair at the back of her neck. I hadn't seen the mannerism in years; it meant she was concentrating very hard. Ten seconds went by. When she opened her eyes, I could see dismay in them. "I doubt it," she said. "It's a *really* hairy problem. I don't think the NSA could handle it. And our window, our margin of error is so incredibly minuscule—we can't be off by more than a few thousand yards or we'll never find her in time. So everything has to be calculated out to a humungous number of decimal places—"

Her voice was rising in pitch, speed and volume; time to interrupt. "Yeah, but didn't you tell me you had some way to steal as much computer power as you'd ever need, honey? Something about word processors on bicycles?"

The feeble attempt at humor did not go down well. "Jesus, Daddy! Yes, Solace taught me a way to access just about all the unused processor cycles of nearly any computer that's connected to the Net, without being caught at it. That's basically what she did to live. Yes, in theory that's more computing power than the U.S. federal government has, or anyway knows it has—"

Again I tried to interrupt her climb toward panic. "There you go—we'll take our best shot, and—"

She was shaking her head. "You don't get it. Raw computer power isn't enough, not nearly enough. Every step of the way you have to make assumptions, ones that could introduce whopping errors if they're wrong—"

"You'll make the right assumptions. Your intuition has always been good; you're good at this stuff."

She shook her head harder. "I'm *terrible* at it. Mike or Lady Sally could do it, no sweat—they solve trickier problems all the time. Uncle Nikky would probably just get the right answer in a flash of light, like always. But my brain isn't like theirs."

"Come on—I saw you hop from an orbiting shuttle to that pool over there—"

Her glare was withering. "Daddy . . . I haven't *done* that yet. Not from my point of view."

Shit. "Yeah, well, you will."

She grimaced. "Fine. Okay, by now you've lived with me for, how long? Eleven years?"

"Close enough," I agreed.

"You tell me. In all that time, do you *ever* remember me Transiting any farther away than High Earth Orbit?"

"Well, I remember one admittedly short visit to the moon when you turned ten."

"Big whoop. Daddy, Mike and Uncle Nikky hop across the baryonic *universe* whenever they happen to feel like it! I'm out of my depth. God, I wish one of them were around!"

For the millionth time in the last ten years I wondered where or when the hell Mike and Sally and Nikola and Mary and Finn all were, what they were up to, why we hadn't heard from them, and above all, why they weren't answering the emergency phone number Mike had once given me. It is perilously easy, I've found, to come to depend on time-traveling immortals to solve your crises for you. It suddenly made sense to me for the first time why Mike would leave us to our own devices. Imagine being Superman—with more than a hundred pain-in-the-ass Jimmy Olsens and Lois Lanes pulling on your coattail every other minute. . . .

After a moment of depressed silence, big Jim Omar spoke up. "Have I got this right?" he said. "You're saying we could maybe solve this, if we only had more computing power than the rest of the world put together?"

"Well . . . maybe, Uncle Omar," Erin said. "Not for sure . . . but it would really really help a lot."

"Hell, for a minute there, I thought we had a problem."

I saw where he was going, and started to get excited—and so did most of those present. "He's right, princess," I said. "We took this class once before. Well, you haven't, yet, but the rest of us have. I won't tell you why, but it doesn't matter now. What we need is a neural net. No, excuse me, I mean we need an interconnected *bank* of dedicated neural nets."

She blinked. "Have they built any good ones by now?" she asked dubiously. "Things weren't looking promising back in my time. And how can we possibly get access to some right away—by which I mean, in the next hour or two?"

"No problem," Omar said. "We roll our own."

"Huh?"

"Out of real neurons. The wet kind."

"Oh," she said, and then *"Oh!"*

Human brains, he meant. Telepathically interconnected, and placed under the control of a single directing intelligence.

All it required was temporary group ego-death.

"Jesus, Jake," Long-Drink said, "I don't know. I don't want to rain on the parade, but we haven't been telepathic in ten years—"

"—maybe we just haven't needed to badly enough—"

"—and everybody's scattered all over town—"

"—town my ass, it's just barely big enough to be a neighborhood—"

"—in the middle of fucking Fantasy Fest!"

He had a point there. At just about any other time, I could probably have stood at the corner of Duval and Flagler with a bullhorn and raised more than half the troops. But tonight, and for the next week, everyone in downtown Key West was trying as hard as they possibly could to attract the attention of everyone else. "We'll just have to do the best we can," I snapped back at Long-Drink, but even I knew it was a crummy answer.

Doc Webster's voice was calm, sane, and reasonable. "All right, friends, let's be calm. Our group has been in rapport several times now, over the years—and we've spent most of the intervening time loving one another. We're all sensitive to one another, psychically attuned. I suggest we all shut up, close our eyes, join hands, and try to send out a Call—the way the MacDonald brothers did the night Finn's Master showed up."

On that memorable occasion, the MacDonalds had broadcast the telepathic message *Mike Callahan needs you*, and the response rate had been 100 percent, even though it cost some of us dearly and forced a couple of us into severe risk of life, limb, or liberty.

"Can we pull that off?" I asked dubiously. The MacDonalds had been Special Talents, mutants: practicing full-time telepaths since adolescence. For all I knew, they'd had amplification assistance from Mike himself that night. And they were both long dead now, their brains burned out by the monster they'd enabled us to destroy.

"Let's find out," Doc said. He seemed to have tapped some inner vein of strength himself; he hadn't made a spoonerism in several sentences now.

So we all looked round at one another, and took deep breaths, and moved closer together, and joined hands.

"What's the message?" Long-Drink asked. "Does 'JAKE NEEDS YOU' work for everybody?"

Half a dozen of us opened our mouths with some suggestion for a nit-picking change—looked at one another—and chorused "Fine," together.

"Okay, on three," Omar said. "One . . . two . . ."

<<<JAKE NEEDS YOU>>>

11

NEED IN A HAYSTACK

To a mind that is still,
the whole universe surrenders
—Chuang-Tzu

An hour later, attendance exceeded 100 percent, and everybody had been brought up to speed. Every single one of my regulars was there, and some had brought along neighbors or new friends just in case more warm bodies might be useful. And they'd managed to get there discreetly, without bringing a traveling riot along in their wake; the rest of Fantasy Fest proceeded out there, oblivious of anything but itself. We had just over 125 brains assembled in that compound, available for our neural bank. Perhaps two dozen more than we'd had the last time. But last time we'd had a less intractable problem to solve than this one. . . .

Outside the compound: universal anarchic tomfoolery. Inside the compound: quiet, calm purposefulness. Outside: joy unrestrained. Inside: muted fear, stoic endurance, cherished hope. It kept reminding me of a time when I had spent New Year's Eve in an emergency room.

The house lights were on, at their lowest setting. We spontaneously formed into a circle—actually a large ragged ellipse—all the way around the pool. Nobody gave orders or stage directions; nobody seemed to feel like making a speech. People adopted whatever posture they felt they could maintain without effort for a time—some sitting zazen, some reclining on lounge chairs, some lying on their backs looking up at the stars—took last sips or tokes and set down whatever they'd been holding, and began to join hands. Down at the deep end, Lex's hands appeared above the water, and each was taken by somebody; he was new to this telepathy business, but game. (Long-Drink said something about him being a game fish, and got splashed for it.) Ralph von Wau Wau sat on Omar's lap, touching paws with Alf on Maureen's lap, and Pixel on mine. Harry the Parrot, uncharacteristically subdued, perched on Double Bill's shoulder, making him look more like a pirate than ever.

One person stood apart: Field Inspector Ludnyola Czrjghnczl, who had politely but firmly refused all invitations to join in. She didn't want to leave the compound, but she declined to join the circle, saying that it would be like a crack skydiving team making an important jump with a beginner who was terrified of heights. We pressed her as much as politeness required, and then let it go—she was right. Telepathy is not for the reluctant. It's scary enough as it is.

Erin sat beside me at the shallow end of the pool, seated on one of the tall chairs I use instead of bar stools. In front of her were two music stands tilted back as far as they would go, with a laptop computer on each one: a PowerBook and a Dell. She had a hand poised over each keyboard and was physically connected to our human circuit by my hand on her right shoulder and Doc Webster's on her left. She was deep in final consultation with Doc and those nearest to him: Acayib, Omar, Merry, Ben, Jaymie, Allen, Doug, Guy, Jim,

Herb—every one of us who had ever worked at, played with, or studied one or more of the hard sciences, especially math, astronomy, physics, biology, or medicine. ("Their heads are already formatted properly to process the data," she'd told me.)

"We're agreed, then," Acayib was saying. "We'll use the Cosmic Microwave Background *as if* it were an absolute reference frame for position in the observable universe."

"Effectively, it is," Jaymie said. "The CMB is isotropic to about one part in a hundred thousand. We can see the reflex Doppler shifts due to the motions of the earth, the sun, the galaxy, the Local Group, and the Local Supercluster—"

"That should allow us to measure velocity deviation to a high degree of accuracy," said Acayib. "With a reliable predictive model of solar system and solar galactic orbit motions—"

Erin nodded. "I was able to find those in Uncle Nikky's toolbox."

"—well, then, I think we have an excellent chance of extrapolating Zoey's location."

Jaymie nodded vigorously. "With enough velocity data from the CMB, we should be able to factor in models of even galactic and supergalactic motions, as well."

"There's something else crucial to consider, don't forget," Doug put in. "When you materialize out there, your velocity amplitude and direction may well be different enough from your mother's that there could be a very high kinetic energy difference. You'll want to try to predict that so you can compensate for it."

I had a horrid mental picture of what he meant might happen. Erin Transits with superb accuracy, pops into existence at just the right instant—with Zoey only ten feet away. Behind her, traveling away at a thousand miles a second. Or there was an even funnier variation. Do you know the true story about how, way back when there were only two automobiles in the entire town of Kansas City, they collided at an intersection? Yeah, that would be hilarious. . . .

"I wish I could examine that belt," Acayib said. "It may be that some measure of inertial compensation is built into it."

"I've studied it," I said. "What would such a system look like?"

He shrugged helplessly. "Anything—or nothing at all."

"That's what I remember seeing besides those two dials and the GO button," I said. "Nothing at all."

"I still say," Herb put in, "we're neglecting the most important problem. Let's say we do our mind-meld thing and become God's own wetware supercomputer and work this all out to so many decimal places that, miraculously, we can plop Erin down as close as half a mile to her mom, and let's even assume we can match course and speed perfectly. That still leaves us with the question of, *How the hell do you find a person in street clothes half a mile away in space?* A great big flashlight? Wait for them to occult a star? I can see you teleporting a portable radar ahead of you, I even know where there's a radar we could steal that's probably in working condition—but humans show up *lousy* on radar. Too soft."

"An X-ray interferometer—," Acayib started to say.

"No," Doug said. "You want IR—"

"Excuse me, Doug," said Erin, "but I'm going to table this. No, you're Canadian, aren't you?—take if *off* the table, then. Rule it out of order. We'll have to deal with that problem before I Transit—but we don't have to solve it *now*. First let's see if it's even possible to pin down the target."

I was very pleased to know that people could form thoughts, construct sentences, create and follow logic chains while Zoey was in danger, because if Zoey was in danger, those things certainly needed doing. I could not seem to do any of them. Maybe because I had nothing useful to contribute—except the use of the wetware in my skull.

Then I remembered something useful I could contribute. Leadership. Brains not required. I took my hand out of Fast Eddie Costigan's long enough to put my thumb and pinkie in my mouth and give a cabdriver's whistle. Murmured conversations broke off everywhere, and my friends gave me their respectful attention. That's a heady drug; it helped to steady me down some. I'm no Mike Callahan—as Jim Rockford once said, on my best day, I'm borderline—but I'd been playing him in the road company for over a decade now. I was the best Mike Callahan we had around at the moment, and nobody I saw seemed to feel that I sucked. I gave Eddie my hand again and took a deep breath.

"Thank you all for coming here tonight," I said. "You know what we're trying to accomplish. Basically we want to build a big calculator out of brains, just like last time. It's a paradoxical situation. We want to blesh our minds . . . but then *not* have a conversation. We want as little thinking to take place as possible, really. We want to touch and interpenetrate and enfold one another enough to provide support, stability—"

"—bliss—," Erin put in.

"—and bliss, yes, thank you, Erin. But this is not the time to swap life stories, or marvel at each other's most intimate secrets, or compose poetry together. In particular . . ." I sighed. "Look, I know this is gonna be difficult, okay? Tell people not to think about something, and it's hard for them to think about anything else, I *know* that. We all know that. Nevertheless, I have to ask those of you who were present for our last symphysis, or have heard about it, to please try to avoid thinking about *why we were doing it*. This Erin, who sits here next to me, has not yet experienced those events—and they were so heroic, it would be a shame if she had to experience them as a déjà vu. She knows we saved the universe together, but not just how or even when, so let's all try to leave it at that in our thoughts, if we can't manage to leave it out of our thoughts altogether."

"I'm not sure it matters that much, Daddy," Erin said. "I've already had a little experience living through events I knew in advance would happen. It's not terrible."

"You didn't mind the feeling of being trapped in clockwork predestination, losing your free will?"

"Well . . . some, yeah, sure. That's why I never peek if I can help it, now. But there are worse things. I don't want to get this calculation wrong because some people are clamping down their mental sphincters to keep the Bad Memories from leaking out. All right, everybody?" she asked. "What we're looking for here is more like what the Zen Buddhists call no thought. The state where you're not even aware that you're not thinking about not thinking. Those of you who are new to this . . . remember what John Lennon said: If you turn your mind off and float freely downstream, *it isn't dying*. Don't be afraid. We float together."

Nobody said anything for ten seconds or so.

Finally I said, "We haven't done this in ten years. We haven't got an experienced telepath to help us, but we didn't have one the last time. What we did have last time, and the other three times, was a life-and-death emergency. Well, we have another one now. Please—" I stopped, gulped, got control. "—please help us get Zoey back."

Many voices were raised in the affirmative.

"Fast Eddie," I said, "would you start the Om, please?"

"Sure ting, Jake."

His hand tightened on mine. He straightened a little on his piano stool, filled his chest and belly with air, and then began to empty them again:

"AAAAAAAAOOOOOOOOOOOOOOMMMMMMM—"

We all jumped in after him.

I'm not trying to say Om'ing will make you and your loved ones telepathic, in and of itself. Countless groups of people have chanted Om together since time began—thousands of them back in the Sixties alone—and I doubt many achieved telepathic symphisis, no matter how long they kept it up; if they did, they kept it to themselves. (Well, but then . . . they would, wouldn't they? *We* had.)

I will say, though, that any group of people that does chant Om together will, if they all have a sincere desire to make it work, defintely end up more telepathic than they were when they started. How much more? Depends on the people.

All it is, really, is just the simplest possible activity that humans can share, and keep sharing. Inhale deeply, use the syllable *aom* to empty your lungs, and repeat. Nothing else to it at all. No prayers, no prescribed methods. Generally everyone holds the same note, in whatever octave they're comfortable with—but in our group if anyone feels moved to pick the dominant harmony instead, or to jam around the central drone a little like a sitar or a shehnai, that's cool, too.

It doesn't matter whether your language uses clicks, grunts, glottal stops, whistles or tones: any human mouth can make an *o* and an *m*—open mouth/closed mouth—and oscillate back and forth between them in a drone. Even the profoundly tone-deaf can usually pick *some* note and stick with it fairly closely—if there are enough people in the Om, the odd sour note actually enhances it, gives the overall sound a sort -

of shimmy that seems to resonate directly with something in the human central nervous system. Each participant has to fall silent briefly while taking in the next breath, so the sound is always changing, but everyone does so at a different moment, so the sound is always constant. Any monkey will find sustained deep rhythmic breathing to be hypnotic, calming, centering, relaxing . . . and at the same time energizing. In a large group, the effect can be enhanced exponentially.

We knew how by now. Most of us were conditioned to associate chanting Om with removing our scalps, melting our skullbones away, and letting our minds out to play together. One by one, in no hurry at all, we began to do so now.

I was sitting on my chair, beside my pool, with my whole family, watching house lights and poolside Japanese lantern lights dance on the water . . .

. . . . .

. . . and then each of us *was* one of those points of light, dancing in a place where there were no chairs or pools or gravity or bodies to be affected by it . . .

. . . . .

. . . a boundless place where we could touch/join/feel/ learn at will, without fear or embarrassment or hindrance . . .

. . . . .

. . . a peculiar pocket universe where a hundred soundless voices could all speak, be heard and be understood simultaneously . . .

. . . . .

. . . where distance between minds did not exist, and misunderstanding was no longer a viable strategy, and defensive armor was not even a concept . . .

. . . . .

This is it/here it is/oh I reMember now/YES/we're back/we're here/it's still here/it was always here/we made it/it made us/how could we have forgotten?/how could we have remembered?/Ready?/I'll never be ready/I've always been ready—

{**Then LET'S GO!**}

I am he as you are he as you are we and we are all altogether together in the altogether, so gather ye chestnuts Willie Mays me when you say the word and yule bee free for all good men to come in an aide of the party animal instincts to high heaven help the guy wire the money lenders from the temple to the bridge of the nose candy cane and able to leap from tall bildungsroman Empire State of the art for art's sacrum and coke deal gone sour you doing these dazed and confused into a single elemental patients is a virtual environment to say that if you're everly brothers' keeper or toss her backgrounded for a weak signal to the public offering a bell tower above the rest room to move your asterisk everything on one role-playing game warden off a cold front tooth and nothing butt the two things I hate the worst case of beer should be enough of this chit for the chatroom service industry standard deviation from the norman mailer-daemon knight Gracie Mansion family doctor the book's a trip and a half, isn't it, man?

{**see? everybody can keep up. take a solo, long-drink!**}

—*Tristram Shandy, Amos & Andy, and Mahatma Gandhi were readin' CANDY, so they all got randy and had a brandy with a girl named Mandy who was fairly handy, and her legs were bandy but her top was glandy; her hair was sandy, like Jessica Tandy*—

{**dandy, grandee! double bill, blow a chorus for us!**}

—*He was a straight head. He was straight ahead. His head was straight, and if you was too straight to GET straight, he was the head could STRAIGHTEN you, see what I mean, if you was in dire straits, didn't matter in the dire front or in the dire rear, he was the straight goods, too first-rate to frustrate, and that's the straight of it, straight up, we straight on that? Right on—*

{okay, round the circle now, everybody take a line:}

Afghanistan banana-stand
A Ceylonese camel with
A Balinese gamelan
Mandalay Brahmin an' a
Ram-a-lam-a-ding-dong
Bing bong Ping Pong
King Kong Donkey Dong
Cheech 'n Chong in Hong Kong
Sing along a strong string
single with a dingleberry
jingle got to mingle Kriss
Kringle on a shingle as
a polonaise mammal
Colonel Rommel had to pummel
on the pommel for a
Simulated summer as a
Ceylonese camel with
A Balinese gamelan
Mandalay Brahman an' a
Ram-a-lam-a-dung-dang . . .

{okay. we're in. we're on. we're networked. good connection. excellent bandwidth. now:}
{enough words.}
{enough thoughts.}
{enough selves.}
{no more words.}
{no more thoughts.}

{no more self.}

{close ranks.}

{those of you who know about no-thought, teach the rest of us. let us be one, and be still.}

Sssshhhhhhhh—

Mmmmmmmmmmmmmm—

A hundred twenty-seven minds hugged.

A million years passed.

Then another.

No problem. In company like this, I could do another billion standing on my head.

Or anybody's, for that matter.

I (wildly misleading term) was from time (as it were) to (so-called) time briefly aware (without ever thinking about it) that large (but not important) portions of what it amused us to consider Jake Stonebender's brain were being put to strenuous use by a two-year-old supergenius, processing zeros and ones at such a stupefying rate of speed that they blurred, superimposed, and became spoked wagon wheels spinning faster than hard disks . . . and every (let's call it) time I did (metaphorically speaking) come to that (for lack of a better term) awareness, I (also metaphorically speaking) always turned around and went the other way, like a first-class passenger avoiding the engine room. That was someone else's pidgin. And besides, *all* the brains here were doing that. . . .

Another million years.

And another, marinating in the warm embrace of nearly everyone on earth I cared about—

{jaymie, acayib, merry, check my figures. everyone else, hold on, please.}

Three or four aspects of myself went somewhere else for a while. The rest of me continued to bask. But only millennia later,

{we've got an answer. time to put our selves back on and go use it. thank you all. . . . }

"—AAOOOOOOOOOOMMMMMMMMMMMMM."
My lungs empty, I drew in another deep breath . . . and let it out slowly. The Om came to a gently ragged ending. There was silence save for the subsonic rumble of Fantasy Fest a few blocks distant. We were back. I was being me again—so convincingly that within seconds I had even me fooled.

"God damn it," Long-Drink murmured blissfully, "*one* of those days we have got to try that when we have time to *stay* there for a while. Maybe just a week or so to start, and then build up—"

"*Did it work*, princess?"

Everyone fell silent for the answer.

"I think so, Daddy. I've got a solution in which we have a high degree of confidence. If I've made the correct assumptions, and Pixel observed the time accurately, I think I know where Mom was when she rematerialized, close enough to exactly that with a little luck, I should be able to rescue her."

A ragged cheer went up. I was glad I was sitting down; nobody knew how close I came to passing out.

"How far away are we talking about?" I asked, when I could speak again. "Orbit of Mars? Oort Cloud?"

"Oh, God, no!" she said. "Sorry, I thought you knew. I

could have given you an approximate answer hours ago. It had to be roughly 68,400 miles from where she started. Nineteen miles per second times sixty times sixty. That's, like, a quarter of the distance from here to the moon."

"Ah," And Erin had *been* to the moon. Well, once, anyway. I felt a little bit better.

"Of course, that was seven hours ago—so from *here*, I've got to Transit roughly seven times that far. A little over half a million miles."

I felt a little bit less better. "Ah. And you're confident?"

She smiled. "Hit a target half a million miles away, with an error no bigger than a few hundred yards? NASA was doing that back in the Seventies, Daddy. Are you saying I'm not smarter than NASA?"

"As long as you're luckier," I said, and then wished I'd bitten my tongue off instead. At that point in history NASA was having some of its worst luck since the *Challenger* Tragedy: a run of maddening disasters like that Mars lander that went silent only seconds before touchdown.

Our luck had generally been notoriously good in the past. But then, in the past we'd often had considerable help in that direction, from the paranormal powers of our friend the Lucky Duck, who is the mutant offspring of a Fir Darrig and a pooka. Unfortunately the Duck had dropped out of sight without warning a few years back, leaving us a brief note in which he explained that right now Ireland needed him more than we did. I can't say I disagree. But *damn* I missed him that night.

"Okay," Herb said. "We have a good target. Now did I hallucinate it, or did we all formulate an actual plan together while we were in rapport? For what you're going to do to find and rescue Zoey once you finish the jump, I mean."

"We'd better have," Omar said. "She's only going to get the one chance. With a window twenty seconds wide."

"I think so," Erin agreed. "I'll be right back."

Pop. She was gone.

"She's just gone up to Titusville to do a little shopping," Acayib assured me.

There's a guy just off Route 1 up in Titusville, whom you could call a fanatic collector in the same sense that the Great Rift Valley is an interesting geological feature; he specializes in esoteric radio and aerospace stuff, and his collection covers over a dozen acres along the side of the highway. Double Bill calls it the Surplus Store of the Gods: there you can find everything from eight-foot dishes on tracking mounts to a complete three-story optical tracking station blockhouse to— I swear, he took me there and showed me once—an honest-to-God Titan booster. We've had occasion to shop there in the past, and Erin has always maintained a good relationship with Gordon.

Pip. A piece of gear appeared on the poolside concrete next to Erin's empty chair. *Pop.* She was back, too. "This is the best I could find," she said, and Acayib, Doug, and Herb began inspecting the device together. It looked to me like an unpainted Magic 8 Ball with an antenna and a few other bits sticking out of it, with its own remote control.

"That's a Zoey-detector?" I asked.

"Close enough," Acayib said. "It's a programmable IR scanner with telemetry." He shut up and started working on it.

"Zoey is small, dark, soft, and nonmetallic," Doug said, watching over his shoulder. "For purposes of detection in free space, the only good thing she is now is *warm*. Erin is going to teleport this ahead of her, to a point a few feet from her own arrival point, programmed to look for warm things.

Once she gets there, she'll have the scanner zigzag via teleportation jumps every second or so along a search trajectory. In twenty seconds . . . Merry, you were in my head watching as I did the math; do you check my figures?"

"Yes," she said. "If Zoey is anywhere within a cubic mile of Erin, the device should locate her within twenty seconds."

"Once it does, I'm there," Erin said. "Then I use this."

"Jesus!" She was holding up an odd-looking pair of scissors. "What for?"

"Well, I thought of bringing along some kind of pressure bubble and stuffing Mom into it—NASA has developed some prototypes I could borrow. But neither Mom nor I has had any experience with them at all, and I'm really dubious about my chances of getting her into one and sealing it within twenty seconds. She's likely to be in a state of panic when I get to her. So I think the best way to go is, once I locate Mom, I Transit to her side and just teleport her back home ahead of me—well, to some location above Earth but within atmosphere, after which I can take her the rest of the way back down to the ground in safe easy hops. But to teleport her ahead of me, *she has to be naked.* So the scissors are to get her that way in as few seconds as possible."

"Remember," Herb said, joining the scanner's telemetry readout and the scissors together with a pair of rubber bands. "When you arrive, first thing, locate this stuff—and for Christ's sake hang on to it! *After* that, you look around for your mom."

"Right."

I had a sudden horrid thought. "Holy shit, don't forget to take off her wedding ring!" I said. I felt a twinge of regret at its loss, but I'd have given a thousand rings to have my Zoey back; I could always buy her another.

"I won't," she assured me. "Good thing she doesn't wear earrings or a watch; that'll save seconds."

"And listen—the release for that belt is right on top, in front. You'll see it. Just pull up on it and the belt opens right up. I suggest you leave it there in space."

"I will," she said. "Thanks."

"Excuse me," said a quiet voice from outside the circle.

We turned and there was Field Inspector Ludnyola Czrjghnczl, looking embarrassed but determined. *Now?* I thought.

"Yes, ma'am?" Erin said.

"Do I understand this correctly? You intend to be exposed to hard vacuum yourself, for the entire twenty seconds of your search window? Because it seems to me that with your smaller size, decompression would kill you faster than it would her."

I stared at her. I should have thought of that.

Erin smiled at her and nodded. "It would—but no, I won't be exposed continuously. I'll have the IR scanner spinning so that it'll take it about two seconds to complete a 360-degree scan; that's the fastest it can process the data. Then I just keep skipping forward two seconds at a time and looking at the readout until I get a hit. Or don't. My total max exposure should be under five seconds."

"Ah," said the bureaucrat. "Thank you."

"No, thank you," Erin said.

"Yes, thank you," I heard myself say.

Ms. Czrjghnczl started to say something in reply, then changed her mind and stepped silently back into the shadows again.

I could feel my heart hammering. "Okay. When will you do it?"

"Right now, Daddy," she said. "Every second I waste is another nineteen miles I'll have to Transit. And I'll never be any readier."

I closed my eyes. A theologian would probably quarrel if I

said I prayed, since I wasn't aiming it at any particular being. Say I wished real hard, if you like.

"Okay, everybody," I said, raising my voice, "we're ready to do this thing."

More than a hundred voices all wished Erin well at once, and then fell silent.

Time seemed to come to a halt for me. All my senses became enhanced. I could hear cicadas, and my friends breathing, and two drunks arguing with a cop up near Duval Street, and some boatman having trouble with his engine somewhere off in the Gulf of Mexico, and a single-prop plane of some kind lining up for its approach to Key West airport, and the hammering of my own heart in my chest. I could smell the sea, coffee from The Machine behind the bar, islands food cooking over in Bahama Village, fried food from Duval, a car with bad exhaust going right by outside, and my own armpits reeking with fear. I could see all around me over a hundred well-known faces filled with concern and support, and all around them the splendid home Zoey and I had built for them and ourselves down here among the palms and poincianas at the end of the world. I could feel air rushing down my windpipe, and blood racing through my veins, and feces making its slow way through the middle of me; I could have sworn I felt my hair growing all over me. I had been frightened every single second since midnight. Now all at once I was so terrified, I wanted to vomit my heart.

I showed my daughter my teeth. I tried to say, "Go get her, honey," and discovered I couldn't trust myself to speak. Instead I nodded, touched her cheek one last time, and stepped back.

She smiled back. That smile had had all its teeth for only a few months, now, I recalled. "Don't worry, Daddy," she said.

"I won't," I lied hoarsely.

Pip. The Magic 8 Ball and its remote vanished.

"I'll be right back."

Pop.

And of course she was.

Idiotically, I had for some reason expected that there would now be an interval of nerve-racking suspense that, whatever its actual duration, would seem to take years. Call it proof that I wasn't thinking clearly. When she reappeared right where she had just disappeared like the Cheshire cat changing its mind, the scanner once again at her feet, there was a split second during which I was relieved, grateful to be spared the burden of waiting even one more second on tenterhooks.

Then I saw that she was still alone.

Then the expression on her face registered.

She drew in a gasping, shuddering breath. "Oh, God, Daddy," she said hoarsely, *"she wasn't there."*

I heard a roaring in my ears, and I started to faint. But my sobbing daughter literally climbed up me into my arms, and I knew this was not a good time to drop her on concrete and fall on top of her. I locked my knees, locked my arms around her, and promised myself that I would become unconscious just as soon as I got a chance.

"Okay, don't panic," Acayib called sharply. "Remember our initial assumptions. Zoey either jumped one hour, or twenty-four. We've eliminated the first one. Now we try the other, that's all."

Of course! We'd failed to find Zoey at 8:03 this evening . . . but for all we knew we might still find her at 7:03 *tomorrow* evening. All was not lost—

Erin's skin felt feverishly hot against mine. Moments ago she had been in space, twice as far away as the orbit of Luna. "You don't understand," she said. "It's not just a matter of multiplying everything by twenty-four! Slippage we could neglect for a span of one hour, effects we could safely ignore get too big to ignore over that long a time—and too slippery to pin down precisely."

"So we'll do another brain orgy," I said.

She shook her head. "Even if we could get everyone back in rapport now that we're all this agitated—and I doubt we could—it wouldn't help." She looked up at me with those huge eyes. "It's just not the kind of thing that more calculating time will improve. It's . . . it's indeterminacy. The part that can't be computed."

"But you're gonna *try.*"

"Of course I am, Daddy! And it may work."

"It may," Doug agreed.

"But the odds are way lousier than they were for a one-hour jump."

"They are," said Doug.

I felt a powerful impulse to rip my beard out of my face. Instead I sighed deeply and looked at my watch. "Okay, 7:03 P.M. this evening is more than twelve hours away, pumpkin. Do you want to take a break before you try again? Use the toilet? Eat something? Nap a few hours?"

She shook her head. "Let's just do it. Put me in my chair."

Deep breath. "Okay." I set her down before her two computers, and her fingers flew over the keys for a minute or so. Then she looked at the figures on the screens for ten long seconds, took in a long deep breath, and shut off both machines.

The crowd quieted down.

"Okay, everybody," she said, standing up on her chair. "This is my last shot. Keep your fingers crossed."

Universal murmurs of support, encouragement, confidence, love.

She glanced over at me and smiled. "I'm really scared, Daddy," she whispered.

I tried to smile back, and couldn't. "You'll get her this time."

She nodded, faced forward, took a deep breath.

Pip. For the second time, the IR scanner vanished.

Pop. So did Erin.

Pop. She was back.

Alone.

Crying her eyes out.

12

GOD'S IDEA OF SLAPSTICK

In the last analysis, it is our conception of death which decides
our answers to all the questions that life puts to us.
—Dag Hammarskjold

I simply have *got* to stop killing wives," I said. "They spot you
the first one—anybody can fuck up once—but two in thirty
years is just sloppy performance. It's starting to cause talk.
Hear it?"

One of my eyelids was peeled up, and the other rose
halfway to join it. Doc Webster, inches away, held up something that ignited and became a star.

"Oh, hi, Sam. Déjà vu all over again, huh? What are you
gonna do for me *this* time—send me to a bar called Callahan's Place? I think you're a little late." I giggled. "I think
we're all a little late."

The sun died. He put a handcuff on me. No, took my
pulse, more likely. Possibly my blood pressure.

"You must think I'm crazy, huh? You'd probably give anything to have another year—even a bad one. Zoey would have
given anything for five more minutes. Thirty more seconds.
And here I am, pissing and moaning because I probably have

another couple of decades of good health to spend feeling sorry for myself."

"Tragedy has no pecking order, Jacob," the Doc said. "Pain is pain, and all pain is infinite and eternal."

"You've got stuff that will put me out," I said dreamily.

"Yes. You can't have any."

"I *can't?*"

"Not yet."

"Why the fuck not?"

"I want you to have a debate with your daughter first."

"Huh?"

"Sit up."

I was so irritated, I let him help me do so. I was on a lounge chair at poolside. Erin sat in a deck chair on my immediate right. Doc stood to my left. A few other people stood around solicitously, but I didn't even bother to register who. "What debate?"

"Which one of you killed Zoey?"

"I did," Erin and I said simultaneously, and at once we were yelling at each other.

"—if I'd gotten the goddamn calculations right—"

"—if I hadn't opened my stupid moron mouth and *suggested* using the fucking belt to her—"

"—if I'd just had the sense to Transit straight home instead of—"

"—if I hadn't been too lazy to find a goddamn *telephone in the city of Miami*—"

"—if I hadn't been careless enough to let that gorilla get cuffs on me—"

"—if I hadn't decided to let my little girl fight my battles for me—"

By now we were both at the top of our lungs, but Doc Webster has a superior instrument; he overrode us both easily. "—if Zoey hadn't done something uncharacteristically *stupid*—"

We both shut up, shocked.

"If I hadn't been silly enough to ignore classic early-warning diagnostic clues of brain tumor—a subject I've *lectured* on, for Chrissake . . ." He dropped his volume back. "People make a hundred mistakes a day. Every once in a while the punishment is wildly disproportionate. No invisible hand makes it just or fair. Jake, a few seconds ago you referred to the circumstances of our meeting."

"Yeah." Over a quarter of a century ago, now. I'd been in a car wreck. The brakes had failed. Trapped in my seat, I had watched my first wife, Barbara, and our daughter, Jessica, burn to death. Sam Webster had been the ER resident who treated me for attempted suicide that night. His prescription—a visit to Callahan's Place—had saved my life, and changed it forever.

"Whose fault was that crash?"

The day before the accident, I'd done my own brake job at home, using one of those Chilton auto repair books. I'd saved almost enough money to buy my daughter a birthday present.

"How many *years* did you walk around believing the crash was your fault?"

I shrugged. "Ten. A hundred. A thousand. One of those."

"And then one day Mary Callahan *proved* to you that the brakes you replaced weren't the ones that failed. Right?"

"Yeah, so? I was mistaken then, so I must be now?"

"You sentenced yourself to ten years of mortal guilt you didn't deserve, because you rushed to judgment, and because something in you decided even guilt was easier to bear than your naked grief. So in the first place, the universe owes you ten years you prepaid . . . and in the second place you should maybe use it to make damn sure of your facts this time.

We've already *climbed* these stairs together, you and I, Jake—and I won't be around for the next flight. Why don't you learn from your mistakes: this time try just assuming that you're *not* a worthless piece of shit and get on with your life, and see how that works out?"

I hadn't often seen the Doc this angry; it would have been startling, if I'd cared. "What difference does it make?"

His eyes flashed. "If you had broken, bay whack when I first met you, it would have been the tragic waste of lun more wife. If you break now, it's the end of The Place and you fucking nell wo it . . . and you will *not* dishonor my memory that way or I *will* haunt your ass, you binny skin of a such!" He turned on his heel and strode away. Mei-Ling, whose presence I had failed to note, went after him.

Nobody else said anything. I had no idea what to say or do. I looked over at Erin, and she was as clueless as I was.

Long-Drink McGonnigle dropped into a chair next to me and put his feet up on my thighs. Someone gasped. "Look at it this way, Jake," he said. "First time out, you croaked a wife and kid. This time you still got the kid." He spread his hands. "Clearly you're improving."

I stared at him and then stared at his feet across my lap and then stared at him, and just then, deadpan, he let loose a fart they must have heard up on Duval Street, that went on long enough to plant beans in it.

I roared with laughter. I didn't want to; I just couldn't help it. After a moment of shocked silence, several other people lost it, too. "Chuckles the Clown," someone said, and the laughter redoubled.

Somehow Drink knew or guessed how long it was going to take me to segue from laughing helplessly to sobbing like a baby; when that happened, he was kneeling beside me with his long wiry arms around me, and he held me until I had accomplished all I could that way. Somewhere in there Erin joined the huddle from the other side, crying just as hard as I was, and I managed to get an arm around her, too.

Finally we all pulled apart and located tissues or sleeves. "I'm sorry, Daddy," Erin said, in a way that meant not *I admit blame* but simply *I am sad*.

I nodded. "Me too, honey," I said, and just then Field Inspector Ludnyola Czrjghnczl sat down heavily on my lap. The tall mug of Irish whiskey in her hand slopped over, and a goodly hot dollop landed on my hand. I winced, drew in breath to swear . . . and let it out again. Suddenly something was clear to me, for the first time—several things. "You know," I told her, licking my hand, "I think I understand why you piss me off so—"

"Shut up," she said. "Please." She held up her mug, emptied it as if it were so much hemlock, and tossed it into the pool. "I cannot drink any more courage than this or I shall throw up, so I must do this now." She paused to wipe whipped cream off her upper lip and sat up straighter on my lap. "I realize I am the lashed—the last person here you want to talk with now. And I am certain I understand less about what went on here tonight than anyone present. But it seems to me that you people are not being very scientific."

She had managed to engage my attention. My attitude toward her had been evolving lately, but—

"Not scientific? Lady, we saved the universe once. And the world *twice*. Nikola Tesla hangs out here, when he's on earth. Why—?"

"What is the scientific method?" she interrupted.

"Find puzzle. Form hypothesis. Perform experiment. Revise—"

"Stop right there!" she commanded. "Why have you not *experimented?*"

"We did," Erin said mournfully. "Twice."

Ms. Czrjghnczl shook her head violently. "Not what I mean." She lurched up off my lap, reeled over to Erin, and took her hand. "Look, I like your logic for one hour or twenty-four, right? Nothing else makes sensological—makes psychological sense, okay? Only it didn't work. So there's got to be something you're missing. Something, maybe some *little* something you don't understand about the way that belt works. Like some cars pull to the left."

Erin stared up at her.

"Fine," I said. "So what the hell are we supposed to do about it?"

"*Experiment*," she insisted, still looking at Erin.

Erin's eyes widened. "Oh, my God," she said slowly. "Oh, I am a major fool." She turned to me. "How long have you had that damned belt?"

I was lost. "I don't know. Fifteen years—twenty, maybe. You'd have to—" I shut up. On automatic pilot, I'd been about to say *"you'd have to ask Zoey."* Suddenly I could see that my future was going to be an infinite series of such unexpected knifings in the back of the heart.

Erin failed to notice. "But way before I was born, right?"

"Sure. Since well before I opened Mary's Place and met your mother."

"Where in Mary's Place? Where did you keep it?"

"In an old footlocker under the bed."

"Always? Even before you met Mommy?"

"Yeah, sure. Why?" But even as I asked the question, the answer was beginning to come to me. "Holy shit. *There wasn't an Erin around then.*"

"Right," she said. "I can go back to then and get the belt, and *experiment* with it at my leisure until I understand exactly what I got wrong, and then put the belt back right where I got it!"

"But—but—but you've already used up your windows—"

"No, I didn't! I stutter-stepped, remember? To minimize my own exposure. Out of every two seconds, I was only there for half a second or less. I still have seventy-five percent of each window left! I'll have to do some fancy timing, but—" She broke off, stood up on her chair, and kissed Ludnyola Czrjghnczl on the cheek. "Thank you!" she said. Then suddenly she was on my lap, without having covered the intervening distance. She was a hell of a lot lighter than the Field Inspector had been. Her smile was so beautiful, I felt an impulse to shield my eyes. "Wish me luck, Daddy!" she said, and kissed me on the mouth, and by the time I could get my mouth open again to say good luck, she was gone.

No, I was mistaken. *There* she was. Over there by the side of the pool, standing next to that big good-looking naked broad yelling "H-O-L-Y *SHIT!*" who was my wife, Zoey. I tried to get up and found I was paralyzed; she had to come to me.

It took a ridiculously long time to explain to her what had just happened—even after I could talk again. From her point of view, she had pushed the button on the Meddler's Belt . . . and then for a second or two it got very dark and cold and she felt just terrible all over . . . and then she was standing naked by the pool, and everybody she knew was staring at her and grinning and crying and applauding. (I've had dreams like that.) When she finally got it, she hugged me and Erin so hard, I heard bones creak in all three of us. It was something like ten minutes before we could stand to stop hugging, even for long enough to go to the bathroom.

So as you can probably imagine, there then ensued a certain period of celebration, raucous enough that a few cops came down from Fantasy Fest to see what all the fuss was—and ended up staying, fascinated by Alf, Ralph, and Pixel . . .

. . . and then, a few hours after sunrise, after most of the wounded had tottered off to their homes, Zoey and I held a somewhat shorter but just as gratifying period of private and most personal celebration, raucous enough in its own way that Fast Eddie next door threatened to turn a hose on us and Pixel the cat thereafter regarded me with a new respect . . .

. . . and then there was a fairly *long* period of unconsciousness bordering on clinical coma . . .

. . . and finally an informal group gathering around the barbecue table, which started out as a walking-wounded-taking-light-nourishment-with-their-medication sort of thing, and then, as the medication began taking hold, evolved into the first brunch I'd ever attended that began at sundown and would still be going strong at midnight. Erin was finally thirteen years old again, as God had clearly intended from the start, and it was so wonderful to have her back, Zoey and I couldn't stop smiling at each other; it was so miraculous to have our Zoey back that Erin and I couldn't stop smiling at each other. I kept bumping into things, cross-eyed because I could not bring myself to take my eyes off either of them for a second. You don't know what you've got until you lose it. If you then get it back, you're Lazarus on laughing gas.

So it wasn't until sometime well after 9 P.M. that Ludnyola Czrjghnczl was able to get me aside and say, "You never got a chance to tell me what it is about me that—"

"Pisses me off?"

She blushed and nodded. "I presume you mean something beyond the obvious, something other than my job and the . . . trouble I've been making for you." She dropped her gaze. "Something personal."

I tried to blow it off. "Look, somebody comes up with the idea that saves my wife from certain horrid death, that's all they have to do to get a free pass from me. You can piss me off any time you feel like it."

"I'd still like to understand."

I thought about it. "Pull up a chair," I said, and we took a table behind the fireplace, where we were unlikely to be interrupted by merrymakers. Along the way I signaled Tom for two coffees. We've evolved a fairly sophisticated signal system over the years. When he dropped the coffees off at our table and she'd taken a sip of hers, she looked up at me and said, "This is just the way I take it."

"One sugar, regular milk, touch of nutmeg," I agreed. "I noticed earlier. Comes with the job."

She nodded slowly, sipped more coffee, and said, "Go ahead."

I sipped some myself. Two sugars, 18 percent milkfat cream, half a shot of the Black Bush. "You're right, it *is* something beyond your occupation, and its intersection with my little scene here. But it isn't personal. Exactly. Well, maybe, in a sense—"

"I see," she said, deadpan. Was that a little dry wit in there?

One more gulp of coffee. Should have asked Tom for a whole shot. *Spit it out, Jake. No, not the coffee, the apology— and don't call me Shirley.* "Here's the thing," I said. "Every time I see you, I get pissed off, but it isn't you I'm getting pissed off at. I mean, I hardly even know you, you know? And as I *get* to know you, I kind of like you. Even before you saved my world, I mean. What I keep getting p—" I saw her expression. "What I keep getting angry at is not you. It's me."

"I don't understand."

"Every time I see you, even now, you remind me of a hole

in my bucket. A burr under my saddle. A piece of unfinished karma—"

"Ah. Now I understand."

Yeah, that was dry wit all right. I *did* kind of like her. "Every time I see you, you remind me of your—your—Oh hell, I have no idea what the word is. What do they call the aunt of one's third cousin twice removed, do you know?"

She frowned—and then her eyes opened wide. "Oh—you mean Tante Nyjmnckra! Cousin Jorjhk's aunt."

"Jorjhk Grtozkzhnyi, yeah."

She tilted her head. "Your pronunciation is very good."

"Thank you. Accent on the *zkzh*, right?"

"And remembering her makes you angry because she drove you from your home in Long Island."

"No, God . . . bless it. It makes me angry because the whole feud was my fault, from start to finish. I deserved everything she dumped on me. My friends and family didn't—but I did."

She sat back and drank more coffee. "Now I really don't understand."

I tried to drink more of my own, but the mug seemed to be empty. I didn't want to signal Tom for more and interrupt this now. I licked the rim, and it helped, but not enough, so I set it down. "Look," I said, "it was a very busy morning. Zoey was *way* overdue to give birth to Erin, and we had to run daily urine samples to the hospital. It was the crack of dawn, I was half asleep, I'd banged my head a couple of times already. We were out of sample containers, and all I could find to use was a Bavarian beer stein with a lid. Then the buddy who was supposed to come pick up the urine sample rang the wrong doorbell, way over at the other end of the building, and I stormed all the way over there, cursing under my breath and flung the door open, and your *tante* Nyjmnckra and I screamed at each other." I licked the rim of the mug one more time.

"Why?"

"Huh? Oh. Well, I assume she screamed because I was naked."

"Ah."

"And in part I suppose because I was screaming at her."

"Ah. Because you were naked."

"No. Well, yes, I suppose, a little. But I've been startled naked before; usually I just make a little squeak sound. Why I screamed . . . Ludnyola, have you ever actually met your *tante*?"

"No."

"Seen a photograph, perhaps?"

She shook her head.

"Ah. Then I must ask you to trust me on this, until such time as you can verify it for yourself. Your *tante* Nyjmnckra is, almost beyond doubt, the ugliest woman presently alive on this planet, and I mean no shit."

Her eyebrows raised. "Really?"

"Was over ten years ago, and I don't see her for a late bloomer. Honestly, my first impression was a pit bull with a fireplug up its ass."

"Ah. So—"

"So what with everything, anxiety for Zoey and the kid, a couple of fresh lumps on my head, bad temper, surprise, embarrassment, truly eye-watering ugliness—"

"You screamed."

"And dropped the urine sample."

"Ah."

"On my bare foot."

She winced. "Ow."

"And most of the contents ended up—"

She closed her eyes. "On—"

"Tante Nyjmnckra," we said together.

She opened her eyes again, looked at me . . . slammed her palm on the table and whooped with laughter. Whooped and hooted and cackled and shrieked, and when somebody laughs like that, what are you gonna do but laugh, too?

"And somehow a feud developed from this?" she managed to choke out a while later, and while that made us both laugh harder, it also helped me to taper off again soon.

"Do you see?" I said finally. "There were a few other subsequent incidents I won't go into, even *less* plausible, that poured gasoline on the flames—but yes, basically the whole feud began right there. A feud violent enough that within a year more than a hundred people had to pick up their entire lives, pack them into converted buses, and move them more than a thousand miles down the coast to Key West. Ten years later, the general consensus seems to be that we all gained more than we lost by it. But my point is, it was necessary. Why? Because Nyjmnckra and I loathed each other on sight. Why? Well, she hated me because I was rude, stupid, clumsy, and naked. And I hated her because she had been pissed on by God, and because she objected to being pissed on by me. Who had the high ground there?"

She sat up straighter.

I took my glasses off, held them up to the light, saw that they were filthy, began polishing them with a napkin. "Do you see—*huff! huff!*—what I mean? She and I have invested a decade of prime hatred in each other. I taught my damn wife and child to hate her, and all my friends. She taught her nephew to hate us right out of town, and ultimately it all trickled down, like the upstairs neighbor's leaking toilet, onto *you*. And now whenever I see you, I remember that half of what she hated me for was my fault, and nothing I hated her for was hers."

My wife's splendidly familiar voice came from just behind me. "You keep this sort of shit up for *another* fifty years or so, Slim, and you're in serious danger of maturing." Her wonderfully familiar hand settled on my shoulder and squeezed gently.

I tilted my head all the way back, until I could see her magnificently familiar face upside down, and grin at it. "I ain't worried. Eavesdropping, eh?"

"Hear my old man laughing that hard with another woman, bet your ass I'm eavesdropping," she said. She was wearing her favorite kimono, the purple silk job with the dragon on the back. Her other, equally gloriously familiar hand settled on my other shoulder. "I'm glad I did. You nailed it, Spice. Tante Nyjmnckra has been a hole in everybody's bucket. And now we can finally start mending it."

Even upside down, it was a rapturously familiar, totally satisfying kiss.

She dropped into a chair beside me and took both of my hands in hers. "I have a couple of holes in my own bucket to deal with," she said.

I thought of six funny replies, and shut up.

"First of all, I know you would never say it at gunpoint, so I will. *You told me so.*"

I said nothing.

"I don't know what the hell possessed me to do something so stupid. Forget risking the universe—screw the universe—I risked my life, and Erin's life, and I don't have the right to do either without consulting you, because they both involve you—"

I squeezed her hands. "Whoa. I can see you're mad at yourself—"

She smiled wryly. "Let me put it this way. Every time I put myself in hard vacuum, it really makes my blood boil."

Ludnyola barked with involuntary laughter, then swallowed it hard.

"Well, okay," I said. "But I'm *not* mad. You did what you had to do. What with one thing and another, raising Erin has never really given you much chance to use your maternal protective instinct. Right from birth, she just hardly ever gave either of us any reason to be frightened. Not only did you suddenly acquire a perfectly good excuse to be scared shitless for her, but you also probably knew somewhere deep inside that it's never likely to happen again—that this was your very last chance to freak out. Having just done a little freaking out of my own, I can empathize, you know?"

She looked at me for a long moment and then said, "Will you marry me?"

"Repeatedly," I said.

"How long have you two been married?" Ludnyola asked.

"Not long enough," we said together, and squeezed each other's hands.

Suddenly something struck me about her grip. I looked, and sure enough. "You still have your ring! I thought it'd be halfway to Neptune by now."

She glanced down at it. "Oh No, Erin did have to take it off my finger to teleport me home, but she sent it home first, under separate cover, as it were. She was in a bit of a hurry, so she just dropped it in the pool; Lex found it and gave it back to me a few minutes ago. There are a zillion teeny tiny little pits on the surface now; I think it's cool."

"Stick with me, baby," I said, "and I'll get you a ring of space-burned gold . . ."

Another in a soul-satisfyingly familiar series of kisses.

"I still have one more hole in my bucket," she said then.

"I'm going to leave that line alone," I said.

"Yes, you are." She released my hands and turned in her

chair to face Ludnyola. "I thought some hard thoughts about you, these last few days. I've been doing a little more thinking since I found out I'd be dead if it hadn't been for you."

"I only—"

Zoey overrode her. "I have no more business hating you than my husband had hating your *tante*. Your job, what you have to see, what you have to do . . . what you must burn to do and can't . . . the bullshit you must have to listen to, the empty-eyed children, the crushing caseload and the pathetic budget . . . it almost *has* to make you cold, formal, efficient, suspicious, profoundly cynical, aggressive, stubborn, and rigid, if you were a decent human being to start with. Almost anyone doing any kind of social work is like an inner-city cop armed with a slingshot and armored with cellophane—never mind the ones who have to cope with children. You become a bureaucrat or you get your heart torn out, those are the choices. Add in the family pressure your cousin and his aunt put on you . . ." She held out a hand, and Ludnyola hesitantly took it. "I ask you to forgive me for judging you, before you accept my thanks for saving my life."

The Field Inspector blinked and blinked and blinked at her. Finally she said, "Don't mention it, you're welcome, if only I met a few more people like you two—and Mei-Ling and all your friends—in the course of my work, I think I'd be a much nicer person to be around."

"We've got a guest bed," Zoey told her. "If you phone ahead, it'll even have clean sheets on it."

The matter of the state of Florida versus Zoey and me dried up and blew away the next day. Field Inspector L. Czrjghnczl filed an Annual Evaluation report in Tallahassee stating that in her opinion, the homeschooling of the minor child Erin Stonebender-Berkowitz adequately and appropriately demonstrated educational progress at a level commensurate with her intellectual age and ability, as required by statute, and that while it had been mutually agreed that the inspector herself would serve as the regular Annual Evaluator in the future (every year at Fantasy Fest time), no further formal written reports would be deemed necessary.

That same afternoon, I mailed brief but sincere letters of apology, translated into Ukrainian and then handwritten, to both Nyjmnckra Grtozkzhnyi and Smithtown Town Inspector Jorjhk Grtozkzhnyi. I had thought to send a few pounds of exotic chocolates along with hers and a case of good vodka with his, but at the suggestion of Ludnyola (who'd also kindly done the translating for me), I reversed them, and by golly, each of them eventually sent me back a letter accepting my apology. Tante Nyjmnckra actually came down for a visit, a year later—during Fantasy Fest—but that's another, and far more ridiculous, story.

Two days after that, Bert the Shirt came by, resplendent in a cobalt-blue silk shirt with fire opal cuff links that were older than he was, and sat at the best table in the house with Don Giovanni wheezing dryly on his lap and a crowd gathered around him, anxious to hear the word. And the word was that nearly all the ten million dollars had been recovered, and while Tony Donuts Junior was apparently still alive, his net worth and his life expectancy were both very close to zero.

"Tony's no Einstein," he told us, "but the third time in a row he breaks a hundred, an five minutes later guys shoot at him, even he figures out this ten million is no good fah spendin. So basically he abandons it ta slow the hunters down, an keeps runnin—in effect, he gives it back to Chollie, see? Chollie smiles so much lately, sharks are gettin jealous."

"Where do you figure Tony is now, Uncle Bert?" Erin asked.

Bert was dipping his aged fingers in a glass of ice water and sprinkling Don Giovanni. The dog sighed every time droplets hit a good spot. "Well, nobody's brought Chollie his head, so he might be on earth. But if he is, it's someplace where they don't have booze, dope, hookers, gambling, unsecured loans, hotel linen, garbage collection, airports, thieves, cops, lawyers, TVs, or telephones. There was one reported sighting up at Baffin Bay, but the thinking now is it was probably a polar bear. I think ya can fuhgeddaboutim."

So we did.

Lex's skin rash and scale infection both finally cleared up, and we trucked him back home to the Florida Strait on the last night of Fantasy Fest. He sat up in the back, waving like the Queen of England and rippling his gills. Everyone who saw him as we drove by assumed they were hallucinating him.

Doc Webster seemed stable for a couple more months. Bouts of Spoonerisms came and went; he seemed to get tired a little more than usual, but not less merry; it became possible to tell a joke around him without being topped, but it was never a sure thing. He and Mei-Ling did seem to work extra hard at savoring every golden moment, but then they always had.

Then with the coming of spring, he went into decline. He started losing weight rapidly, first. Then the Spoonerisms started to cluster and get a bit compulsive. I heard him introduce three strangers he'd just met with, "Jim Thompson—excuse me, Tom Jimson—I'd like you to meet Tim Preacher, a prim teacher and a trim peacher; Treacher, this is either Will Johnson, John Wilson, Jill Wansen or Juan Jillson; Ginseng, say hello to Tim Johnson . . ." They didn't stay long.

A few days later it went beyond Spoonerisms; his unit of meaning began to shrink. He went from funny jokes to funny sentences to funny words, and finally he began to get hung up on individual syllables. I don't mean he got dumb. One night I was behind the bar, trying unsuccessfully to fix a jam in the conveyor belt of The Machine with orders backed up to Mars, when he came up and slammed his fist on the bar top until he had my and everyone else's attention. Then he held the fist in the air, and used it to count syllables, as he said, "Bot but bit bot but bite, bait boat boot bought beat Eleven. Ah?"

I nodded cautiously. "Mm-hm."

He zeroed his fist and started over. "Met mat mitt mott mutt might mate moat moot mought meet—eleven? Eleven."

"Uh-huh," I said.

"Ah—but"—this time he counted slower—"cat kit cut cot kite Kate coat coot caught . . . *nine*. No *keet* or *ket*, you see?" Before I could respond, he went on, "Set sat sit sot site sate suit sought seat . . . nine! No *sut* or *sote*. But check *this* out: get gat git got gate gut goat . . . seven, only seven, no *gyte*, *geet*, *goot*, or *gawt*, isn't that amazing?"

I felt my smile congealing, and tried to think of another noncommittal grunt besides *uh-huh* and *mm-hm* . . . and then all of a sudden light dawned. "Oh, I get you, Doc. You're saying there are a whole fistful of basic one-syllable words, just as simple and memorable as they can be—"

"—*that aren't being used at the moment*, right," he agreed. "There's gotta be money in that somewhere."

You see what I mean? His brain didn't so much break down, exactly, as come adrift, or at least begin steering by a map nobody else could read. And still it managed to find interesting places.

Here, for the record, is the last coherent joke I ever heard him tell. "Researchers say they are baffled by a newly discovered discrepancy: While only forty-three percent of husbands say good-bye to their wives when they leave the house, over *ninety-nine* percent of men say good-bye to the house when they leave their wives."

And here, from a little later in the same impromptu mock newscast, is the last pun I ever heard him make: "Asked how a student dressed entirely in black, wearing a mask, and brandishing a sword could have gained access to the building, school officials cited their new Zorro-tolerance policy." Several people got up and left his vicinity, crying out in disgust; he looked over at me, winked, closed his eyes, and smiled.

One day Fast Eddie and I were trying to set up a live recording of some new music he'd composed, which I wanted to send as a present to some relatives back up on Long Island. As we were making the final sound checks, Eddie nudged me, pointed over to where the Doc was sitting at poolside with his back to us watching his wife swim, and murmured, "His elevens is up." It's an old British colonial expression, from the days of the Raj. What they meant was, when the tendons at the back of your neck stand out like a number eleven, you're a goner. With a stab of sorrow I saw that Eddie was right; Doc's elevens were up.

Just then he suddenly stood, turned around, and came shuffling up to me and Eddie, his eyes glowing with excitement. "What's up, Doc?" I said, partly because I just love saying that.

"Vamp," he said to Fast Eddie, pointing at the piano, "Blues ballad," and he hummed a few bars of "Try to remember/that kind of September . . ." to indicate meter and tempo. "Fill," he said to me, and pointed to my guitar. Eddie and I exchanged a glance, shrugged, and went for our instruments, and thank God left the tape running as Doc Webster, off the top of his head, in a single take with no fluffs, tunelessly declaimed the following, his last twisted masterpiece:

PRUZY, THE NEWSIE WITH A CHARTREUSE UZI

Hugh's an intrusion who sues cows for moos:
He will cruise avenues to woo slews of new stews,
So the cooze of the floozy he screws is a doozy;
The brews and the booze he abuses till woozy
Excuse what he chooses, confused, to refuse:
The queues in the pews, all the falses and trues . . .
So, amused by confusion, we use rendezvouses
To enthuse over news of shrews snoozing in flues
Who confuse their infusions with views of
    illusions
Whose Muse eschews dues through the tissues of
    clues
And the ruse that glues mews imbues yews with
    tattoos
While gnus in igloos contuse crews of yahoos . . .
Chu's baby Suze coos: she has Terrible Twos
She spews slews of grues, and strews shmoos that
    she shoos;
Youse ooze goos and muse, right through Lou's
    don't's and do's,
To the hoos of two zoos, because two twos till Tues
day are clues to defusing the losers who bruise:
If you shmooze about boo-boos and fuse cootchy-
    coos
With the issues of thews for the Jews and the
    Druze
Syracuse would refuse, with fondues in your
    shoes,
Dr. Seuss can peruse any cashews he chews,
                 so you lose:
                    Louis,

*you is
got the blues*

And then as people were applauding and whistling, his nose started to bleed, his eyes rolled up in his head, and he went down.

At his insistent request, we broke him out of the Stock Island Hospital the next day and brought him home. He never left The Place again. We set up a round-the-clock home care rotation system, and within a week it was clear it was a deathwatch. With an almost eerie appropriateness, considering it's Sam Webster we're talking about, it turned out to be one of the very few silly deathwatches of all time. I've asked around: at no time did any of us ever see him frightened, or depressed, or angry, or even particularly sad. If anything, he laughed more than usual, at less excuse, with each passing day. Everything amused him. His own deteriorating physical condition struck him as a riot, and I honestly believe his deteriorating mental condition escaped him. I, for one, found it much easier to deal with in consequence, and I'm sure Mei-Ling did, too, but I don't think he was bravely faking it for that purpose. Basically, he just got a little goofier every day, until one day he got so goofy, he neglected to take the next breath.

There was no deathbed scene. He went in his sleep in the middle of the night. I thought that a special mercy. Then a few days later I was going through some of the oldest letters he'd sent me, so old the stamps had single digits, and I ran across one where, in discussing the recent passage of a friend, he'd written, "Me, I'd *hate* to go in my sleep. Miss the whole thing!"

Well, there you go, Sam. One last joke on the funniest and

kindest man I ever knew. It's been over a year now, and I miss you every day.

We all do.

Mei-Ling is doing well, and misses you every second, and her new boyfriend has sense enough not to have a problem with that.

Every few months, I pick up the phone and dial Mike Callahan's number. I never get an answer, a busy signal, or a machine. It always makes me feel a little like Manuel Garcia O'Kelly Davis did after *his* friend Mike stopped answering the phone. My sole comfort is that so far at least I still get a ring, instead of a not-in-service recording. I can't seem to shake the notion that I have to tell Mike the news about Doc. Which is silly—he's from the far future and the ass end of the universe, he can zip around space and time better than my daughter—why does he need me to tell him about a matter of public record that, it seems to me, he probably had available to him the day he met Doc?

(I wonder what that must be like. Partying with people whose date of death you can just look up. I think I'm glad I'm not a time traveler . . . or an immortal.)

I waste an occasional idle moment wondering what the hell Mike and his family are up to, Out There, that's so relentlessly pressing they can't spare an hour to visit past friends on Earth. But in the first place, Mike Callahan doesn't owe me a God damned thing—it's *way* the other way around: I owe him every single thing I care about. And even if he did, my best present understanding is that what he and Lady Sally and Mary and Finn and Tesla and their whole posse basically *do* for a living is keep the universe intact, crash-protect the cosmos, preserve this fragile reality in which I am privileged to watch and help my beautiful daughter enter puberty and my beautiful wife enter menopause and my presentable self approach the dotage I've trained for all my life.

If that has to take priority over taking phone calls from old combat buddies . . . so be it. Perfect or not, it's a universe worth preserving.

Readers who can, are urged to make a donation to:

The American Brain Tumor Association
2720 River Road
Des Plaines, IL 60018

phone: {847}   827-9910
fax: {847}   827-9918
e-mail: info@atbta.org
URL.   https://www.abta.org/donations.htm